To

with love!

Sawyer Bennett

THE PECKER BRIEFS

By
Sawyer Bennett

All Rights Reserved.

Copyright © 2018 by Sawyer Bennett

Published by Big Dog Books

This book is a work of fiction. Names, characters, places, and incidents either are products of the author's imagination or are used fictiously. Any resemblance to actual events, locales or persons, living or dead, is entirely coincidental.

No part of this book can be reproduced in any form or by electronic or mechanical means including information storage and retrieval systems, without the express written permission of the author. The only exception is by a reviewer who may quote short excerpts in a review.

ISBN: 978-1-947212-02-2

Since the release of her debut contemporary romance novel, Off Sides, in January 2013, Sawyer Bennett has released multiple books, many of which have appeared on the New York Times, USA Today and Wall Street Journal bestseller lists.

Find Sawyer on the web!
sawyerbennett.com
twitter.com/bennettbooks
facebook.com/bennettbooks

Table of Contents

CHAPTER 1	1
CHAPTER 2	15
CHAPTER 3	25
CHAPTER 4	38
CHAPTER 5	51
CHAPTER 6	64
CHAPTER 7	80
CHAPTER 8	95
CHAPTER 9	106
CHAPTER 10	119
CHAPTER 11	131
CHAPTER 12	143
CHAPTER 13	157
CHAPTER 14	168
CHAPTER 15	183
CHAPTER 16	196
CHAPTER 17	208
CHAPTER 18	221
CHAPTER 19	233

CHAPTER 20	245
CHAPTER 21	257
CHAPTER 22	266
CHAPTER 23	277
CHAPTER 24	291
EPILOGUE	300
Connect with Sawyer online	308
About the Author	309

CHAPTER 1

Ford

NORMALLY, THE SOUND of an incoming text—that tiny, single note—doesn't cause me anxiety. But when it's followed by another "ding," then another, and finally another, I can feel my pulse pick up slightly. It takes a lot to rattle me, even though I'm not rattled now.

Just… perturbed.

I snag my phone off the passenger seat, letting my fingertips briefly drag across the buttery leather. Drawing in air through my nose, I let the scent of brand-new Mercedes wash through me and it makes it palatable when I see Alison is the one texting me as I thought. She has the most annoying habit of splitting up whatever she wants to say in a flurry of multiple texts.

My glance at my phone is brief, because I'm not about texting and driving. I've represented far too many people injured, maimed, or killed by some dumbass who believes they have the mental and physical acuity to operate a vehicle and carry on a conversation with their fingers at the same time.

After tossing the phone back down on the seat, I drum my fingers lightly on the steering wheel. It's wrapped in the same, supple black leather as the seats. I'd just bought this AMG G63 three days ago, and it's absolute perfection.

Five-point-five liters, V8 biturbo with 563 horsepower under the hood.

Totally puts Alison and her annoying texts out of my mind, although I will have to deal with her at some point. I'd cut things off with her over two weeks ago, and she just doesn't seem to understand. I still get perky snippets from her several times a week—split into multiple messages of course—and despite the fact I stopped responding five days ago, she doesn't seem daunted.

I might be concerned she was stalker material except her texts are nothing more than friendly greetings or funny little things that happened to her. Friendly, light, and in no way suggestive that she's upset we're not dating anymore.

Or fucking.

Whatever you want to call it. I'm sure she saw things differently than I did, but I was never anything but honest with her from the get-go. I'm just not long-term boyfriend material.

Don't get me wrong.

I'm a monogamous man. Loyal and focused on the

woman I'm with—for the time I'm with her.

But that time often isn't very long. My interest always wanes, and it could be for a variety of reasons. Sometimes, it seems like no reason at all. Leary says I'm merely in a rut, and I don't want to put forth the real effort.

And I disagree with her wholeheartedly. While I don't give her the down and dirty details—because that's not the way our relationship is anymore—she knows me well enough to know that when I'm with a woman, I'm *with* that woman. I give it my all.

Until I just can't anymore.

Or don't want to, rather. That would be the honest thing to say.

My phone rings, but I don't need to grab it from the seat to answer. I tap a button on my steering wheel. Through the convenience of Bluetooth, I answer, "Ford Daniels."

It's a formal greeting, but most people who call are clients or business associates. I don't recognize the number, so whoever it is gets my best "attorney" voice.

"Ford…" It's a rumbling voice with a thick southern drawl. "I need you to get down to the site."

No need for me to ask what "site". Drake Powell is the president of Landmark Builders and one of my larger clients. He's referring to a sixteen-hundred-acre tract of land he's breaking ground on today to build a new subdivision on the north side of Raleigh.

"What's going on?" I ask as I approach a red light. I slow my vehicle, enjoying the purring vibration as my G63 idles.

"What's going on is that some crazy bitch has tied herself to a pine tree, claiming it houses some fucking endangered species of bird. I can't very well just run her over, so you need to get down here and handle it."

He grinds those words out with almost an anticipatory relish because Drake Powell likes to run over people.

Metaphorically, that is.

"Or *can* I run her over?" he asks, undisguised hope in his voice.

"No, you can't run her over," I say sternly. "But can't you just… I don't know… cut her out and gently escort her away?"

"She says she's got legal papers. An injunction," he mutters, and then he yells at someone. Not me. "Can you go any slower, you jackass?"

"Where are you?" I ask.

"On my way to the site," he growls, laying on his horn for several seconds. "That's right, Grandma… get out of the way."

My eyes shift briefly to the dashboard clock. My first appointment isn't until ten, and it's not even eight yet. It would be a very short detour to meet Drake and help him with this. Plus, I charge him attorney fees of $575 per hour, so I can't really complain.

It only takes me about fifteen minutes to reach

Swan's Mill since I'm going against the flow of the morning rush. Drake was the one who named this subdivision, and it fits with the whole *It's a Wonderful Life* vibe this place is going to have. Charming and unique houses that will have secretive courtyards and second-story balconies. Gas-lamp-styled lighting set every thirty feet on every sidewalk will create a cozy glow at night. There will be low, wrought-iron fences bordering each yard, making it easy to chat with your neighbor or pass that cup of sugar across. The absolute perfect place to raise kids, or at least make people think they were in the safest place in the entire world by the neighborly vibe Drake's aiming for. The plans and architectural renderings that I'd seen were quite impressive.

It ought to be for the millions of dollars that are being invested in this project.

But right now, Swan's Mill is nothing but sixteen-hundred wooded acres off a two-lane road just three miles north of the city limits. So close to the city of Raleigh, yet seemingly in the middle of nowhere. I park near the road as what little bit of clearing that's available is filled with several trucks, bull dozers, backhoes, a flat-bed tractor trailer to haul off tree trunks and one small beat-up Volvo station wagon.

I lock my vehicle, even though it's probably not necessary, before making my way through a group of workers waiting around. Some sit on tailgates, others sip on drinks and tell jokes. Drake is talking to one of his men. By the way he's waving his arms and leaning in aggressively, I don't need to hear the conversation to know he's pissed.

His head snaps my way as I approach. Drake spins on his heel and jerks his chin in a silent demand I follow him. We step into the copse of trees that were scheduled to be cleared today, walk thirty paces, and then I see her.

I'm not quite sure what I was expecting, but a beautiful woman in chains was not it. I guess I figured some hippie tree hugger who had a few screws loose was what we'd be facing. Maybe in jeans, a flannel, and with a granola bar clutched in one hand for sustenance.

Instead, the woman chained to the tree is absolutely exquisite. Her blonde hair is so pale it's reminiscent of moonlight. Long and braided into a pattern that resembles herringbone, it hangs over her left shoulder. She has a heart-shaped face, high cheekbones, and full lips. Her eyes are pale blue, filled with intelligence and defiance. Most striking is the way she's dressed, and it's most definitely not the outfit of a granola muncher.

It's a mid-April morning. There's a tiny nip to the air, but I feel comfortable in my suit jacket, so I doubt she's uncomfortable in what she's wearing. Her black pencil skirt comes to her knees. She's wearing a form-fitting white blouse with her sleeves rolled up, and the best way I know she's not cold is because her nipples aren't poking through.

More's the pity.

Black pumps adorn her feet—legs bare of panty hose. The heels to her shoes are quite sensible, unlike most women who use fourspiked inches to ratchet up their sex appeal. But this woman doesn't need it because, by my guess, she stands around five-ten without shoes on her feet. Very tall for a woman, but she's also filled out in all the right places.

"Holy shit," I murmur under my breath. Gorgeous woman in chains. I had no clue my day would start off so fucking awesome.

Drake isn't swayed by her beauty in the slightest because the man is only motivated by money, pure and simple. He stomps up to her, sweeps a hand in her direction as if I can't see her for myself, and barks, "Do something about this!"

The woman's gaze shifts from Drake to me, and oh yeah… she's smart as a whip. I can see it shimmering in her defiant stare. There's no doubt she has a very purposeful agenda here today.

Stepping forward, I sweep my eyes down the length of her. The chains are massively thick, and I'm not sure regular bolt cutters would work. They wrap around her from just above her breasts to below her hips. I take a slow walk around the tree, observing a thick padlock at the back that's heavy duty, but could easily be cut. Clearly, she had someone help her out because there's no way she did this by herself.

When I get back to the front, she stares at me with

an unrepentant smirk. I wait for her to say something, but she remains quiet.

"I'm Ford Daniels," I finally say by way of introduction before pointing to Drake. "He's the owner of this land, and I'm his attorney. You're impeding a building project that's supposed to start today, so want to tell me what this is all about?"

The woman's lips tip upward, and she gives me a challenging smile. Bright white teeth that are almost mesmerizing in their perfectness are revealed before she says, "I'm Viveka Jones. And your client, Mr. Powell, cannot start clearing today. This tree and several others in the vicinity house the red-cockaded woodpecker, who, unfortunately for you, is on the endangered species list."

My head tips back to stare up the length of the tree, seeing nothing unusual.

"It's on the other side, about thirty feet up," Viveka says. "They burrow out their holes to live in. It takes them years to create a nest."

I don't bother walking around to confirm. It's obvious she's telling the truth. But since I don't know fuck-all about the red-cock-whatever-pecker, I don't bother with it.

Instead, in my sternest, most lawyerly voice, I say, "You're trespassing. If there's an endangered species here, there are proper judicial channels you can go through—"

"In my purse," she interrupts.

"In your what?" I ask, befuddled.

Her eyes cut to the ground. There's a black leather purse that's big enough to be considered a briefcase. She turns back to me. "You'll find I've already gone through the proper legal channels."

I cock an eyebrow.

Her smirk gets bigger, and Christ… it makes her sexier.

Shit.

I bend down, pull the edges of the black leather apart, and see a document I assume is the one she wants me to read. Nabbing it, I straighten up and turn my back on her, walking a few paces away.

As an attorney who represents Landmark Builders, I should be affronted by whatever this ploy is.

But I'm not.

I'm amused as I read the legal order entitled "Temporary Injunction". It's brief and to the point, but essentially says the red-cockaded woodpecker has been recognized by the federal government as an endangered species and may be inhabiting the sixteen-hundred acres known as Swan's Mill.

A hearing has been set for next Tuesday for further review, but until such time, any construction on the property of Swan's Mill—in particular, anything that could potentially damage or endanger any tree—is hereby forbidden until such hearing.

Although this presents a legal dilemma for my client and me, what I find most fascinating about this strange morning is the certificate of service—that page at the back that lists all the people who will get notice of this document—lists one especially gorgeous attorney by the name of Viveka Jones.

I turn to glance over my shoulder at her for a moment, deciding I very much like the intelligence, challenge, and bit of ego shining back from those gorgeous eyes.

Turning to Drake, I motion him over. When he reaches me, I incline my head toward the document in my hand and say, "This woman has a temporary injunction to stop you from doing anything until we have a hearing next Tuesday on the matter. Apparently, there is an endangered woodpecker here… or some shit like that."

I wait for a good thirty seconds while Drake curses and bitches. He spews about how time is money, and he's losing both because of this bitch—his words obviously, not mine. Since he does nothing to lower his tone, Miss Jones and every other person standing around can hear him.

When he's done, I calmly say, "I suggest you let the men know what's going on. They might as well clear out. You can't do anything today. You and I need to talk about this, though, to prep for the hearing next week."

More cursing and glares aimed at Viveka Jones, who is still chained to the tree and when Drake mutters the word "cunt" loud enough that a few men standing nearby definitely hear it, I stop his tirade.

Taking him by the elbow, I turn him toward his truck and start marching him that way. "Enough, Drake. Get everyone out of here. I'll call you later."

To my surprise, he obeys, but I've learned over the years he's comprised mostly of hot air. Once properly deflated, he's easier to deal with.

Turning back to the tree, I approach the attorney who managed to stop an entire construction project.

"Viveka Jones," I say when I'm almost toe to toe with her. "Interesting spelling of your first name."

"It's Swedish," she says. I tilt my head, my ears straining. Does she have an accent?

"Jones doesn't sound Swedish," I point out.

"That's my married name."

There's not a word to describe the surprising disappointment I'm feeling over that. "You're married?"

"Divorced," she clarifies. "I kept Jones because it's a lot easier to spell than Sjögren."

And yes, I do hear the accent now. Can't say I would have been able to pinpoint it was Swedish. It's very faint and very subtle. I'm guessing Viveka Sjögren may have been born in Sweden, but she's spent a lot of time in the States.

"Want help out of those chains?" I ask dryly.

"Key's in my purse," she replies with a grin and another nod to the bag at her feet.

It's not a chore to squat to retrieve the means to

unlock her, not since I get an eyeful of her beautiful bare legs. After I retrieve it, I round the tree and open the padlock. The chains are heavy and once I loosen the top strand, they slither down her body to pool around her feet.

I walk back around the tree and offer a hand to her. She smirks and places her fingertips against my palm. My fingers curl around hers. She steps gracefully out of the pile of chains while saying in a flirty tone, "Very gentlemanly of you."

"My pleasure," I reply with just a touch of innuendo because everything about this exchange has been delightful. "So… your accent is very faint."

I'm hoping to elicit more dialogue. We're technically adversaries now, but that means nothing right in this moment.

Next Tuesday in court, the fight will be on.

Today… right now… I'm talking to a very attractive, sexy, and intriguing woman. No harm in flirting.

"I worked hard to get rid of it," she says. She squats gracefully and with knees pressed together to retrieve her purse from the ground.

"And why is that, Viveka?" I ask in a low voice, wondering if I could convince her to go to dinner with me tonight.

Miss Viveka Jones, though, is all business when she stands back up and pins me with a hard look. "Only my friends know that story, and we're not friends. Those people in my life who are privy to such things either call me Viv or Veka."

She pronounces Veka with a long *e*.

Veeka.

Pretty. Unique. Sexy.

She's also not interested in my flirting, and I know this meeting is winding down. Still, I can't help but ask. "Why the chains? I mean, you could have just been waiting here and handed Drake the injunction."

To my surprise, those pale eyes light up with mischief. She gives a subtle nod at something behind me. I crane my neck to peer over my shoulder, seeing what appears to be a reporter and cameraman standing near a white crossover with the logo for one of the local news stations emblazoned on the passenger door. The cameraman is clearly filming us as we speak, although they're too far away to hear anything.

When I turn back to her, she grins. I'm momentarily dazzled by her spectacular smile. She leans toward me. "Wouldn't be nearly as dramatic without the chains, and Mr. Daniels… the media coverage on this matter is extremely important. You'll find that out soon enough."

I can't help but laugh.

At her audacity and her ingenuity. Her sass, cunning, and clear enjoyment of the win she is relishing here this morning. Good for her.

I nod and turn my body, opening a direct path to the reporter. Viveka gives me a wink and pushes past me, shoulders held back and a sway to her hips. Her arms swing slightly as she walks, full of confidence and poise. Her ass is fantastic from behind.

"Miss Jones," I call. She stops and turns to me. "Who chained you up?"

This is not an attempt to flirt again, but is a definite curiosity.

She gives me a grin that pops out two perfect dimples. Inclining her head, she replies, "Someone who calls me Veka."

My laughter follows her until she reaches the reporter and cameraman. If I stick around, they'll want my statement. I don't know nearly enough about whatever the fuck this is to sound intelligent, so I make my way to my G63 and head to my office to start my workday.

CHAPTER 2

Viveka

Turning my wrist over, I take a quick glance at my watch.

4:59 PM.

"Shit," I exclaim. I roll my feet off my desk, and then push out of my squeaky secretarial chair.

Snatching my keys off the corner of my desk, I jet out of the front door of my law firm and quickly lock it behind me. I've always been comfortable in high heels, though the ones I'm currently wearing are only two and three-quarter inches high. It's nothing for me to run down to the next business in this little strip mall and practically throw myself through the swinging glass front door of Do or Dye, a hair salon.

Because Frannie has a set of cowbells tied to the interior door handle and given the thrust and momentum of my entrance, Frannie and the woman who she is working on both jump in surprise.

"Good Lord, child," the woman sitting in Frannie's

chair says.

I give an apologetic smile to Mrs. Dewberry as I rush to the reception desk. Throwing open the right-hand drawer, I pull out the remote control.

Turning toward the TV that is mounted in the corner of the salon, situated so the women sitting under the hairdryers can watch TV with close captioning if they wish, I push the power button and flip through the channels to find what I want.

Frannie ignores me, going back to putting fat curlers in Mrs. Dewberry's iron-gray hair. She comes in every Thursday, rain or shine, for the same wash and set. She's a sweet old lady struggling on a very small retirement income, so Frannie only charges her half-price.

This is something that Frannie does routinely for many of her customers. It's why she can only afford to set up her shop in this cheap strip mall in the bad part of the city. It's not hard to figure out my situation is not all that different since I'm her next-door neighbor here.

"How did it go today, Veka?" Frannie asks, rolling another lock of Mrs. Dewberry's hair.

"How did what go today?" Mrs. Dewberry interjects herself into the conversation. That's par for the course though while in a hair salon.

I stand in front of the TV, gazing at it with my arms folded across my chest.

"It went perfectly," I say, shooting a grin over my shoulder. "Just like we planned."

Frannie was my accomplice this morning. She accompanied me to the Swan's Mill construction site just before daybreak. She's the one who chained me to the tree and left me there to battle the wolves on my own. Frannie would've totally stayed with me, but I didn't need her help to serve the injunction and she had an early appointment set for eight.

The well-known jingle signifying the start of the five o'clock news program for WBCT comes on, and Frannie's eyes go to the TV. I turn around and wait anxiously as the news anchors do their welcome spiel.

I sense a presence to both my left and right. Craning my neck one way, I see Mrs. Dewberry standing there with the plastic cape around her shoulders and half her head in rollers staring intently at the TV. I turn the other way to see Frannie standing beside me, excitedly watching as well.

My dear, sweet Frannie. The best friend I've ever had.

My only confidant.

My sister from another mother.

In fact, Frannie's mother is more of a mother to me than my own.

I take in her plump face and her kind eyes, counting myself blessed to know a woman such as her. She's five years older than me, but she doesn't look it. She wears her hair short and spiky. It's usually always multicolored. Currently, she has streaks of blue, purple, and shimmery gray throughout. I'm thirty-six, and I've been wearing my blond hair the same way for most of my life. Parted down the middle with light layers cut into it, but mostly I keep it in a braid or a ponytail to keep it out of my way.

Maybe I should have Frannie put in some pink streaks or something.

"We now turn it over to Angela Halpern, who is reporting on a legal battle that is unfolding over a woodpecker," the news anchor, Chad Gibbons says in his smooth, rich voice.

Hurriedly, I snap my head back to the screen. Chad Gibbons is exactly what's expected from an aging news anchor who was never good enough to make it past the five o'clock slot. Blond hair that is so expertly cut, styled, and sprayed it resembles a football helmet. He has spent way too much time in the tanning booth over the years, and his skin looks like leather. His teeth are bleached so white it's hard to watch him when he smiles on the TV.

The camera cuts from Chad to Angela, the reporter who interviewed me this morning. She taped this portion earlier after we talked, and she's standing at the tree where my chains still lay on the ground. "That's right, Chad. Today, there was a standoff between real estate developer Drake Powell of Landmark Builders and local animal rights attorney, Viveka Jones."

The camera cuts away to prerecorded coverage of me chained to the tree. Drake is visible, waving his arms and cursing, though his words aren't audible. It was when Ford told him about the injunction, and I can't help the smile that comes to my face.

This morning was a lot of fun.

"Miss Jones served an injunction upon Landmark Builders today, prohibiting them from starting excavation of this property. It's currently slated to be a multimillion-dollar subdivision known as Swan's Mill. Ms. Jones sought the injunction in court late yesterday afternoon after an anonymous tip came in that the red cockaded woodpecker was found to be nesting on the property."

The video coverage fades away, and generic video of the woodpecker in question begins to play. The bird is small and black with white stripes on the wings. The male is distinguished with two tiny red triangles on either side of its head, hence the name red-cockaded.

"This type of woodpecker is on the endangered species list, which is curated by the federal government. The bird typically makes its home in trees such as this longleaf pine that Miss Jones chained herself to. Now, according to Miss Jones, the court has ordered a hearing to be held next Tuesday to determine what will happen next. We called Mr. Powell's office, but he declined to comment. As of the time of this broadcast, we have not received a response back from his attorney, Ford Daniels of the law firm of Knight and Payne."

Next, they engage in drivel-type chatter between

themselves, but I tune them out when Frannie's arms lock around my neck to pull me into a stranglehold of a hug. "Veka, I am so damn proud of you."

Mrs. Newberry pats my shoulder gently. "So am I. Although I really don't understand what's going on."

I aim the remote control at the TV after Frannie lets me go, turning it off. While she settles Mrs. Newberry back in her chair and begins rolling her hair again, I plop in the swivel chair right next to them. I feel giddy with my success today, using my long legs to push me around in circles while Mrs. Newberry asks me questions.

I tell her all about how I was approached just yesterday morning by the animal rights activist group known as Justice for All Animals. A group of their birdwatchers had been on Landmark's property—they were trespassing of course—and they noticed the red cockaded woodpecker nests.

They also knew there was imminent construction, so they rushed right to my office in a desperate plea to help them. Now, Justice for All Animals is a small local group. They are led by a veterinarian by the name of Alton Granger. He was the one who sought me out. Even though he really couldn't afford to pay me, it didn't take much to sway me to take the case.

Seeing as how I have devoted my entire legal practice to the protection of animals, it was kind of a no-brainer. Again, it's why my office is in a cheap strip mall rather than a fancy glass building downtown.

"Can we just take a moment to talk about how hot that attorney is who was out there this morning?" Frannie says as she dramatically fans her hand in front of her face.

Mrs. Newberry, who has to be at least seventy, nods her head and says, "Mmmm. Hmmmm."

And well… she's right.

Ford Daniels is H-O-T.

So hot, in fact, he had me a bit flustered when he first approached. Given I stand right at 5'10", the first thing I notice about a man is his height. Because I am totally self-conscious about mine, I always find it an utter relief when I have to deal with someone that is taller than me. And Ford Daniels has me by at least seven inches.

Once I got over the fact he made me feel small, I noticed how incredibly gorgeous he was. He's older than I am, but probably not by much. He wears his hair cropped very short and brushed sort of forward in a stylish way. It's light brown or perhaps dark blond, but the part that got my tummy fluttering was a slight bit of gray focused at the temples and interspersed lightly throughout. His brown eyes were warm and sexy, and there was no doubt that he was flirting with me.

There was no doubt I was flirting back. I mean, the man filled out his designer suit nicely.

I'm still spinning my chair in slow circles going counterclockwise when I realize it's utterly silent. I bring my chair to a stop and find Frannie and Mrs. Newberry staring at me expectantly. Frannie's hand is poised with a curler in one hand and a lock of Mrs. Newberry's hair in the other.

"What?" I ask.

"He's really hot," Frannie prods.

"Very handsome," Mrs. Newberry adds.

I shrug my shoulders. Although I agree with both wholeheartedly, it's really kind of irrelevant. "If you say so. I think he'll be a formidable adversary."

Frannie rolls her eyes at me and I know without a doubt if Mrs. Newberry was not sitting there listening to us, Frannie would have said something like, "Veka... girl... You need to fuck that boy's brains out."

And I would have to agree. It's easy to tell just by looking at a man like Ford Daniels that he knows what he's doing.

I shake my head in a silent refusal to give her more information. She reads the message in my eyes.

We will discuss this over wine tonight.

She nods at me and resumes rolling Mrs. Newberry's hair.

I go back to spinning my chair around in slow circles, thinking about the next time I'll see Ford Daniels, which will be in court next Tuesday. I think I'll wear my red suit because it's the sexiest thing I own that is still acceptable to wear inside a courtroom without offending a judge.

I spin, staring at nothing in particular as the interior

of the salon passes by. Frannie and Mrs. Newberry, the reception desk, the large bank of glass windows at the front of the store, the chair beside me, there's Frannie and Mrs. Newberry again, the reception desk—

Holy shit… There's Ford Daniels across the street getting ready to cross and head this way. He glances left, then right waiting for traffic to clear. When it does, he jogs across, aiming straight for my law firm.

I fly from the chair and stumble three paces to the left because I'm so dizzy from all the spinning. Planting my feet, I hold my arms out to get my balance and ignore the way Frannie is snickering behind me.

"That's Ford Daniels," I say, watching his foot come down onto the sidewalk.

"Oh, Veka," Frannie says in a breathless voice. "That man is coming to see *you*."

I hastily smooth down my skirt, and then tuck stray locks of hair behind my ears. This morning Frannie had done an intricate fishtail braid that she started at the right side of my neck, so it can drape over my shoulder. Throughout the day, the shorter locks around my face and jaw have come loose. Why I'm feeling compelled to put them back in place is beyond me.

Ford Daniels is just a man.

A hot man, but no different from any other I've encountered in my life.

Besides… technically, he's my enemy.

I suck in air through my nose and let it out softly

through my mouth. Throwing my shoulders back, I walk toward the door and tell Frannie over my shoulder, "I'll be right back."

That would actually turn out to be a lie.

CHAPTER 3

Ford

"Fuck." The groan that follows tears free from my throat and sounds about as desperate as my need was to come.

But I came, and it was incredible.

My forehead drops down to touch to hers. I feel another ripple of ecstasy working its way up my spine and then back down again. She dislodges her fingernails from my ass as she hums some type of approval or agreement with my last sentiment.

Just… fuck.

Lifting my head up, I find Viveka staring at me with those big blue eyes. The pupils are larger than normal, a sure signal she enjoyed that just as much as I did.

"That was…" she murmurs, sliding her hands up my back, along my ribs, and around to press into my chest.

I smile down at her. "Amazing is a good word."

But who in the fuck am I kidding?

That was beyond amazing.

Hell, it's beyond reasoning that Viveka Jones is in my bed, a mere sixteen hours after we met this morning at Swan's Mill.

Admittedly, I hadn't planned on fucking her. Maybe fantasized about it, but never thought it would happen. No, I went to her law firm because I was curious about her and I had the perfect excuse as Landmark's attorney to seek her out.

Her office is in a bad section of town and although I hardly know her, I hated she had to work there. I was surprised when she walked out of the hair salon next door and approached me with a friendly enough smile.

"What are you doing here?" she asked.

"Came to get my hair done," I quipped, pointing to the salon named Do or Dye.

Cute.

Viveka rolled her eyes at me, so I fessed up. "I want to talk about the case."

"Okay," she said carefully, motioning her hand toward her office.

I shook my head and fessed up some more. "Let's go have a drink and talk about the case. It's quitting time."

My body braced for a fight and I had counter arguments worked up in my head if she insisted we stick to the professionalism of an office setting. But Viveka surprised me for what would not be the first or the last time that day, by giving me a bright smile. "Even better. There's a bar two blocks down—"

"Let's go The Capital Grille," I rolled right over her. "We'll grab dinner, too."

And I swear—swear to God Almighty—I did not suggest Capital Grille because my apartment was in the same building. They really have good food.

She readily agreed, and so we went.

We had drinks, dinner, and talked about the red-cockaded woodpecker. I know more about the damn bird than I care to, but what she told me would at least help me to prepare somewhat for the hearing on Tuesday.

One drink turned into two, and then three. The flirtation was obvious, and neither of us needed innuendo. The attraction between us was palpable, and it had only grown since our first meeting while she was chained to a tree. When she glanced at her watch and made a clucking sound of dismay that it was getting late, I had no hesitation.

"Stay the night with me," I said.

Her head snapped my way, and her eyes lasered onto mine. There was no question or confusion in her expression, only consideration. She knew I wasn't asking for a sleepover, but rather to go upstairs and fuck.

She said yes and it was one of the happier moments in my life that I can recall.

And now, I'm inside her and not wanting to lose that feeling. Viveka's eyes soften as she stares back at me, curling a hand around the back of my neck. She's not shy when she pulls me down for a kiss, but it's only a brief touching of her mouth to mine. Then both hands are back to my chest and she is giving me a slight push. "It was definitely amazing, but I've got to go."

I don't budge an inch. She pushes a little harder, but I give a slight shake of my head. "You don't have to run off."

She grins, giving a harder push while at the same time wiggling her body out from underneath me. My half-hard dick slides out of her, and I blink in surprise as she rolls gracefully right off the bed. "But I do."

"Veka," I call, testing the nickname for the first time.

Her head snaps my way, causing her long hair to fall over her bare shoulder. Her fucking nipples are still hard, and I want them in my mouth again.

She gives a playful wag of her finger and shakes her head. "I told you that name was reserved only for my friends."

I plop my head in the palm of my hand as I watch her walk around my bedroom to pick up her clothes. "I made you come twice tonight. I think that makes us friends."

Her laugh is husky. "I'll give you that."

"Or do you prefer I call you Viv?" I ask her.

Her eyes come to me, and I can see them clearly even though she's across the room. That's because even though it's after midnight, the lights are on in my bedroom. When we had stumbled our way in here, kissing and clawing at each other, I asked her if she wanted me to turn the lights off.

She had laughed and said, "Hell no. I want to see the goods."

I think in that moment, if I were capable of such a thing, it would have been the moment I would have fallen in love with her. I enjoy looking at the goods, too, and let me tell you… Viveka Jones has them in spades.

I'm mesmerized as she walks to the bed, stark naked and completely glorious in her nudity. She clutches her silky white panties in one hand. Viveka comes to a halt by the side of the bed and I scoot closer to her, staring at the short-cropped hair that covers her pussy. She's a natural blonde, but I figured as much.

Given she's Swedish and all.

When I finally let my gaze travel slowly up her body, lingering on those hard nipples and wanting like hell to reach out and pinch one, I find her eyes aren't on my face. Instead, she's doing her own leisurely perusal of my body.

I let her study me, not in the least bit self-conscious I have a condom still clinging to my dick filled with what felt like buckets I unloaded just minutes ago.

When she raises her eyes to mine, I give her a seductive smile. I run a finger up the inside of her leg, hearing her breath catch, but I watch my fingers progress. Goose bumps follow in my wake, until I reach those soft lips with wetness still clinging to her pale curls.

Fuck, she was drenched when I first put my hand up her skirt in the elevator to my apartment. She only got wetter the harder we fucked.

I push my finger in and tap her clit lightly. Her hips jerk, and I finally glance up. Her pupils have grown large, obliterating the pale blue like an eclipse.

"Or, I could just call you 'V'," I murmur, giving her pussy a slight rub. "Because this is the 'V' I like most on you. Right here."

I give another tap, and she moans.

The hand holding her panties flies out and wraps around my wrist. I can feel the silk against my skin, along with the tight grip of her slender fingers. I think she means to push me away, but instead, she violently pushes my hand deeper between her legs.

My dick starts to respond, thickening inside the used condom.

And well, that's never happened before.

"I really have to go," she pants, moving my hand between her legs. "But get me off first. Okay, baby?"

"Fuck," I mutter because that is goddamn hot as hell. She came twice tonight, and she wants it again from me.

She demands it of me, actually, and while I'm the alpha dog in bed—always—I don't mind a woman expressing her needs. I love being able to give Viveka what she craves.

I lurch up from the bed, swing my legs out, and plant my feet on the floor. Viveka gives a cry of surprise when I grab her and make her lay over my thighs.

Her stomach presses against my dick, which is ready to go for another round, but that's not what interests me at this moment.

That beautiful round ass sticks up in the air, begging for attention. I give it a light swat, then delve in to push my fingers between her cheeks. They graze over that sensitive little hole I'd like to claim at some point before sinking into her cunt.

Viveka moans, and my breath seems to freeze in my lungs. She's soaked. Fucking dripping.

And she's a squirmer.

I bring my other hand to spread wide over her back, holding her down while I finger fuck her. I drive one, then two fingers in deep, all the way to the third knuckle.

Viveka starts grunting in pleasure. It's not ladylike at all, but it's hot as fuck. My dick feels like concrete, and it starts to ache under the pressure her stomach is putting on it.

I find out quickly, though, that this woman gives as good as she gets. She doesn't stay in place for long, but rather plants her feet hard onto the floor and pushes slightly from my lap. My dick springs upward, announcing its randy presence. My fingers don't miss a beat, still lodged into her from behind and pumping hard. She groans and presses the hand holding her panties into my thigh. The other pulls the condom off me.

"Goddamn… yes," I bark out as her hand closes

around my cock, which is still slick with my cum from our last fuck. She starts to jack me hard and fast, matching my strokes.

The noises we're making are like a symphony for my ears. Grunts, moans, wet skin sliding and slapping. Her ass jiggles because my hand is working her so hard from behind, and her tits sway as she rocks while leaning over my lap.

Most guys—and hell, I'm most guys—would beg a woman in this position to lean a little further and take my cock down her throat, but this frantic hand job where she jerks my cock roughly is making me see stars. This may be my new most favorite thing.

Thrusting and pumping and moaning and those grunts… from me… from her. Feels so fucking good we can't keep quiet about it.

And then her pussy tightens around my fingers. Arching her spine deeply, she throws her head back as she cries out her pleasure. All that glorious moonlit hair that had come free a long time ago flies in an arc and floats over her back.

The orgasm takes me unaware, coming on so fast and viciously I can't even move or make a sound. I erupt, splashing her tits, which are hanging just inches from the tip of my cock as her hand still moves on me.

"Now that was amazing," Viveka gasps when I slowly draw my fingers out of her.

"I have no clue what the fuck that was, but I want to

do that again soon."

She laughs, straightening to peer down her at her breasts. My cum looks beautiful there but to my disappointment, she uses her panties to wipe it off.

Raising her head, she gives a lopsided grin that pops only one of her dimples before leaning over to bring her face close to mine. Dropping the panties onto my lap, she gives me a light kiss.

"You can keep those," she says as she pulls back.

I watch her for a few moments as she once again starts to gather her clothes. She pulls that slim black skirt up her legs, and the thought of her without panties is something I like very much. I pick up the white silk laying across my spent dick, then rub the material between my thumb and forefinger as she dresses.

"Why do you have to go?" I ask, because even though I'm pretty sure I've got nothing left in the tank, I just… well, I don't want her to leave.

Viveka Jones… Veka… Viv… V… I want her to stay. She's perhaps the most unique woman I've ever met, and I'm not just saying that because we fucked about sixteen hours after meeting this morning.

"I wish I could," she says while she slips her blouse on over her bra. "But I've got my dogs at home. While my friend went over and let them out for me, I can't leave them alone all night."

I glance at the clock. Getting close to one AM now.

"Why not?" I ask, turning back to her.

She smirks as she works the last of the buttons on her shirt. "You're not an animal person, are you?"

I can't help the slight grimace. "I don't actually have much experience with them. Except my best friend Leary has a dog. Well, she married into the dog. It was her husband Reeve's before they met. It slobbers a lot."

Viveka laughs. She nabs her heels from the floor, and then comes to sit beside me on the bed to slip them on. "I have to say, Ford, I've thought everything about you was hot as hell up until this moment. But if you don't like dogs, there's just something weird about that. I'm not sure we can sleep together anymore."

She's teasing.

I think.

"We're not sleeping together now," I point out. "You're leaving."

She smiles, leans over, and pecks me on the cheek. "Okay, you're still hot. Adorable and hot, but I have to go."

Viveka pushes off the bed and I follow, walking to one of my dressers to get a pair of jeans. I slip them on commando while she steps into my master bath. She runs her fingers through her hair, trying to tame it somewhat, but there's no helping that wildly fucked hairstyle.

When she turns back to me, she seems surprised to see me getting dressed. "What are you doing?"

"Walking you down to your car, of course," I tell her.

"You don't have to—"

"Not letting you walk into that parking garage by yourself," I cut in. "So I either walk you down, or you get your pretty ass back in bed."

Viveka stares at me a moment as if weighing the words in her head. Something about my offer has taken her by surprise, but I don't see why. It's plain good manners, and something any man should do for his woman—I mean, his current fuck—if he's got a pair of working balls.

I pull a t-shirt over my head, and she still just stares at me from the bathroom.

"What?" I ask curiously.

She gives a small shake of her head, as if I'd pulled her out of some deep thoughts, and gives me the sweetest of smiles. "You can call me Veka or Viv if you want."

"V it is," I tell her with a smirk.

"Okay… V," she agrees with a laugh.

I put on a pair of tennis shoes, but I don't bother lacing them. I walk her down to the parking garage, right to her very old Volvo station wagon. She insisted on following me here with her car, which was smart on her part. It offered easy escape in case things hadn't gone all that great between us.

But Jesus… it had been so great. So much so I consider begging her to stay.

She won't, though. I could see it on her face and hear it in the tone of her voice. Her dogs are an important obligation to her, and she won't budge.

After she unlocks her door, she turns to me and tucks a lock of hair behind her ear. I'd think it's a nervous gesture, but her gaze is confident as she looks me in the eye. "Tonight was totally unexpected, but I really had a good time."

"Me too," I tell her. I use my fingers to brush back her hair on the other side of her face, pushing it behind her ear.

"I need you to know something," she says softly, and it's the first hint of vulnerability I've heard from her since I've known her, which has been for about half a day.

"What's that?"

"I don't do this," she says, waving her arms outward.

"What?" I ask teasingly. "Stand in a parking garage at one AM?"

"Fuck virtual strangers," she corrects sternly.

"No judgment here," I assure her.

"I didn't say that because I was afraid of judgment," she corrects, and I blink at her in surprise. "I told you only because I regret nothing about today. I think coming to your apartment was one of my better decisions."

"Oh yeah?" I ask her, slightly confused by this admission, but not put off by it in the slightest. Some men might think that was a woman getting a little too close… a little too serious, way too fast. But I love her honesty and confidence.

Viveka nods. "Yeah."

And that's all she'll give me.

Despite her height, we are not eye to eye, so she goes to her tiptoes and presses her mouth to mine for a soft kiss of goodbye. When she drops back down, she says, "See you in court on Tuesday, stud."

"See you then," I reply.

But deep down inside, I already know I don't want to wait that long.

CHAPTER 4

Viveka

My eyes drift from my computer screen to the front window that looks out on the street. My law firm is very small. As in, I'm the only one employed here. I didn't need much room when I hung my shingle eleven years ago after I moved to the area with my now ex-husband Adam. Because my office is sandwiched in between Do or Dye on my left and a bail bondsman on my right, the only windows in the space are the front lobby. As such, I parked my desk there to have some natural light, even if the view wasn't all that great.

It consisted of a similar strip of offices across the street, all the same as the one I occupied. Dulled and yellowed brick that was once white but is no more. Black shutters to the sides of the front windows, the paint cracked and peeling on the edges. The doors are commercial glass with aluminum handles to pull them open, with the business names painted on the glass windows.

When I first moved in, Adam surprised me by having my front window painted with fancy gold block lettering trimmed in white.

Viveka Jones, Esquire
Animal Rights Lawyer

Eleven years later, the paint is peeling just like the shutters and I don't have the money to have it freshened up. Besides, any person who needs to hire an attorney of my ilk isn't going to be checking to see how fancy my office is.

I turn back to the computer screen, my eyes scanning the outline of the brief I'll be handing in to the judge on Tuesday when I ask for the injunction against Landmark Builders to protect the vulnerable and totally cute red-cockaded woodpecker to be made permanent. Ford will be submitting his own brief in opposition. In my twisted mind, I've dubbed these documents The Pecker Briefs.

Of course, every single time I've thought about wood*peckers* or the word "red-*cock*aded," I naturally think of Ford.

And his pecker.

Cock.

Dick.

Shaft.

Eight inches of make-me-wanna-scream his apartment building down.

Last night was intense. I was impetuous, rash, and bold in my decision to sleep with him. True to my word to him last night, I regretted not a minute of it. Ford is the absolute sexiest man I've ever been with. He's completely unfettered in his sensuality, and he made my body do things last night I didn't even know was possible.

I certainly didn't know it was possible to come twice just with cock and no stimulation to my clit. I'm thinking the thick eight inches had something to do with that.

Of course, my only comparison is to the three men I'd been with prior to Ford. The first was a nineteen-year-old male model I lost my virginity to when I was sixteen. I fashioned myself in love with him. He'd just wanted to bust a nut, and it wasn't a good experience at all. Three thrusts and he was done.

The next was a guy I dated while in Florida getting my undergrad. We lived in the same dorm, and we were together for two years. The sex was mediocre. Of course back then, I thought it was the best ever. We broke up when I went off to law school, and he went off with another girl he'd been banging behind my back.

The last was Adam. I met him at Emory during my first year of law school. He was in his second year of medical school there. It worked out nicely since we both graduated at the same time. Adam really liked Emory and accepted his residency there. I wasn't so crazy about

Georgia, but I loved Adam.

I took the Georgia bar exam and went to work at a slick corporate firm, because Adam felt that type of law would be a nice complement to him being a neurosurgeon. He was all about appearances. I was in love with him, so I let it be about appearances for me, too.

That all changed one night on my drive home from work. We lived in a relatively nice neighborhood given we were just newbies in our careers, but it was full of professional-type people just like us. It was summer, and there was still plenty of light as I drove slowly down our street. Three houses before I reached ours, I saw a man on the sidewalk trying to walk a reluctant dog. The dog was pulling back—almost in fear—from the man.

To this day, I can remember the cramp of pain that hit my chest over the look in that dog's eyes. And then to my utter disgust and shock, the man hauled off and started hitting the animal. Hard blows to the dog's head and back, until the dog just rolled over and went belly up on the man.

Later, Adam told me he'd never seen me so mad in his life. I don't remember much about the entire incident, but from what neighbors told Adam, and from what he, in turn, told me, I stopped my car in the middle of the street, jumped out, and went after the man. I had my briefcase with me, and I pulled it out of the car. It was one of those hard ones with sharp corners, and I started whacking the man on the back as hard as I could.

He stopped beating the dog. Only by the grace of another man who was jogging down the street did I come out unscathed, too. He apparently had to pull the man beating the dog away from me. I wasn't cowed or scared, though. I merely picked up the dog's leash and told the asshole, "I'm taking your dog."

He screamed and cursed at me, threatening to call the police.

I told him to "bring it".

He never did come for the dog, but he did threaten Adam with a lawsuit since I'd hit him with my briefcase.

I didn't care.

I had a dog, and I named him Stanley. He loved me beyond measure, but he never really warmed up to Adam. And from that day forward, I knew I wanted to be an animal rights lawyer.

Adam was not happy, but when he transferred residency to Duke two years later and we moved to the Raleigh-Durham area, I talked him into letting me venture out on my own as a solo practitioner seeking justice for all sorts of furry and feathered animals.

But I never really had his full support. It was more of a "pat me on the head" and tell me to have "fun with my little hobby." I didn't care, though. I was doing what I was meant to do. I moved into this dingy office eleven years ago, and Stanley came to work with me every day until he died.

As always when I think about Stanley—my very first

furry child—I get a little misty-eyed. I'm immediately blinking back the tears when the door opens, as it is never very professional for a potential or current client to see me crying.

Luckily, it's just Frannie strolling in, so I don't worry about it. She takes one look at me and says, "You've been thinking about Stanley, haven't you?"

She knows me that well and doesn't even wait for me to respond. Plopping down in the modest—okay, cheap—guest chair on the other side of my desk, she leans forward expectantly.

"What?" I ask with raised eyebrows.

"Don't you play stupid with me," she says, pointing her finger at me. "I've been dying to hear how last night went."

"Oh, that," I say casually, knowing it will irritate her. I've actually been waiting for her to wander over so I could tell her all about last night. She was the one I'd called from the restaurant, asking if she'd go let my dogs out and feed them. I was currently a proud mom of another rescued golden retriever—from the pound, not from a man beating the poor thing—and a tiny Pomeranian, also rescued from the pound.

Settling into my chair, I kick my feet up on my desk. I dressed casually today because I don't have court, depositions, or clients. Casual means jeans, a frilly blouse for a hint of femininity, and a pair of strappy sandals with a low heel.

Placing my hands over my stomach and lacing my fingers, I try to keep my expression serious. Frannie is about ready to fall out of her chair as she leans forward, waiting for my story.

Finally, I break the silence and grin. "I had three orgasms last night."

Her eyes go round, and her mouth drops open. "Three? You had sex three times with the man?"

I shake my head, my grin getting bigger. "Only once. Well, only once with penis in vagina. He gave me two orgasms, and then after… well, just with his hand."

"After?" She gasps.

I nod exuberantly. "He was amazing. I mean… Frannie, I've never experienced anything like it."

"Did he have you barking at the moon?" she asks sagely.

I giggle, having no clue what that even means. "Let's just say he had me making all kinds of sounds I didn't even realize were possible. No way could I try to replicate them right now."

She wiggles her butt, moving it to the edge of her seat. Her voice lowers. "And when are you going to see him again?"

"In court on Tuesday," I tell her, my smile slipping a bit.

"Whoa, whoa, whoa," she says, dramatically holding both hands up, palms toward me. "You do not have sex with a man you just met, let him wring three orgasms out of you, and not have plans to hook up again."

"Well, we didn't make plans." I raise my chin up in defiance, really as a fake show of confidence in how I let it play out. The truth is, though, I wish he'd have asked for my cell number or gave some hint he might want to see me again.

But he didn't, so the only thing I can think is it was just a one-night stand. I knew going in that was probably all it would be, but coming out on the other side?

With my body feeling like jelly and my knees weak as he walked me to my car?

I wanted another night, damn it.

"So call him," Frannie suggests.

"Nope," I say with a hard shake of my head. "Not going there. It sounds desperate."

"Girl, if I had the night you had, I'd be desperate for more," she mutters.

And yeah… I feel the same. But that's not unusual. Frannie and I are so much alike, despite the moderate age gap. And it's more than just age. Frannie's been married to her husband Billy for twenty-four years. They have two kids, ages twenty-five and twenty-one. Not hard to do the math on that one and figure out the first baby came before marriage.

But the very first day I'd opened my law office beside Do or Dye, Frannie came over and introduced herself. We hit it off like I'd never done with another woman before. I expect that's because in the modeling industry, for those three wretched years I was doing that type of work, all the women were catty and competitive. After that, I was serious about college and law school, as well as Christopher. There just was never a time in my life that was conducive to developing a friendship of my own.

Until Frannie.

"Call him," she urges. "Just pick up the phone and dial his office. You're a modern, progressive woman. You can totally call him up and invite him out. Or to your house. Or here… desk sex is good, too."

I snicker. "You're so bad."

"Do it," she demands, pointing to the phone on my desk.

"Seriously?" I inquire, still very unsure. What if he thought last night was horrible and wants nothing to do with me?

"Yes, I'm serious," she says. She stands from the chair and reaches out to pick up the receiver. When the phone rings, it startles us both. She gives a yip and jumps backward, and I start laughing as I reach for it.

I take in a deep breath and answer, "Viveka Jones."

"Vivvy…" My mother's voice hits my ear, and I can't help the grimace. Frannie's eyebrows rise in concern.

I lean forward and put the call on speaker, laying the receiver back in the cradle so Frannie can listen.

My mother continues. "I've left you several messages on your cell, but you haven't called me back."

Frannie rolls her eyes and settles into the guest chair,

glaring at the phone. She doesn't like my mom, and she makes no apologies for it.

I, on the other hand, love my mom, but that's because I feel obligated to. I mean, we're blood. I have to love her, right?

"I've been busy," I say, forcing my voice to soften and not sound so guarded. Can't help it, though. My mother causes my defenses to lock into place every time we speak.

"Well, I'm going to be visiting the area, and I wanted to set aside some time so we can get together," she says, her Swedish accent still fairly thick even after twenty-two years in the States. While I worked to soften mine over time, she has actually made hers more pronounced.

She once told me that all rich men love exotic, foreign women so she really hammed it up sometimes.

My stomach sinks. The last thing I want to do is visit with my mother, and oh God… I'm going to hell for even thinking that. I suck it up, put on a brave face, and ask, "When will you and Stephan be arriving?"

Stephan is husband number three—some tycoon who makes his money in things I don't understand. He's also eighty-three years old.

My mother sniffs. "Oh, good God. You don't think I'd bring Stephan with me, do you?"

Well, yes, Mother. He's your husband after all.

"Then you'll be coming by yourself?" I ask, which means she might want to stay with me, although that's a long shot. She prefers luxury accommodations, and my little house is as about as far from luxury as possible. She'll spend the entire time berating me for not making my marriage work because while Adam doesn't make the type of money Stephan does, being married to a neurosurgeon is still quite respectable.

"No, I'll be traveling with a friend," she says evasively.

"Who?" I ask. My mother has no friends. She doesn't care enough about people in general to develop a sincere friendship.

"Just a friend," she clips out, and my eyes shoot over to Frannie's. She gives me a knowing look.

It means my mom will be traveling with a boy-toy.

I wrinkle my nose at the thought. My mother is fifty-three, but she likes her men young. I'm guessing her "friend" will be in the late twenties to early thirties range.

So gross.

"I'm thinking the end of next week," she continues. "Carmine wants to try some deep-sea fishing off the coast, so I'll hang out in Raleigh while he does that."

Frannie mimes gagging by sticking her finger in her mouth and silently retching. I nod in agreement.

"I'll call you in a few days once we make our flight reservations," she says, not even bothering to ask if this is a good time in my life for a visit. "Chat later."

And she hangs up.

Frannie shakes her head, giving me a pitying look.

"How someone as sweet, caring, and humble as you came from those ovaries is beyond me."

The bark of laughter that escapes is well warranted. Frannie never fails to brighten my day, even on the heels of a telephone call with Tilde Sjögren. Of note, she refused to take her husbands' last names because she didn't want to lose the exotic nature of hers. She about had a cow when I married a man with a simple name like Jones, and she tried to talk me in to keeping my maiden name.

I give Frannie a wry smile. "You know, I think that call would have actually bothered me more had it not been for those three fantastic orgasms I had last night. I'm feeling all kinds of loose and relaxed, even after that."

"Girl, I need to talk to Billy," she says as she pushes up from her chair. "I love my husband, and he makes sure I get my happy ending. But after almost a quarter-century of marriage, I think I deserve three in one night."

I have to drop my feet to the floor from my desk, doubling over in laughter. I practically wheeze, "A quarter of a century? God, that makes you sound as old as Methuselah or something."

Frannie stares down her nose at me primly, tapping her finger on my desk. "I'm just saying… knowing that's possible, I'm going to be educating my man on the wonders of a woman's body and what she might be capable of with the right effort."

"Oh, God help poor Billy," I say, still chuckling.

"You going to call Ford?" she asks, getting us back on track with what we'd been originally talking about.

"I don't think so," I say, having lost all my fire and gumption she had me worked up to before my mom called. It's just not in my nature to be so forward.

Frannie plants her palms on my desk and leans over, her expression going somber. "You should call him. You're amazing, and I bet it would make his day. But I also get it might be hard for you. So I'm going to make a prediction."

"And what's that?" I ask dryly.

"You'll hear from him by the end of the day," she says with a firm nod of her head. "Mark my words."

I don't think it will actually happen, but I enjoy the fluttering in my belly over the prospect. Regardless, I have to get to work on my pecker brief because no matter how magical Ford's dick or hands are, he's still my enemy come Tuesday morning.

CHAPTER 5

Ford

I LEAN TO the right and whisper, "Seriously, Leary... did I really need to come here with you today?"

"Yes," she hisses from the side of her mouth. Her eyes are glued to a large, flat-screen TV at the front of the classroom. The blinds are closed and the lights are off, but it's not totally dark in the room as some of the morning light filters in. "I didn't want to be the poor pathetic woman all by herself in the first class."

"But this is something your husband should be doing," I mutter, knowing it's pointless to argue since I'm already here and stuck for the next hour.

"And he would be here if he hadn't been called into court for an emergency restraining order," she replies. I knew this, too. Reeve needing to bail on his and Leary's first Lamaze class couldn't be helped.

Leary being Leary just marched right into my office and said, "I need your help."

I thought she was talking about a legal case, so I

readily agreed. Next thing I knew, I was at a community center in a small classroom with ten other pregnant couples hoping to gain some sort of Zen perspective on childbirth.

I guess there are no lengths people won't go to for their best friend. And Leary is undoubtedly mine. We are partners at the law firm of Knight & Payne, and we are also former part-time lovers. The lovers part changed two years ago when she met Reeve Holloway and fell head-over-heels in love with him. I had known Reeve before they met. He's a really decent guy, so I wasn't bent out of shape or anything. I'm also beyond happy for Leary, but I do like to grumble about some of the shit she puts me through.

There's an instructor standing at the front of the classroom making some welcoming remarks. Leary is seven months pregnant and because her husband is in court, I am the substitute father today. Leary assured me I would not have to do anything stupid because the first class was usually informational.

I lean toward Leary again. Pregnancy has filled out her face some and despite the obviously rounded belly, she's still an incredibly beautiful woman. But that beauty does nothing for me now. There was a time I lusted after it, just as she did me. It all seems so long ago, and I'm grateful our friendship always stayed intact over the years while we were on again and off again.

We chose the table at the back of the classroom, and

I'm speaking low enough I can't be heard. "Didn't you get enough humiliating satisfaction when you made me the maid of honor at your wedding to Reeve?"

Leary snickers and leans into me. "You were not a maid of honor. I just asked you to stand by me during the wedding. I even called you the best man to everyone."

That was true. It wasn't even awkward.

"Besides," she adds with a chuckle. "If I had wanted to torture you, I would have made you wear a peach dress with big puffy sleeves and a satin bow on your ass."

My answering soft laugh lets her know that I really can't be mad at her for much. Leary is about the best person I've ever known, and I'd pretty much walk through fire for her. So, if she wants me to attend a Lamaze class, I'm going to do it.

The instructor is not what I expected. I thought somebody a little bit younger would be teaching this class. Instead, Mrs. Craig is matronly and old-fashioned looking. It has to have been at least three decades since she's given birth—if she has, in fact, actually experienced childbirth. I just assume they would have someone teaching this class with practical experience. Still, I guess most of this is just medical and scientific. Anyone could probably teach it.

"Okay," she says in a calm, serene voice. "How many of you in here have actually seen a child being born?"

Being at the back of the class, I can tell exactly who is

in the same boat as I am. Practically no one raises their hand.

Mrs. Craig beams. She has found her fledglings to teach all the mysterious ways of childbirth. "Well, we're going to rectify that right now. I have found that often our biggest fears stem from the fact that we don't know what to expect. Now you can read textbooks, literature, and talk to your doctor and friends who have given birth, but there is nothing like seeing it happen, so you know exactly what you are facing."

Another whisper to Leary with a tinge of faux fear to my voice. "We're going to watch somebody give birth?"

"I suspect it's going to be on the TV," she returns sarcastically.

Well, I suppose this could be interesting. I've always been fascinated with how the human body works. There was even a time while I was an undergrad that I was torn between law school and medical school. I think I would've been a good doctor. Of course, knowing what I know now and having had an amazing legal career, I know I made the right choice in going to law school. A lawyer is what I'm supposed to be.

Mrs. Craig walks over to a laptop sitting on a small table below the TV. It's apparently hooked up with an HDMI cable, and that means Mrs. Craig isn't as old-fashioned as I thought. She taps a few keys on the keyboard, and a video starts running on the screen.

At first, I'm all into it. This is clearly a professional

production, and I'm assuming it was shot with the idea in mind to be instructional. There is a husband and wife in a private room, and she seems to be okay. She's not doing any of that huffing and puffing breathing I've come to associate with the term Lamaze, and she and her husband are smiling at each other.

The video goes to show the doctor coming in to check how far along she has dilated. Her feet go up in stirrups, and the cameraman walks right around so I get a good shot of what pregnant pussy looks like. Other than the fact the pregnant woman doesn't do much maintenance down below—although I will chalk that up to her probably not able to reach it—it looks like any other pussy.

I lean toward Leary and whisper, "That's a brave woman right there."

Leary mutters, "You're not kidding. I'd never let anybody put a camera that close up between my legs."

The video continues, and I start to get bored. As has happened several times since last night whenever my brain is given some respite, I start to think about Viveka. In particular, I keep replaying over and over again that amazing fuck followed by the best hand job I've ever had in my entire life. At forty-three, I can say it's not natural for a man that age to bust a nut twice so close together.

And because I'm thinking about sex and how sweet her pussy was, my dick starts to get hard.

Even though I'm sitting at a table at the back of the

darkened room with my crotch out of sight, I do not want to go full-blown hard-on. For one, it's just icky sitting next to Leary now that we are only in the friend zone. I also don't want the frustration of having a hard dick and not being able to do anything about it.

I prepare to cycle through my usual storage of memories or images of horrific things to get rid of my pecker problem. Nuclear war, starving children, and that one time I watched the film Xanadu. All of those have proven to be effective in the past, and I decide to think about Olivia Newton John. But then my eyes seem to focus on the TV screen, and I realize the woman is now in active labor.

I know this by the fact that she is sitting with her legs spread wide and held up on one side by her husband, and on the other by a nurse. Her face is beet red as she pushes. The doctor is sitting on a stool that's rolled up right in between her legs, and the cameraman deserves some kind of Oscar because he has managed to find an angle over the doctor's shoulder so everything that's happening is visible.

And it's absolutely fucking horrifying. The woman's vagina is stretched beyond limits. Bile coats the back of my throat when the doctor uses a scalpel to cut her open even further—as in he widens her vagina with a scalpel.

I swallow hard to avoid vomiting.

There's a lot more coaxing, a lot more bearing down by the poor woman who seems to be in excruciating pain, and then something starts coming out. Dark hair, blood, and nasty clotted yellow shit. The doctor starts easing the baby out, and the woman pushes so hard she starts shitting herself right there over the edge of the table.

"Holy fuck," I mutter, and it's loud enough even Mrs. Craig heard it. I lower my voice and tell Leary, "That is the most disgusting fucking thing I have ever seen."

"I'm right there with you," she says, her voice sounding awestruck and horrified at the same time.

The baby comes out. After a few more pushes, what I'm guessing is the placenta slithers from her. I start to gag and squeeze my eyes shut. I try to think of Viveka and will my hard-on to come back, which had been deader than a doornail once the doctor took the scalpel to that poor women's pussy.

The image of Viveka's beautiful, model-esque face helps. Thankfully the nausea subsides. I take deep breaths—the kind I expect Leary will receive instruction on at some point during this course—and I start to feel a little better.

I'm absolutely terrified though, of what Leary is going to have to go through when she gives birth in a couple of months. I grab her hand and whisper, "Please get drugs. Don't try that shit without them."

She turns to stare at me with wide eyes and nods. "Oh yeah… I'm asking for all the drugs."

♦

LEARY WALKS THROUGH the café carrying two cups of coffee. After sitting through what may have been the absolute worst hour of my life, I felt the least she could do was buy me a cup.

I have to admit, she looks apologetic when she sits in the chair opposite of me, pushing the cardboard cup of an Americano toward me.

"I'm thinking I definitely want an epidural," Leary says with a huff as she eases back in the chair.

I nod. "Can't they just knock you out or something?"

"I actually think I can schedule a cesarean section and be completely unconscious through the entire thing," she says, and I can't tell if she's joking or not. Given that Leary is probably the strongest woman I have ever met, I know she's not going to be afraid of a little birthing pain. Still, I guarantee you she doesn't want to shit herself in front of everybody either.

Leary picks up her cup and takes a sip. She grimaces and sets it back down.

"What's wrong with it?" I ask.

"It's not coffee, that's what's wrong with it. I can't have caffeine, so I'm stuck with some decaf herbal tea shit."

I grimace in commiseration. That would suck to have to give up coffee.

"What's new with you?" she asks as she puts her

elbows on the table and rests her chin in the palms of her hands. Leary's face is not only fuller from the weight she's put on with the pregnancy, but her features are softened in a way that's almost magical. Like she's filled with some type of weird inner peace that makes everything in her world rosy. She's going to be such a good mother. I can just feel it.

I toy with the edge of my cup. "I had something interesting happen to me yesterday."

"Does it have to do with Drake Powell getting shut down at Swan's Mill?"

My eyebrows shoot up. "How did you hear about that?"

Leary smirks and pushes from the table, settling back into her chair. "Who do you think? Midge."

Of course. Midge Payne, the senior partner and matriarch of the law firm. She knows everything that happens within that practice, although how is quite the mystery. She never leaves her office, rarely talks to any of us, and is reclusive. Yet, she knows things.

But then it hits me how Midge found out. She has a financial interest as she is a silent investor in the Swan's Mill development. In addition to being one of the best lawyers the state of North Carolina has ever seen, Midge is also real estate royalty when it comes to the capital area. She actually owns the building that houses our law firm, which is one of the larger ones downtown. Like she herself owns a fucking twenty-six-story building.

"So what happened?" Leary asks.

"Apparently, there's a woodpecker on the endangered species list nesting there. The attorney got a temporary injunction to stop Drake from progressing on the construction."

"That doesn't sound all that interesting," Leary says, and she makes this observation because she can tell by the tone of my voice and the set to my body when a legal case really excites me.

And I'm sorry, but helping Drake in this scenario doesn't interest me all that much. I couldn't give two fucks about the red-cockaded woodpecker.

"There was a woman…" I hedge. She nods in acknowledgment of the fact that with me, it's almost always about a woman.

"Go on," she urges.

"She was chained to a pine tree when I got over to the site."

Leary's eyebrows shoot up so high they almost disappear into her hairline.

I grin. "A really sexy, blonde Swedish woman."

Her face twists in disbelief. "You're making that up."

"Am not."

Leary starts chuckling and shaking her head. "Only you, Ford."

I laugh right along with her for a moment before it fizzles. My tone gets serious. "She represents an animal rights group, and she's the one who filed the injunction.

I fucked her last night."

I'll give Leary credit. She has one of the best poker faces around. She doesn't so much as let a facial muscle tick in response to that.

I continue, "And I really don't want to get involved in this case."

That causes Leary to have a slight reaction. By that, I mean her expression gets very worried. She tilts her head. "Because there's a hot woman involved who you fucked?"

I muster up as much professionalism as I can. "It's a serious conflict of interest. After last night, I really have no business staying on this case."

Leary just cocks an eyebrow.

"It would be the professional thing for me to do… step down from the case. Let another attorney handle it."

Leary leans across the table and murmurs, "Do you intend to continue to see her?"

I shrug. I have no clue whether I should or shouldn't. I believe Viveka Jones could be very dangerous to get involved with. There's just too much I actually like about her.

"Maybe," I admit.

"If it's just about fucking, there really isn't a conflict. You can continue to bang her and still represent Drake adequately."

I snort because Leary is wrong about that. It would be a huge conflict of interest. The reason why she's downplaying it is because that's how she met her husband. She and Reeve were on opposite sides of a case, and they were doing a whole lot of hanky-panky while battling each other in the courtroom.

And truth be told, I'm not much for the rules either. There has been an occasion or two over my career that I've banged opposing counsel. Never lost a moment's sleep about it.

Leary's gaze narrows, and she gives a slight shake to her head. "There has to be more to it than just a conflict of interest. What is your real hesitation?"

I hate to admit anything that makes me seem vulnerable. Then again, this is Leary sitting across the table. There's no one safer for me to let in on my secrets. "Maybe I don't want her to lose."

"You're not much of an animal lover, Ford. So I know you're not looking out for the woodpecker's best interest."

"I'm aware of that," I reply dryly.

"That means you like her then," Leary surmises.

"I don't even know her," I return blandly.

She levels me with a knowing smile. "You know her enough."

She would be right about that. In the last twenty-four hours, I learned enough about Viveka Jones to know she's different from any other woman I've been with. I would like to say it's probably because she's the most beautiful woman I've ever seen, but that's not exactly it.

I'd also like to hypothesize that her beauty in combination with her clear intelligence and passion about what she does makes her attractiveness unparalleled.

But that's not quite it either.

I think it all boils down to that one moment where she took my hand, shoved it roughly between her legs, and asked me to get her off. It was probably the first time I remember feeling needed by a woman.

I'm talking about a true, genuine need that wasn't exaggerated or done with any ulterior purpose. It was a pure request.

And for some reason, I really like that feeling.

CHAPTER 6

Viveka

WHEN MY EYES start to glaze over, I know it's time for me to put the legal research aside. I'm normally a whiz at this sort of stuff, but I've been having a hard time concentrating. That's because the area of law I am researching pertains directly to the injunction I got against Landmark Builders, and I can't think about this case without thinking about Ford Daniels.

I have come to the point where I need to admit it was stupid to have slept with him. Not that there's anything wrong with a one-night stand. But they are meant to be over and done with and you don't think about them anymore.

Now the sexy litigator from uptown is doing nothing but occupying my thoughts.

I back out of the North Carolina Court of Appeals case I had been reviewing where an injunction was upheld when developers tried to encroach on land that held an endangered tadpole. Amazing that such a tiny creature could cause such a ruckus.

I decide to sift through my emails, which have been accumulating for the last few hours while I did my online legal research.

I have a few from some existing clients wanting to know the status of their cases. Since I know every single case by heart and don't even need to pull the files, I'm able to answer them swiftly. I also respond to an email from one of the assistant district attorneys who is going to be prosecuting an animal cruelty case. I'm often asked to consult because these cases are fairly rare and obscure, and animal rights lawyers such as myself have a better grasp of the law.

Hell, I've helped state congressmen draft some of the laws that are in effect today in North Carolina.

I read an email from a concerned citizen that her neighbor, a pig farmer, isn't slaughtering his livestock in a humane way. Although the thought of it brings tears to my eyes, there is no way I can help on this case. I have my limits, and cruelty cases involving inhumane slaughter techniques is it for me. I respond by giving a recommendation for a fellow attorney here in Wake County who handles cases such as these.

When the door to my office opens, I don't even bother raising my head. My walk-in traffic is almost nonexistent, and I have no appointments scheduled today. I assume it's Frannie stepping over while she's on a short break, so I merely hold a finger up and say, "Give me a minute to read this last email."

"Take your time," I hear, and my head snaps up in recognition of that deep, sexy voice belonging to none other than Ford.

He stands there casually in a designer suit with his hands tucked into his pockets, giving me a roguish grin.

"What are you doing here?" There's no time to analyze my voice, which comes out all breathy and curious at the same time.

"It's quitting time," he says.

I glance down at the clock on my computer screen, quirking a brow when I return my gaze to him. "It's only four thirty."

He gives me a mischievous grin. "It's the perfect time to go have a drink. What do you say?"

I want to say *yes, yes, yes*. The man I've been fantasizing about all day is now standing before me looking even better than I remembered him the night before, and the night before was spectacular.

Still, I narrow my eyes and ask, "Is asking me for a drink code for a booty call?"

Ford doesn't answer me. He doesn't laugh and shoot me a wink. He doesn't come back with a witty remark filled with the appropriate amount of sexual innuendo.

Instead, he turns away and walks over to the wall that borders Frannie's hair salon. If I put my ear up to it, I can sometimes hear people talking on the other side.

With his hand still tucked in his pockets, Ford casually peruses the items that are hanging there. That would include one framed news article that was written about me seven years ago, my undergraduate and law degree, and a cheap print of a basket full of Golden retriever puppies in a plastic gold frame. That's probably my most favorite because it was given to me by a little boy whose parents hired me to successfully wrangle away a dog who was being abused next door to them.

Ford stands before it, examining it as if it were a Degas in the Musée d'Orsay. He lifts his chin up, indicating the picture of the puppies. "This is humbling."

I cock my head. "How so?"

He cranes his neck to glance over his shoulder briefly before turning back to the basket full of puppy goodness on the wall. "I've got about twenty thousand dollars' worth of sculptures and art in my office, yet I bet this one little picture has more meaning than the entirety of my office."

My mouth drops open over his observation, but nothing seems to come out. I knew Ford had to be loaded since he was a partner at Knight & Payne. I'd also went to his fancy high-rise apartment that would fit my entire little house in his living room. With wealth comes luxuries, so I'm not surprised the art in his office constitutes almost half my yearly income.

I am surprised, however, that he understands that what's hanging on my wall tells a very important story about me and the career I've chosen.

Ford moves over to the news article I'd had framed. It was one of my prouder moments, helping Congressman Irving in our district to beef up the animal cruelty statutes here in North Carolina. The article only mentions me in one line, and I'm not even quoted, but the congressman gave me most of the credit for drafting the new statutes. It was sweet and very rewarding.

Ford stands before the article and reads it. I don't say a word.

When he finally turns to face me, he says, "So you protect endangered species and you help draft legislation. Past that, though, I have no fucking clue what an animal lawyer does."

My head falls back to make room for the unbidden laugh that comes over the consternation in his voice. I lean back in my chair, completely amused. He doesn't ask for an invitation, but moves over to elegantly sit in one of my guest chairs opposite my desk.

"I do a lot of different things," I explain because my area of law is indeed quite obscure. "I work on animal cruelty cases. Sometimes, I'll help the D.A. prosecute abusers, or I'll sue for custody of an animal that's being mistreated. I review contracts related to animals—like sales contracts or even divorce custody clauses over who gets the cat and the dog. I've taught some law courses and helped set up a few nonprofits. Really, I'll do anything that relates to the protection and safety of animals."

"And that's all you do? No other type of law."

"Just animal law," I say proudly.

"I'm guessing it doesn't pay a lot," he muses, but not in a snobbish way. More like he's testing the weight of my career. It's non-monetary value.

"Let's just say I don't have twenty grand worth of art," I say with a chuckle.

Ford doesn't reply. Rather, he slaps his palms on his thighs and stands from the chair. "Okay… let's go get a drink and then grab some dinner."

My head starts spinning slightly over his domineering ways, and God help me… it turns me on, too. But I can only shake my head. "I can't. I have plans tonight."

"What type of plans?" he asks in a low voice, not quite irate but clearly not liking my answer.

I could tease him or tell him it's none of his business, but I don't want to play games. "With my bestie. She owns the hair salon next door."

"Do or Dye," Ford murmurs, and I'm surprised he even noticed something like the name of the business next door. "Very clever."

"She's a very clever person," I reply softly.

"No matter," Ford says almost jauntily. "It's Friday, four thirty, and we deserve a drink. Let me buy you one before you meet…"

"Frannie," I supply.

"Frannie," he affirms with a nod. "What are you two

going to do tonight?"

"Mud masks on our face, wine, cheese, and a corny eighties' movie," I tell him. All true and completely lame. "I know it sounds weird, but it's our thing."

"I attended a Lamaze class with my bestie today," he returns. That catches me off guard. In a million years, I couldn't imagine Ford in his impeccably groomed suit at a Lamaze class. I'm also a little surprised his bestie is a woman, and I'm not quite sure how that makes me feel.

Before I can process that, though, he jerks his chin toward the door. "Come on… we can talk all about it over a drink. You can choose the place."

♦

"Sorry this isn't very fancy," I say, swirling the piece of celery around my Bloody Mary.

His brown eyes sweep around the bar, before coming back to me. "Who doesn't love TGIF Friday's?"

I cock my eyebrow. "Have you ever been in one before?"

The guilty expression on his face says it all. Still, he admits, "Can't say I have."

"Well, cheers," I say, holding my drink up to him. He raises his Jack and Coke, and our glasses clink before we each take a sip.

When Ford puts his glass down on the small round table we had taken in the bar area, he says, "Okay… I know we don't have but about an hour before you leave to go meet Frannie of Do or Dye for mud masks, wine, cheese, and corny movies, but let's utilize the time wisely and start with you giving me a rundown of your life's history."

Amazement covers my face. "So this really isn't a booty call? Or an attempt at one?"

His lips curl in a sly grin. "I am more than willing to come over to your house after Frannie leaves for a booty call if you want."

I can't help but laugh, but I don't admit I would open my door to him if he came over.

"What do you want to know?" I ask as I start to slowly stir my celery around my drink again.

"How did you get from Sweden to the United States?"

"A plane." I keep a neutrally bland expression on my face.

Ford rolls his eyes at me, and it's a completely endearing maneuver. The man has to be in his early forties by my calculations of stalking him on his firm's website, but that immature display makes him completely sexier for some reason.

I don't make him ask the question again, just give a very brief rundown of my transition from a Swedish citizen to an American citizen. "When I was fourteen, I was approached on the streets of Stockholm by a talent agent. An American talent agent. They wanted me to sign with their agency to do fashion modeling."

Ford places his forearms on the table and leans forward, listening intently. "Not surprised."

I take that as the compliment it was meant to be. Obviously, he has made his attraction to me known in more ways than one. And with those few simple words, he tells me he believes I'm beautiful enough to be a model. It's crazy how I've always doubted that about myself even if I was in a Vogue fashion spread or walked the catwalk in Milan. I never saw in myself what others did, I guess. I also think it was probably the fact I was so young and hadn't had time to let my confidence develop.

I continue my story. "My mother was a model in Sweden. She's a beautiful woman and loved that lifestyle, although she was never quite successful at it. When I was offered the chance to pursue what was really her dream, she sort of forced me to take it. So she and I moved to the States."

"And your father didn't come?" He asks.

"Never knew who my father was," I say with a wry smile. My gaze drops down to my drink for a moment before returning to him. "At least not at that age."

Ford nods, and it's obvious he's filing away further questions about my father. I continue. "Let's just say my modeling career was very good for my mother and me. Actually, let me amend that. It was very good for my mother. I made a lot of money and she managed it, and by manage, I mean spent most of it. She led a very posh lifestyle on my coattails."

There's no mistaking the sympathy in Ford's gaze. I am utterly shocked when he makes an astute observation about a woman that he doesn't know. "I guarantee you she didn't do that for long, though, did she?"

That simple question tells me Ford has figured out in a very short time I'm not the type of woman who will be walked all over for long. He knows enough to realize I would never let anybody take advantage of me, even if it's my mother. It means a lot he recognizes that, because it's probably the personality trait I'm most proud of. If I have a daughter one day, it's what I will encourage her the most in.

I shake my head and give him a smile. "When I was seventeen, I got myself emancipated from my mother. I stopped modeling, got control of what money was left—which wasn't much—and because I had graduated high school early with homeschooling, I went off to college, much to my mother's dismay."

Ford cocks his head curiously. "Was your mother's dismay in the fact you chose an education over modeling or that she'd lost her gravy train?"

Laughing, I point my finger playfully at him. "Both. You win."

Ford picks up his drink and takes a sip. He sets the glass down, and his words are measured. "Let me guess… college at seventeen, graduated at age twenty and went off to law school. Had your degree by about the time you were twenty-three, and then was well on your way to becoming an animal lawyer."

Chuckling, I roll my fingertip around the edge of my drink glass. "Almost. I started out doing corporate law in Georgia. It wasn't until I saw someone abusing a dog out on the street that my career path changed."

"What did you do?"

"I beat the guy up with my briefcase and stole his dog," I say simply.

I'm not prepared for the bark of laughter that erupts or the respect shining in his eyes. He gives an amused shake of his head. "You are something else, V."

He picks up his glass to take another sip, and I do the same. When we set our glasses down, he asks, "What brought you to North Carolina?"

"My ex-husband transferred his residency from Emory's university hospital to Duke. When I passed the North Carolina bar exam, I used that as an opportunity to start my career in animal law."

Ford's eyebrow raises. "You were married to a doctor?"

I nod. "A neurosurgeon."

"And how long have you been divorced?"

"About two years." And I can't believe it's been that long. I also can't believe it had been more than two years since I'd had sex. I'd been through a rather dry spell after my marriage fell apart, but Ford has proven it's kind of like riding a bike.

"Have you ever been married?" I ask.

Ford laughs and shakes his head a little too vigorously. "No way."

If I were sitting beside him, I would probably give him a playful punch on his shoulder. Instead, I have to say, "You say it like it's a disease or something."

Ford shakes his head a little more vigorously, and his expression turns slightly apologetic. "No, it's not that. It's just… marriages are forever and well… Let's just say a few months for me is a long time."

My eyes widen, and I drawl, "You don't have a lot of staying power."

"I haven't so far," he says. "And to be clear, we're talking about relationships—not my stamina in the bedroom."

"At least you're honest," I say, and I mean it as a true compliment. Ford has his ways, and I can't necessarily say that they are wrong knowing what I know about marriage now. Still, I can't help asking. "You don't feel like you're missing out on anything?"

Ford shrugs, and it's not casual in any way. If anything, it conveys he's given this some thought. "I'm not sure. It's not like I'm anti-relationship or anything. I guess I've just been so busy with my career. There's never been anyone I've met who has held my interest for very long or who I wanted to share my life with."

I can't help but tease. "So what you're saying is I shouldn't be making any long-term plans with you?"

I had hoped he would get I was joking. Instead, his

expression remains somber. "Do you want to get married again?"

I give the same type of shrug Ford had just given me. I honestly don't know the answer. However, unlike Ford, I have not really thought about it. There's been no reason to. "What is marriage anyway? A piece of paper. What does that even mean in today's day and age with the rate of divorce?"

"I've had those same thoughts myself," Ford admits, but then leans even closer over the table. "But I watched my best friend Leary fall in love with a man a few years ago, and they've actually given me hope for humanity."

My insides melt over the affection in his voice for his friend. I grin. "Maybe there's hope for you yet, Mr. Daniels."

He stares at me a moment, and I wonder how this conversation got so serious so fast. I hardly know him at all. The fact we fell so fast into bed leads me to believe there is nothing of substance at this table other than perhaps the two drinks sitting before us. I try to think of something light and airy to say, to bring us back around to a fun, flirty conversation.

But to my dismay, Ford turns his wrist over and glances at his watch. His eyes come back to me, and he says, "Look at the time. We need to get out of here so you can go meet Frannie."

I check my cell phone I had set on the table. I can't believe we've been here for almost an hour talking. The swell of disappointment tells me that my rationale is probably not seeing this as a one-night stand or a booty call. I don't know if he can do anything more after a few months, but I do know I want to see him again.

Surprisingly, there's hardly anything left of my drink. I pick it up and drain the last of it as Ford does the same with his Jack and Coke. After, he pulls his wallet out and leaves some money on the bar for a tip.

Ford walks me to my car, his hand at my elbow as we cross the parking lot. When we get there, he turns me to face him and steps in close. Peering down, he asks, "I've got two tickets tomorrow night to see the North Carolina Symphony? Would you like to go with me?"

I can't help wrinkling my nose. "I'm sorry, but that's sort of not my thing."

Ford's lips tip up. "You don't like classical music?"

"Oh, I like classical music well enough, but my days of fancy dresses and elegant galas are kind of in the past for me. I don't even own a dress that would be suitable enough."

Ford blinks in surprise. "You're kidding me. I get your practice may not be as lucrative as mine, but you were married to a neurosurgeon. Surely you had a cocktail dress or two when you divorced?"

His tone is light and teasing, and that's the only way I can take what he's saying.

"Well, believe it or not… My ex-husband wasn't into that sort of thing either. We never did fancy stuff, and he worked all the time. I think the last time I got to dress up all fancy was my wedding. And probably prior to that was when I was still modeling."

"I don't know whether to be sad about that," Ford says, seeming perplexed.

I laugh and lightly touch his arm. "Maybe we can do something else another time," I suggest.

Ford surprises me by putting his palms against my face and pulling me in for a kiss. It's not soft, but it's not sensual either. It feels more like a claiming. When he pulls back, he murmurs, "I hate classical music and the symphony. I thought I would impress you with the fact I had tickets, which really belong to the senior partner at our firm and are available for the taking if I want. What would you like to do tomorrow night?"

I stare at him a moment before trying to be the mature voice of reason. "You know we're on opposing sides of a legal case. This is probably not a good idea."

"Fuck that," Ford says. "I can be impartial in court next week, and I guarantee you can as well. We're both professionals. When it boils right down to it, this case has nothing to do with what's between us."

"At least not for a few months," I quip, teasing him about his self-imposed deadline where his interest in me will purportedly wane.

Ford grins, and I'm not sure what it means that we can joke around about the fact that this is probably a temporary thing between us. "Exactly. So let's make the most of our time together."

I study him for a moment before I incline my head. "All right then… Dinner tomorrow night."

CHAPTER 7

Ford

It's 6:59 PM when I knock on the front door. She doesn't have a doorbell; I doubt any of these houses do. She lives in an older, slightly rundown neighborhood not far from her office.

It is not exactly the safest area to be in.

Still, her house is cute and well maintained. The cement board siding looks new, and the bright white color contrasts with black shutters, giving it a charming appearance.

The front porch is hardly big enough to hold me but it does have a portico-type roof that extends over it and shields me from the slight mist of rain that's going on.

There's the distinct sound of a deadbolt unlatching and a chain sliding off the track, then Viveka is standing before me in the open doorway. When we made plans for dinner yesterday, I did not give her any indication of what to expect, only that I'd pick her up at seven.

From her appearance, she clearly thought I would be

taking her out to a fancy restaurant. The woman may not own any fancy cocktail dresses, but she rocks a little black dress like no one I've ever seen before. It's simple with a neckline that's cut severely across her chest just below her collarbone so not even a whisper of cleavage is showing. Her bare arms are amazing and the hem is right above her knees, which still shows plenty of her beautiful legs.

That I hope to fucking God will be wrapped around my waist tonight.

Viveka's hair is down—it's wavy and loose, parted down the middle in soft waves that fall all around her shoulders. Her makeup is impeccable and by that, I mean it doesn't look like she's wearing any. Her skin is dewy and flawless. Her blue eyes are sparkling inside a magnificent rim of long dark lashes. Lips with a pale gloss on them but they are full and pink, and I also know what they would look good wrapped around.

While I shamelessly ogle her from head to toe, she is clearly doing the same to me. Her eyes run over me, and she says, "I'm obviously overdressed for whatever you have planned tonight."

I'm dressed super casual in jeans, a well-worn button down, and a pair of chukka boots.

My lips curve, and I tip my head toward the large paper bag I'm resting against my hip. "I thought we'd cook dinner here."

Without hesitation, Viveka pulls the door open wider and motions me in. As I walk past her, she asks, "You're going to cook for me?"

I flash what I hope is a charming smile. "No. I suck at cooking. I was kind of hoping you were good at it. If not, we can order in."

She tips her head back and laughs before shutting the door. Inclining her head to the left, she tells me, "You can go put that stuff in the kitchen. I'm going to go change into something more casual."

"Or… You can just go naked," I suggest with a waggle of my eyebrows.

She smirks before giving me her back to head down a short hallway I assume leads to her bedroom. I call, "Your ass is amazing in that dress. You could leave it on."

She wags her finger up in the air without even slowing her pace. "You're so bad."

You have no idea, V.

My gaze sweeps around her small living room. This house may be old, but some work has been done on it. She's got glossy hardwood floors, and the walls are painted a light, mint green. The fireplace appears recently refurbished to be fit with gas logs. The furniture is simple and modern. A sleek cream couch on one side with two butter-yellow armchairs with chrome accents on the other. There is a simple wooden table separating the furniture and a set of bookshelves on one wall filled to capacity. The style is light and unrestrained. It's like a fucking IKEA showroom, or more accurately, a nod to her Swedish roots.

I walk through an open doorway that leads into the kitchen. It's also been recently remodeled, with pricey cabinets and granite countertops.

Based on what little I know of Viveka's law practice, I have to assume these upgrades to the house came before she purchased it.

I set the bag on a small butcher block table at the end of the L-shaped counter and pull the contents out. I'm folding the bag up when she walks in.

And if I thought she was stunning in a little black dress, let me just say the woman can rock a pair of sweats. Coupled with a simple t-shirt, she looks unbearably sexy. And at the same time, so beautiful she could easily model her outfit on the catwalk.

The last thing I notice is that her feet are bare with pale pink painted toes. It tells me she's comfortable with my suggestion we stay in.

She eyeballs the items I had placed on the counter. Raising a sleek, delicately arched eyebrow of pale blonde, she asks, "A frozen pizza?"

I shrug and lean against the counter, placing one elbow on the granite. "It's a fancy frozen pizza from Whole Foods."

She points at two other small bags I laid on the wooden butcher block. "What's in those?"

"I'm glad you asked," I say. I push away from the counter and reach for the first smaller bag. It's pink with white tissue poking out from the top. I hand it over to her.

She gives me a look... surprise and uncertainty... before she reaches inside and pulls out a plastic bag filled with bath bombs.

"It's not mud masks, but perhaps you would like to take a bath later," I say.

Her lips tip upward as she gazes from the gift to me. "Sadly, I don't have a bathtub."

I wince and take the bag back. "That's just awful. I'll take these back to my apartment and we'll try them out in my bathtub at some point."

Viveka chuckles. "I seriously doubt the two of us are going to fit into a bathtub together."

"Didn't you check out my tub at all when you were at my apartment? It's massive. We'll totally fit in there together."

She gives me the cutest smirk. "We'll see. But what's in the last bag?"

It's a plastic Target bag and I open it, pulling out three DVDs. "Cheesy eighties' films. I figured we could watch one tonight."

Her eyes light up, and Viveka snatches the movies from me. She flips through them while grinning. "*Big Trouble in Little China, Dirty Dancing*, and... hey, *Flash Gordon*. That's actually one of my favorite movies."

"You've got to be kidding me?" I ask in disbelief. Because I seem to remember it being incredibly stupid, although the music is amazing.

"Oh my God… I swear. One of my favorites. We are so watching this one tonight."

Her enthusiasm is contagious, and I realize I'm looking forward to it. Not the actual movie, but just being with her.

Viveka puts the movies down and grabs the frozen pizza, turning it over to peruse the instructions. She walks to her oven while she reads and then turns it on. While she rifles through a lower cabinet, she says, "Help yourself to some beer that's in the refrigerator if you want. I also have a couple bottles of wine, or I might even have a bottle of vodka somewhere."

I move to the refrigerator and ask, "What do you want?"

"Just a bottle of water. Frannie and I overindulged in the wine last night, and the thought of any alcohol makes me slightly nauseated."

Chuckling, I open the refrigerator and pull two bottles out. I hand her one and open the other.

Viveka merely sets the water down on the counter. To my surprise, she hops up to sit down beside it. Because of her height, it was effortless for her to do so. That maneuver along with the way she's dressed—her free-spirit attitude—makes her seem like a teenage girl. And while teenage girls aren't my thing, I can tell you the carefree way in which she carries herself is.

"You seriously have never had a long-term relationship?" she asks. Her eyes cut over to the bath bombs and movies. When she turns back to me, she says, "Because you're really good at the dating stuff."

My tone has a slight censure when I respond. "Just because I'm not big on long-term relationships doesn't mean I can't be romantic and doting."

Viveka shrugs. "I suppose that could be true."

"Be honest," I demand with a grin. "Would you have rather gone out for an expensive and elegant dinner tonight, or would you rather stay in and eat frozen pizza?"

"They're both good date ideas," she hedges. "I would've been happy with either one."

That doesn't tell me what I need to know. I lay it all out there so we can get on to enjoying our evening. "Because I don't want you to think I'm expecting anything of you because we're here in your home and not a fancy restaurant surrounded by other people."

Viveka blinks in surprise, and her face softens. "I don't think that."

"I hope not. Because after pizza and Flash Gordon, I am prepared to walk out of here and go home alone."

"I appreciate the sentiment, but I'm a big girl, Ford. I also don't have any regrets about sleeping with you already, and if you do stay the night with me, I'm quite sure I won't have regrets about that, either."

We stare at each other, the silence that envelopes us quite comfortable as we consider the exchange of words we just had. It seems we both reaffirmed this is casual, and that sex is still on the table. Yet, at the same time, I offered her an out if she didn't want to go there and I truly meant it. I wouldn't be disappointed if we don't end the evening with sex. That is off character for me, especially because this woman completely rocked my world the other night.

The oven makes a small chime, and Viveka slides off the counter. She puts the frozen pizza on a round baking stone.

"This house is really nice," I say as she opens the oven door. "Not in the best of neighborhoods, but it's clearly had extensive remodeling."

She nods as she slides the pizza onto the top rack. When she closes it, she turns to face me. "My ex-husband Adam bought it for me when we divorced. He gave me some money to do the remodeling as well."

"That was nice," I drawl slowly, not really sure if that is a good thing or bad thing.

She smiles. "That was his guilt. He wanted me to have a good start post-divorce."

"Guilt?" Because if that fucker cheated on her, I would so kick his ass.

She gives a hard shake of her head. "He worked a lot. There wasn't a lot of time for me. The marriage just… fizzled. His medical practice was more important than me, so when we finally decided to call it quits, he was very generous in the divorce settlement."

She doesn't sound bitter or broken up about it at all. Not an overly harsh word about him, and I have to assume she must have wanted the divorce to happen.

"Is that why you can afford to have a law practice that doesn't make a lot of money?"

"Not really. I put all the cash settlement into investment accounts. Because I don't make a killing at my law practice, you can imagine I don't have much to put in retirement. So I pretty much live hand to mouth on what I make. But I've made it work for me, and I wouldn't change a thing."

I can't help but be honest. "It seems like a struggle."

Viveka chuckles. "I'm guessing your peer circle doesn't include attorneys like me. It must be shocking to see how I practice and live."

"I find you utterly fascinating," I say truthfully. "So, for example, how much are you being paid to defend this stupid woodpecker?"

I get a chastising look in return. "First, the woodpecker is not stupid. Second, I'm not making a dime. I took the case pro bono. In fact, a lot of what I do is pro bono."

I blink in surprise. Not that she does free legal work, but it would be impractical for any attorney who owns their own business to do a lot of it. "You're kidding me."

"I'm not kidding you. Adam paid for the house. My car is paid for and still running. I'm just a regular person, Ford, who makes do with what she has. I clip coupons, and I shop at Costco for bulk items to save money. Frannie cuts my hair for free. One of the veterinarians I work with on animal cruelty cases treats my animals for free. And if I have frozen pizza at night, it's the three-dollar variety from Food Lion and not the twelve-dollar variety from Whole Foods."

I stare at her with a mixture of emotions coursing through me. I can't tell if she's upset she has to explain these things to me or she's amused by my inability to relate. She doesn't seem pissed or offended in any way. "The expression on your face says it all."

I give a hard shake of my head as I step up to her. My hands go to her waist where I hold her lightly. "It's just... I've never met another person like you. Not an attorney. A person." Viveka looks up at me, and I notice for the first time she has a thin layer of gold separating her pupil from her iris.

Her voice is soft and almost apologetic. "We don't exactly run in the same circles."

I have to agree with that. My world is vastly different than hers, from both a legal perspective and a personal one. "All the attorneys I know are in it for the money."

She tilts her head. Thankfully, there's no condemnation in her eyes. "Including you?"

I breathe in through my nose and let out a pained sigh. "I can't lie to you... I like my lifestyle, but I love the law, too. I would practice law for a lot less money, but I've worked hard to get where I am. The fact I can charge top dollar to people like Drake Powell came through a lot of blood, sweat and tears."

Her warm hands go to my chest, and she's quick to reassure me. "And I think that's amazing. I want you to know I don't hold anything against you because your practice is so different than mine. You have every right to your type of practice, and I think it's great you've got the ability to charge jackasses like Drake Powell an arm and a leg."

I chuckle and tease her. "I'd like to lock the two of you into a room together. I would put money on you to kick his ass."

"That guy is a certified schmuck," she says with disgust in her voice. "You should've heard some of the things he said to me before you got to the construction site."

My body stiffens. "Like what?"

Viveka steps away from me with a husky laugh of amusement as she checks on the pizza. I try not to stare at her ass overly hard when she bends at the waist to peer in the window.

When she turns to me, she gives a dismissive wave of her hand. "Oh, you know… how some men can be. Bullying and sexual innuendo in an effort to assert power and control over a woman."

I shake my head. "No, I don't know that."

How would I know that? I don't do that to women. My male friends don't do that to women. Maybe back in college there were some but—

"It was nothing," she assures with a smile. "Besides I'm a big girl. When I was modeling, I had to grow a very thick skin, very fast. Constantly being told you're just a little too heavy or you're getting a little old looking can get to you."

If she wanted to get my mind off Drake Powell, that worked. I practically sputter, "You were what… like fifteen or sixteen?"

She gives a wry smile. "I know. Crazy, right? But modeling is a brutal business."

I don't even want to imagine, but I'm thankful Viveka escaped it as quickly as she did. I firmly believe she kept her good graces and infectious free-spirited attitude because she did break away. She may have the beauty of a supermodel, which, I'm not going to lie, is what first attracted me to her. But it's the things inside I'm finding that clearly sets her apart from all the other women I've known.

♦

SHE'S GODDAMNED BEAUTIFUL like this.

Palms pressed to her headboard, back arched, and ass tipped up.

Panting for it.

"Christ," I mutter as I fist my cock and feed it into her.

"Oh, Ford," she groans as I bottom out, and her

head falls forward.

All that glorious pale hair curtains her off from me and that won't do. I grab it all up, transfer it to one hand, and pull it so her head comes up. My free hand goes to her hip, and she twists her neck to look over her shoulder at me, eyes glazed and needy.

"I'll give it to you, V. Just hold on."

So she does. Palms slide up, fingers curl over the top of the headboard, and her arms lock tight at the elbows.

It's a good thing because I ride her rough, fisting that silky hair. Her pussy gloves me tight, and her cries echo off the walls all around me.

Frantic, crazy fucking. I'm not sure I know how to do it any other way with this woman. She brings out the animal in me, and more importantly, she seems to enjoy that beast.

Viveka comes without warning, her back bowing and then arching as she slams backward onto me.

"Oh God, oh God, oh God," she chants.

The pressure in my balls swells, and I have a sublime moment where everything just seems to stop. My cock lodged deep, my knuckles holding her hair so tight they graze the back of her head.

One last tight squeeze of her around me and I explode.

A feral growl tears free of me, and it feels so fucking good it almost hurts.

Almost unbearable.

But then, time starts again, and I'm overwhelmed with sensations. The smell of sex, her tiny pants, and the sheen of sweat on her back. My cock pulses inside of her, and a terrible groan rumbles free.

Holy shit, that was…

I don't know what that was.

I release her hair and ease out of her body. She collapses to the mattress and gives a soft, beautiful sigh of satisfaction. "That was… well, I can't come up with the right words."

She can't see my smile, but she feels it when I bend over to kiss her shoulder. "Be right back."

I hit her bathroom up to ditch the condom. As I'm washing my hands, I glance into the mirror and see my hair sticking up all over the place. That brings another smile to my face. Her fingers spent a lot of time in my hair while I ate her out earlier.

When I get back to her room, I realize I don't want to leave. I was pretty sure we'd have sex tonight, but I'd always envisioned I'd leave after.

But Viveka is on her side facing me, one hand tucked under her pillow, the other fingering the sheet she'd pulled over her body. She doesn't say a word, just peels it back and lifts it up. I let my eyes run over her body, lingering on the most fantastic pair of tits I've ever had in my mouth or hands. With some reluctance, I let my gaze move from her breasts to her face.

It's that look right there that has me making the

decision to stay.

I don't take her invitation to get in on that side of the bed, though. I walk around, slide in behind her under the sheet, and pull her into me. Her ass settles against my happy, well-spent dick, and I curl an arm around her belly.

We don't say a word to each other. Before long, I hear her breathing slow down.

I close my eyes and go to sleep with a smile still on my face.

CHAPTER 8

Viveka

I FLIP THE bacon on the sizzling griddle. Cooking always eases my anxiety, and yes, I'm slightly nervous to have a man sleeping in my bed right now. It's been a long time since I've woken up to that, so I did the best thing I could to save my sanity. I slid out from under his hold and decided to make breakfast.

Cooking keeps my hands busy and my mind from overanalyzing things. There's a lot of stuff to be confused about this morning. What I thought would be an impersonal booty call last night took a different direction than I had anticipated.

Now, I don't know what to think.

I give another flip of the bacon before pulling out a plate from the cabinet. After covering it with a few sheets of paper towels, I pull the slices off the griddle to drain. I snag a strawberry out of the bowl of fruit I had cut up earlier and pop it into my mouth.

Then I freeze.

I can hear Ford's footsteps coming down the short hall and through the living room. I brace for what may either be a shameful confrontation or a pleasant greeting.

Ford steps into the kitchen, and I actually get tingles between my legs when I see him. He slipped on his jeans, but that's all he has on. Hair messed up, feet bare, and an unforgettable chest with amazing abs I spent a great deal of time feeling up last night.

Mostly because the two of us slept wrapped up in each other's arms.

My cheeks flush with warmth as I think about the wild and crazy sex we had followed by an intimate cuddle that turned into satisfying slumber.

Ford's eyes lock with mine. I think he will make a quick excuse to leave because that's what you do after a booty call, right? And besides, Ford has on more than one occasion made it clear he's not relationship material. And this is generally okay. I'm not searching for one either.

But I can't deny I like the guy.

Forget about what he does to me in bed, I have absolutely enjoyed every minute of conversation I've had with him. It's been seamless and perfectly natural. Moreover, he has shown a genuine interest in me as a person. For much of my life, I have only been noticed and interacted with because of my looks. Many men don't even want to hear a thing I have to say.

But not Ford. He peppered me with questions relentlessly while we munched on pizza and watched Flash Gordon. In just a few short hours, I can now say he is someone who knows practically everything there is to know about my life, as lamely normal as it has been up to date.

The tingles move from between my legs into my belly when his lips curve up in appreciation as he stares at me. I had thrown on a short silk robe that was hanging on the back of my bathroom door and had put my hair up in a haphazard ponytail.

"How is it that you are sexier and more beautiful every time I lay eyes on you?" Ford asks.

And he is not teasing me. He is absolutely serious with that question, and the tingles spread through my entire body.

"How is it that you manage to say and do things that make me like you even more every time you open your mouth?" I ask in return.

"You had an up close and personal experience with my mouth last night," he reminds me.

I can't control the deeper blush that warms my face. My pale Swedish skin always betrays my embarrassment.

"I like that you like my mouth," Ford murmurs.

God, do I like his mouth. He made me come in under a minute with it before he flipped me on my stomach, pulled me up to my hands and knees, and fucked me from behind.

I think perhaps he might be able to read my face

because his expression softens, and he takes a step toward me. Unfortunately, his foot catches on the huge bowl of water I have on the floor for my dogs. It's stainless steel and makes quite the racket when it knocks into the refrigerator and spills water over the top.

"Shit," he says apologetically. He makes a grab for some paper towels off the counter. "I'll clean that up."

I laugh and point out, "It's only water, Ford. It's not going to hurt anything."

He gives me a sheepish grin, and then starts to bend down to mop up the water when he freezes. "Dogs," he says, sounding completely perplexed.

"What about them?"

He straightens up and turns to stare at me, the fistful of paper towels forgotten in his hand. "You have dogs. Where are they?"

Understanding dawns, and I give him a soft smile. "I had Frannie take them for the night. While I didn't want to assume you were going to stay, I figured if you did I would at least make it a little more comfortable for you. I know you're not much of a dog person."

"You see," Ford grumbles, throwing his hands out, "It drives me nuts that people automatically think that."

"Oh, poor baby," I tease as I turn back to the bacon. "But you're the one who told me you didn't like dog slobber."

"And you do?" he asks me.

Touché.

"It's not my favorite thing in the world," I admit grudgingly. "But the price is well worth the joy they bring to me."

He's nothing but pure stealth because I don't hear him come up behind me. His hands go to my waist before circling around my stomach, and he draws me back into his body. I feel the rough scratch of his jeans against my legs and the warmth of his chest through the material of my robe.

Ford rests his chin on my shoulder and murmurs in my ear, "Next time, you do not have to send your dogs away. I will learn to like them."

Of all the ways Ford has made me feel since I've met him, there's no describing the swelling within my chest over those simple words. My dogs are important to me. They're like my children. And it absolutely killed me to send them away last night.

I had hoped if I had a relationship one day in the future, it would be with a man who was an animal lover. And while I can't say Ford is such a man, the mere fact he is going to try speaks volumes.

I give a cough to clear my throat and reach for the bacon. Ford releases me and says, "Do you have some coffee?"

"The Keurig is right there," I say, jerking my head toward the machine to my left. "I'll take another cup too, if you don't mind. Cups in the cabinet above."

"A gorgeous woman making breakfast on a Sunday

morning?" he says with a chuckle. "I absolutely do not mind making you a cup of coffee."

After I pull the bacon off, I work on mixing up some pancake batter.

"Tell me about your dogs," Ford says. The tingles take over once again when he adds, "Because I guarantee you I'll be back in your bed sooner rather than later."

"Both of them are rescues." I ladle hotcakes onto the griddle. "A golden retriever named Daisy, and my Pomeranian mix is a cocky little male who thinks he's the boss in this house. I named him Butch."

"Daisy and Butch," Ford says as if testing their names to see how they roll off his tongue. "Got it."

"It's a good thing they weren't here last night," I say as an afterthought. "The noises we were making would have freaked Butch out."

"You mean the noises *you* were making," Ford counters.

I flip pancakes and laugh.

I don't know why I feel compelled to tell him, but maybe it's gratitude for his excellent lovemaking abilities. I just know I've never had a man devote the type of attention to me that Ford does when it comes to pleasure. "It's been over two years since I've had sex. I imagine I have been making all kinds of sounds."

Ford doesn't respond, so I'm compelled to look over my shoulder. His face is impassive. "Two years?"

I turn back to the pancakes and say lightly, "Well, I

know for a stud such as yourself who cycles through women as often as you do, it might seem unbelievable, but…"

My voice trails off as I realize this might make me sound overly pathetic.

Ford moves to my side as I continue to monitor the pancakes. His hand comes up, and he slides his knuckles across my jaw. It's a move intended to get my attention, and I can't help but turn my head toward him.

"I don't understand," he says softly. "You're an incredibly beautiful and outgoing woman. You have a lot to offer someone. Why have you remained alone for two years?"

I give a shrug and turn back to the pancakes, sliding the edge of the spatula under one to check whether it's done. It's not so I turn back to him. "I really don't like talking bad about anybody, and please know I'm only telling this to you because you asked an important question. But my sex life with my husband was not all that great. My sex life with the two other men prior to him wasn't all that spectacular either. My knowledge of sex is clearly limited, but it's what I believed sex felt like. Honestly, I didn't feel like I was missing much the past two years. I definitely got more enjoyment out of my vibrator."

A gleam enters Ford's eyes. His voice goes low and husky. "You have toys? Excellent. We'll talk about those later and in more depth, but I have to ask… how do you feel about sex now?"

I don't think he's angling for compliments, but I decide to keep on the straight and narrow and give him my full honesty. "You have to know you're completely different. I mean, you heard the sounds I make right?"

He slides in closer to me, his voice going even lower. His hand comes up to rest on my hip. "Tell me exactly what it is you like about what I do to you?"

My throat feels tight and closed off, but I manage to ask him, "Why?"

My legs practically buckle when he says, "So I can give you more of it. I like pleasuring you, V."

I suck in a sharp breath through my nose, and let it slide out slowly between my teeth. My voice is barely a whisper. "I like that you're so in control. I like that you do what you want and somehow seem to know it's exactly what I like. It's the control you have over me I like, and I'm not sure what that says about me."

"It doesn't say anything particular about you. You like what you like, and I like that you like it."

He leans in and brushes his lips along my jaw. "Your pancakes are gonna burn."

I startle and turn toward the griddle, lifting the edge of a pancake to check. They are perfect and ready to come off.

Ford chuckles as he steps away from me, and I plate up the food for both of us. We walk over to the small kitchen table on the other side of the butcher block island and settle in to eat and sip at our coffee.

"Okay, I'm going to ask you something I swear to God has nothing to do with inflating my ego. But you said you like the control I have over you. I'm just wondering… your ex-husband was a surgeon, which means he's probably confident and has a healthy ego. I guess I'm curious—as sort of a human study—why he didn't take care of you in the bedroom?"

I spread butter over my pancakes. "Well, Adam as a surgeon was definitely in control and confident, but he was also meticulous and efficient. You translate how that might work out with sex."

"He never saw to your needs, did he?" Ford asks, but he doesn't even need the answer. The question was absolutely rhetorical.

I put my knife down and look at the gorgeous man sitting across from me while we have a completely naked conversation about my previous love life. "I didn't know I had needs to be honest. Not until that first night with you when I was getting ready to leave. The way you dragged your finger up the inside of my thigh, and I don't know… I just ached. I actually hurt from the need that consumed me, and I had never felt it before."

Ford's face softens, yet his eyes seem to blaze with heat over the memory. His voice causes me to shiver. "You shoved my hand between your legs. It was one of the hottest things I've ever experienced."

My voice goes to a whisper. "I needed something,

and I never knew it until then."

"Did I give it to you?" he asks me softly.

"Yes."

"I'll give it to you any time you ask me to, V." His eyes reflect the same promise as his words.

I nod, knowing I will ask him for it. I'll also give it to him.

"I'll do the same for you," I say.

Ford gives me a sexy grin and points his fork at me. "Looking forward to it."

I stare at him in fascination from the way he can so easily bounce between serious sex talk and mischievous teasing. With a slight tilt of my head that's swimming with curiosity, I ask, "What is this? Between us, I mean."

"It's definitely not a one-night stand," Ford says, and I'm relieved he doesn't seem perturbed. "I want to keep seeing you, and I hope you feel the same."

"And the fact that you and I have a case against each other?" I ask.

"We agree to leave that out of our relationship."

The tingles ripple up my spine over the word *relationship*. It's not a word that has been important to me for a very long time unless my friendship with Frannie and my love for my animals counts. I'm still amazed how quickly my life has changed in just a few days. Who knew the thought of a relationship with a man like Ford is something that would appeal to me?

I also remember I'm dealing with a man who self-admittedly will want to move on from me at some point. I know I'll end up getting hurt, yet it doesn't scare me away.

CHAPTER 9

Ford

THIS IS ONE of my absolute favorite places to be. Dark paneled walls and the raised judge's bench set the tone for the authority in the courtroom, along with swivel chairs in the jury box and the heavy wooden tables where counsel will sit—the plaintiff's table closest to the jury and the defense table on the other side. It's a typical courtroom. Yet, I never fail to get a thrill stepping into one.

I walk up the main aisle and unbutton my suit jacket. Drake Powell stands in front of the first row behind the defense table along with several of his cronies I recognize. A few other major real estate developers and some of the larger contractors they deal with. They all came here today because this case could potentially affect them all. If the judge rules against Drake Powell, a landslide of cases from the activist groups in this area could increase and target other building projects. A lot of money is on the line.

I will admit, the fact a lot of money could potentially be lost is the one thing that's driving me to stick with this case.

I talked to Midge yesterday after I had finished preparing my brief to hand in to the judge. While my ethical duty is to Drake Powell to ensure he gets the best representation, I have a personal loyalty to Midge. And the fact she's an investor in this project is why I really need to be on my A-game.

Of course, Midge was Midge. Didn't matter she probably had millions riding on this real estate deal; she told me I was not to consider that in any of the legal decisions or strategies I would be making in this case. She demanded I take her completely out of the equation.

Yeah… That's not going to happen. Midge likes to think she can control everything that happens within the firm and among her people, and she likes to think she can take care of herself. I'm not going to overtly disabuse her of that notion, but I'm also going to do whatever I can to protect the financial investment Midge made without deviating in my duties to Drake. Luckily, their interests are the same.

Regretfully, that means I cannot pull any punches when it comes to Viveka. I'll have to fight hard and possibly dirty within the bounds of the law. I'm hoping this won't be a problem, but we both agreed this case stays out of our life and out of our bed. It's going to be a precarious line to walk, but I'm more than willing to walk it. I'm not ready to give Viveka up.

The bigger problem I've had to deal with has been my own client. Drake's been an overbearing asshole the last few days, breathing down my neck about this case.

But I don't need to like my clients. I only need to be legally competent to represent them and make sure their checks won't bounce. I try to ignore the fact that while I've never had any qualms with taking cases I don't necessarily agree with, going up against Viveka is slightly unsettling to me. It's not what I want to be doing with her. I don't want to fight and argue case law. I want to watch corny movies and spend a great deal of time between her pretty legs.

And I don't foresee me getting tired of being between them anytime soon. I spent essentially the entire weekend at her house. When Sunday evening rolled around and I needed to leave, I found it incredibly difficult to do so.

And it's not that we spent the entire weekend fucking. There was plenty of that, but there was other stuff, too. We went to the gym and worked out Sunday morning after breakfast. I then did something utterly preposterous—I went over to Reeve and Leary's house and borrowed their dog to take it for a walk in the park with Viv and her two dogs. Leary wasn't at home when I showed up, but I could tell by Reeve's expression as I was leaving that he was going to relish telling her all about how I came to borrow their dog to impress a woman.

What the fuck ever.

When I showed back up at Viveka's house with dog in tow, the smile she gave me was worth any amount of shit I was going to get from Reeve and Leary about this.

I didn't see Viv yesterday, though.

It was Monday and the start of the new workweek. More importantly, it was one day before the hearing was scheduled where we would battle against each other. We both had to prepare, and we couldn't afford to be distracted by the other. When I left her Sunday night, there was a shit ton of making out on her front porch before I left. It was torture pulling away from her and the only saving grace was that I knew I could have her again Tuesday night.

Assuming nothing terrible happens today in court that would change anything between us.

"Hey, Ford," Drake calls. I set my briefcase on the table as he motions me over to him.

When I reach him, I take a moment to shake everyone's hands. It's a good old boys network of builders and contractors. They stick together.

"Got a joke for you," he says with lewd grin.

"Oh, yeah," I ask, pasting an affable smile on my face. I'm suspicious he's in such a good mood. If I didn't know our presiding judge so well—Lana Boyer—and how above reproach she is, I would have thought he'd paid her off.

"Two trees are next to each other in the forest," he

says with a snicker, and the other guys standing around all snicker. He's clearly told the joke to them already. "A birch and a beech. A sapling sprouts up between them, but they don't know whose it is."

I smile, and it occurs to me that Drake Powell is not only a blowhard, but he's a creep as well.

He continues. "A woodpecker shows up and lands on the sapling. The trees asks, 'We can't tell whose sapling that is. Is it a son of a birch or son of a beech?'."

I'm still smiling, waiting for the punchline.

"The woodpecker says, 'It's neither, but it is the best piece of ash I've ever put my pecker in.'"

Drake cracks up laughing, as do the other men. I force a chuckle and turn toward the table, intent on pulling out my supporting documents to appear busy so Drake will leave me alone.

"Say, Ford..." I turn back to Drake. He doesn't make any effort to lower his voice when he asks, "What's the worst that would happen if I just moved forward with clearing the property? Just cut the damn trees down."

"It's a year in prison for each animal and fifty grand in fines," I say dryly. Drake probably would risk the prison time, but he loves money too much to do it.

"Well, fuck," he grumbles. I turn quickly back to the table to hide my smile.

"Would you look at that fine piece that just walked in?" one of the guys says with clear appreciation in his voice. My hackles rise before I even turn to the courtroom door, knowing it's Viveka who elicited such a comment.

While I would like nothing more than to see her, turning that way puts me in direct collusion with this group of assholes ogling her so I open my briefcase and try to ignore them.

"I'd like to put my pecker in that," Drake mutters, and the other guys start snickering. I ball my fists up, crumpling the fucking brief I'd intended to hand to Judge Boyer.

"Shit," I hiss, trying to smooth it back out.

"You had *that* chained to a tree, Drake, and you didn't take a crack—"

I spin around on the group and growl low. "I suggest you all shut the fuck up. This is a courtroom and a place of respect."

Christ, I sound lame as hell saying that, when what I really want to do is kick the living crap out of each one of them talking this misogynistic bullshit about my woman.

And yet, my hands are tied. I can't do much more than hit them with some harsh words to protect her. Not only would I be arrested for sullying the sanctity of this courtroom, but I'd give away my relationship with Viveka. My hands are thoroughly tied, and I hate it.

Hopefully, this will be the one and only time in my life I feel inadequate when it comes to Viveka.

The men thankfully heed my advice, and a few of them even appear chagrined. Not Drake, though... he stares lewdly at Viveka as she walks down the aisle.

No... she struts.

Fuck, she works the aisle like she's still on the catwalk. I find it sexy and adorable all at the same time. I bet she had that walk so perfected it's like second nature now when she gets on a strip of carpet resembling a runway. She left her modeling days behind a long time ago, but some things stayed with her.

Grinning, I once again turn back to the table and take the remainder of my documents as well as a legal pad out of my briefcase. From the corner of my eye, I see Viveka has reached her own table, so I step over to her for a short word.

Lowering my voice and with my back toward my client, I ask, "You ready for this?"

She gives me a polite nod of her head and the slightest of smiles. It's all for show because her words are sexy and teasing. "Bring it, big guy. Loser has to serve the other in bed tonight."

Jesus fucking Christ. While the thought of Viveka on her knees before me is about the best thing ever, I wouldn't mind losing and doing her bidding. I'd love to see what else she wants to demand of me.

What else I can give her that will rock her world.

"Good luck, V," I murmur.

"Back at ya," she says in the barest of a whisper.

I start to turn away, but she stops me with more soft words. "Regardless of winning and losing, do you want to go out to dinner tonight?"

"Are you asking me out on a date?" I ask.

"Yup."

"Then I'm in."

I get another polite nod of her head. The way it looks to anyone in this courtroom, we just had some cordial and professional words of greeting to each other. I contain my smile on the inside as I move back toward my table, and Drake joins me there.

♦

"Your Honor," I say as I stand up from my chair, tapping my finger on my copy of the brief I'd handed to her. I try not to call it "the Pecker Briefs" in my head because I'm afraid I'll blurt it out to the judge. But Viveka told me Sunday afternoon as we walked the dogs through Pullen Park that's what she named them. I thought it was hilarious, brilliant, and sexy when she said the word *pecker*.

The judge studies me expectantly, and I realize I've just lapsed off into thinking about Viveka. I give a slight shake of my head and continue, "We have not seen proof there are any endangered species on Mr. Powell's land. He has several subcontractors lined up to clear the land, and the losses are mounting. We're talking about excavators, backhoes, bulldozers, and dump trucks.

Thirty plus tree cutters ready to do their job, and they aren't going to get paid until they can do so. Furthermore, every day this job is held up, these subcontractors are going to be forced to take on other work."

I continue, "Mr. Powell has meticulously planned out the scheduling of this project. If he loses these guys, the losses are going to be catastrophic when he can't replace them in a timely manner. We're talking about a multimillion-dollar development, and if the clearing gets delayed, then all the other construction gets delayed. The effect is not only on Mr. Powell and the money he has invested, but it's also for every person who has been contracted to work that land over the next several months. As such, I would respectfully ask the court to lift the injunction until solid proof can be given that there are indeed any of the red-cockaded woodpeckers in actual danger."

Judge Boyer peers at me from the bench, her dark eyes intense with interest and concern for the case before her. She nods and turns to Viveka. "Miss Jones."

As I sit down in my chair, Viveka stands with poise and confidence. She's wearing a simple gray suit—jacket and skirt with a pale pink blouse underneath. Her heels are low, yet she's taller than the men sitting behind me. Who would ever think they could have a chance with someone as smart and beautiful as she is?

"May I approach, Your Honor?" Viveka asks. She picks up a stack of documents from the table.

"You may," Judge Boyer answers.

Viveka steps over to my table and hands me her pecker brief. I don't make eye contact, but start to read it as she steps up to the bench to hand the judge the original. She walks back with the last copy where she lays it back down on the table.

She remains standing as she addresses the court, "Your Honor, I'd like to point you back to my original motion asking for an emergency injunction and the affidavit that was attached by Dr. Alton Granger, a practicing veterinarian here in Wake County and head of the nonprofit group, Justice for All Animals. He identified a nest and visually identified it was occupied by a family. Red-cockaded woodpeckers are non-migratory and cooperative breeding creatures. That means after the female lays eggs in the male's roost, other group members who live there will help to incubate the eggs. While Dr. Granger could not visually confirm eggs, he could see multiple birds in the roost, which suggests there are eggs in there. We are at the beginning of the breeding season, so all of this means it's likely there are going to be hatchlings soon. As such, you have more than sufficient evidence to uphold the continued injunction."

"And what do you propose, Miss Jones?" Judge Boyer clips out. "That Mr. Powell just walk away from the land he paid for and the money invested already?"

"Not at all," Viveka replies smoothly. "But I do think

further study is warranted to come up with a solution. Perhaps a land swap with the federal government to compensate Mr. Powell—"

"There is no law in place," I say, standing from the table to interrupt Viveka, "that will compensate Mr. Powell if that land is sequestered from his use."

Viveka rolls right over me, her gaze never leaving Judge Boyers. "Despite Mr. Daniels pessimistic view of our federal government, the truth of the matter is there's a confirmed sighting of an endangered species, and they are to be protected by the law."

"Fine," I say, turning my eyes to Judge Boyer. "Then Mr. Powell can work around the tree. He can leave it in place and start construction—"

"Have you even done any research on the red-cockaded woodpecker?" Viveka asks smoothly as she turns to me for a moment. Her eyes pin me in place, and it's hot as hell to be honest. She then turns to Judge Boyer, not even wanting an answer to her question. "What Mr. Daniels fails to understand is that because this is a non-migratory, cooperative species, there will undoubtedly be other nests clustered around that tree. They bore cavities exclusively in living pine trees, unlike other woodpeckers that will use dead trees, which are easier to breach. It can take a red-cockaded woodpecker three years to bore out their roost. The average cluster will usually take up approximately ten acres, although clusters have been found to congregate in areas as large as sixty acres."

"That's all fine and good," I say to put in my two cents. "And I did do my research, contrary to what Miss Jones wants to believe. Your Honor, the red-cockaded woodpecker can have clusters as few as one nest in only one acre. As such, we have to consider the possibility this one tree is the only nest that could be in danger."

"And it could be upward of sixty acres or more," Viveka reminds the judge. "And if you let them start tearing down those trees, a significant number of the species could be killed."

Judge Boyer holds up her hand, indicating she's heard enough. "I appreciate that Mr. Powell is in a precarious financial position here, but I certainly can't ignore a federally protected species that could be in danger. You've both made compelling arguments, and I think what we can all agree on is that we don't know enough to make an informed decision. While I'm sure you both have argued the law in these briefs you've handed up, it would make a difference if I knew how many, or as the case may be, how few, birds are present on Mr. Powell's land. As such, I'm going to order that the injunction remain in place for another ten days. In that time, I suggest the two of you hire whatever experts you need to evaluate the land and figure out exactly what we're dealing with. I expect to have your findings presented to me within ten days, and we'll go from there. This court's adjourned."

Judge Boyer doesn't bother rapping her gavel on the wooden top of her desk. Not many judges do that nowadays. Instead, she stands fluidly up from her chair and disappears through a door behind the bench.

Since this is out of the way, my thoughts turn to dinner and another evening spent with Viveka.

CHAPTER 10

Viveka

While I'm not exactly surprised by Judge Boyer's ruling, I'm also not overly enthused about it. She has made this a battle of the expert witnesses. Unfortunately, experts cost money. I know if Justice for All Animals didn't have the money to pay an attorney fee to represent them, they sure as hell don't have it to hire an expert to determine the proliferation of clusters on the Swan's Mill development.

I pack up my stuff, intensely aware Ford is speaking to his client in hushed whispers. While I can't hear the exact words, I can tell Powell is not happy about the ruling by the way his arms are gesticulating. I have no idea who those men are with him. If I had to take a guess, they are other developers who could potentially be impacted by this ruling. I felt their skeevy eyes on me, hot and oppressive as I walked into the courtroom. I spent part of my life strutting down runways in such a way as to make people notice me. I still have that strut as a matter of fact, and I like the confidence it portrays about me. I may not swing my hips with as much exaggeration, but I hold my shoulders back and my chin tilted up so there's no doubt I'm a strong, confident woman. Unfortunately, I have to put up with men watching and thinking all kinds of nasty stuff, but I choose to ignore it.

As I'm closing up my briefcase—which is quite old, battered, and needs to be replaced, but I won't because it's sentimental and the one I beat up that guy to rescue Stanley with—I note Drake Powell and his crew leave the courtroom. That leaves just Ford and me.

He has his briefcase in hand, and motions toward the aisle that leads to the exit doors. "After you."

I smirk and mutter, "You just want me to walk in front of you so you can watch my ass."

"Yup," is all he says.

I can't help the tiny laugh as we exit, Ford just half a step behind me. While I did not enjoy the other men watching me today, I certainly don't mind Ford's appreciative looks. When we exit the courtroom, I come to a halt when I see Drake Powell and the other men waiting for an elevator, their backs to us. I immediately turn right and head for the stairwell. Ford follows along behind me.

We step into the stairwell and as soon as the door closes, Ford has me backed into the wall and is pressing the entire length of his body against mine. It feels really good, all warm and imposing at the same time.

He's the only man I've ever been with that made me actually feel small and vulnerable.

He puts one palm against the wall near my head, the other still holding onto his briefcase. He leans his face in closer to me. "Can I take a moment to tell you how fucking sexy you were arguing your case to Judge Boyer?"

My voice is husky and not my own. "You didn't look so bad yourself."

Ford tilts his head slightly and grazes his lips along my jaw for a moment. "What I wouldn't give to have taken you up to the judge's bench, bent you over it, and fucked you there."

A shudder ripples through my body, leaving my legs weak and rubbery.

"But that would be totally inappropriate," he whispers into my ear. "Just like it would be absolutely inappropriate and scandalous to fuck you right here in the stairwell."

A tiny moan escapes me.

Ford then pulls his head back slightly, so I can look into his eyes. I can tell he is beyond turned on from telling me his little fantasies. If he decided to be bold and adventurous and put his hand between my legs, he would see I feel the same.

But he plays the voice of reason. "But neither one of us should ever risk that. Not while we're on this case together. So how about I take you out to an early lunch?"

My eyes round with surprise. "But I thought we were gonna have dinner tonight?"

Ford winks and steps away. "You're damn right we're going to have dinner tonight. Then you and I are going to go back to your place and get all kinds of creative with each other."

"Or," I suggest with innuendo that is not put on in any way. "We could go to my house right now for 'lunch'."

His face splits into a wide smile. He grabs my free hand in his, pulling me to the stairs that lead down. "As tempting as that offer is, I would rather wait. I think waiting can make things even better."

"I can see that," I say with a laugh.

"Besides," Ford says as we trot down the stairs. "I'm starving."

♦

"Aren't you worried about people seeing us?" I ask, perusing the busy interior of J. Franklins. It's a popular downtown restaurant, and because it's only two blocks from the courthouse, it's frequented by a lot of the court personnel as well as the local bar.

Ford shoots me a look from across the table that says, *I can't believe you seriously asked that.*

"What?" I say, completely offended. But not really. "Yes, to the casual observer we may be having a professional lunch, but you and I have chemical attraction. You can feel it swirling around us. In fact, I'm a little afraid if anybody gets too close to our table, they're going to be overcome from the emotion of it. It could have disastrous effects to others."

Ford stares at me for a very blank moment before bursting out laughing from deep within his belly. I smile and let my eyes fall to the menu as I decide what I want to eat.

After our waiter takes our orders, Ford asks how I think the hearing went.

I give a slight shrug. "I guess it was the correct decision. I mean, how could Judge Boyer make a final decision without knowing the reach of the problem?"

Ford nods with a grave expression on his face. His eyes lock onto mine. "My client has ordered me to use every available resource and to spend any amount of money necessary to hire the right experts for this."

Ford uses air quotations when he said the word *right*.

His message is patently clear. I'm up against some big guns, and I'm going to be outspent no matter what.

Ford continues. "Let's have a brief hypothetical discussion to see if there's anything we can do to resolve this case."

"Like what?" I ask, never having once considered there would be room to negotiate anything. In my mind, there's an endangered species. They can't build. End of story.

Ford crosses his arms and leans them on the table.

"Okay, let's say hypothetically that the experts find out there's only one nest. Would your clients be amenable to letting Drake build around it?"

"But tearing the trees down around it would prevent other woodpeckers from coming in," I point out.

Ford's gaze turns shrewd. I realize I'm not talking to the man who wrings out amazing orgasms from my body. I am talking to a top-notch litigator. "You know the law does not prohibit tearing down trees that are not currently occupied by the woodpecker. Many builders preemptively strike all the timber from their land just to prevent an endangered species from taking up residence."

My stomach flips because he's right.

I turn the tables back on him. "Okay, hypothetically… What if the experts find out there is a large cluster of nests within the acreage?"

Ford doesn't say anything for a moment. I can tell he is weighing how much he should reveal, and I have to imagine it's somewhat of a conflict for him because part of the reason we are able to have this conversation right now is because we are actually fucking each other. With that comes a certain amount of leeway we're willing to give each other in these discussions.

Ford stalls a bit longer by taking a sip of his iced water. When he sets it down, he chooses his words very carefully. "You do understand, V, that the experts I hire are not going to find a large cluster of nests."

I push aside the wave of bitterness that sweeps

through me. It's not something I'm feeling because of Ford but rather because of my circumstances for the type of law I've chosen to practice. What he's saying is Drake Powell's money can buy an expert who will say whatever Drake Powell wants him to say. Hell, he could buy ten experts who will all testify under oath they have seen no other evidence of nests from the red cockaded woodpecker. It's just the way the game is played.

So I tell him the truth. "Then I will accept defeat, because in that scenario, Judge Boyer will rule against my clients. I'll be disheartened and disappointed that several beautiful animals we are struggling to keep on our planet will be wiped out. But I will go on. It's the nature of what I do, Ford. And I do understand I could very well lose this case."

"And how will that affect what's between you and me?" he asks, and I'm absolutely stunned by the concern in his voice and that he's even bothering to ask this question. I thought we had an understanding that this case had nothing to do with our personal relationship.

What I would love to do is reach my arm across the table and take Ford's hand. I would like to reassure him through touch that I understand he is doing what his client is asking him to do. That he has no choice in the matter.

Instead, all I can offer him is a personal promise. "Unless you were to do something dirty, underhanded, or illegal to beat me in this case, I swear I will never hold the results of how this turns out against you. And I trust you will be ethical in everything that you do."

That clearly doesn't satisfy him. "Even if I have to spend a lot of money at my client's direction to find experts who will tell him what he wants?"

On the face, this seems to be unethical. But it's done all the time. Those experts won't get up there and out and out lie, but they will manipulate and massage the facts to Drake Powell's benefit. They are called jukebox witnesses. Put a quarter in them, and they will play whatever song the one with the money wants.

In fact, if I had the money to hire such experts, I would be concentrating my efforts on those who are pro-wildlife and pro-saving endangered species. I know they would do whatever they could to manipulate and massage the facts to *my* benefit. That is just how our legal system works.

But before I can answer, a woman slides into the booth across from me right next to Ford. In fact, she slides in so forcefully she actually bumps against him, forcing him to move to give her room.

I gape, stunned, noticing several things at once.

First, the woman is beautiful. Extremely so. Flowing chocolate-brown hair, a sculpted face, and a megawatt smile.

When she leans into Ford and kisses him on his cheek, it causes an immense swelling of anger to rise within me, despite noting she's quite pregnant. So much so, in fact, her belly barely fits in between the table and the booth seat.

In the back of my rational mind, I realize this is Ford's best friend he told me about. But still, I can't get over her intimate familiarity with him, and one would have to say that's pure jealousy.

What does cause the anger to disappear, only to be replaced with an extreme surge of doubt in myself, is the way Ford regards this woman. Love, affection, respect, happiness, loyalty, and tenderness. So much more than what a typical best friend would look like while staring at their counterpart.

I blink hard as I realize the woman is now staring at me and Ford is making introductions. She sticks her hand out across the table, and I automatically take it for a firm handshake.

"I'm Leary. A really good friend of Ford's. And he's told me all about you. When I saw you two sitting here, I had to come over and introduce myself."

She beams a happy smile, and my eyes cut to Ford. He's staring at me expectantly, almost as if he thinks I might bolt from the table.

I don't, though. Instead, I level a huge smile back and say, "Viveka Jones. But you can call me Viv or Veka. All my friends do."

Leary inclines her head. "I love Veka. Veka it is."

"Hold on a minute," Ford butts in, leaning across the table toward me. He taps his finger on the wooden top and demands, "How come she gets to call you by your nickname right away, but I had to wait for it?"

I give him an innocent look. "Any friend of yours is a friend of mine."

Leary laughs and shakes her head. "You two are absolutely adorable. In fact, we need to get together and go out on a double date soon."

I think this sounds kind of nice. Ford, however, can't resist teasing. "What makes you think we're even dating?"

Leary cocks an eyebrow at him, and her eyes flash wickedly. "You borrowed our dog to go walk with her in the park. You're dating."

To my immense surprise, Ford flushes with embarrassment. It is quite adorable.

Leary scoots back out from the table and says, "I have to get going. I just wanted to pop over to say hello and introduce myself. But I really would love to get us all together."

"I'll call you," Ford says. His face softens with such genuine affection for Leary it makes my nose start to tingle.

We both watch her walk across the restaurant. She sits at a table occupied by two other men in suits. I'm assuming she's on a business meeting.

"So that was my best friend Leary," Ford says in a tone that suggests she's an absolute embarrassment to him, but we both know that's not true.

I turn slowly from staring at her across the restaurant to study Ford. It's not something I really intended to say, but the words sort of tumble out anyway. "She's the one who got away from you."

Ford actually rears back in his seat, his mouth dropping open in surprise. "What do you mean? Why would you say that?"

I give a tiny shake of my head. "No particular reason. Just the way you two looked at each other."

"It's just affection, V."

That's the truth. I can see it in his eyes, and I can hear it in the confidence of his words. It lightens the slight weight I hadn't realized was pressing down on my chest.

But I'm surprised when Ford says, "But there was a time, had a million other things been aligned the right way, she potentially could have been the one."

I'm absolutely blown away by his candor. And oddly, not even a little bit jealous. Nothing is pressing down on me from this revelation. His expression says it all. He's not sad or grieving in any way for what might have been with Leary—which, according to him, was a longshot anyway.

Ford then takes a moment to be even more truthful with me. "We were lovers in the past. It was an on-again and off-again thing, and I was never in love with her. She was never in love with me. But we do love each other as friends. It's been that way for many years now and will continue to be. But I promise you, I have absolutely no feelings for Leary other than friendship. On top of that, she is absolutely head over heels in love with her husband. Who, I might add, knows about my history with Leary as well."

I pick up my glass of water and take a tiny sip, really to force the dryness in my throat away Ford had induced with his revelations. My voice is still slightly hoarse when I set the glass back down. "You didn't have to tell me all that. It's not any of my business."

"It is your business," he replies smoothly. "You can ask me anything, and I'll tell you."

I really should let it go. I should be beyond happy over the level of brutal honesty he has given me. It goes a long way toward building trust, there is no doubt.

But I can't help but ask another question since he gave me full license to do so. "Have you ever explained the nature of your relationship with Leary to another woman you've… um… been intimate with?"

My question doesn't seem to surprise Ford. Instead, he smiles, but it's with respect not amusement. "You are the first."

And I find I don't need to know anything more about Ford and Leary's prior relationship.

CHAPTER 11

Ford

V'S MOUTH ON my cock.

I don't want this moment to end, but I'm getting closer and closer to erupting. My fingers have clenched her comforter so hard they hurt, and I've thought about pulling her off me once or twice so I can prolong this.

But she keeps staring at me with those baby blues while her head bobs up and down, silently begging me to let her continue. Fucking begging me to come in her mouth.

That's exactly what she asked me for not all that long ago. We'd had a great dinner at a little out-of-the-way Italian place before heading to her house. There was not even a discussion about going back to mine because I didn't want her to have to worry about Daisy and Butch.

While I can't say the dogs have grown on me all that much in my limited interaction with them on Sunday, Viveka has very much grown on me. When I'm invested in a woman, I'm all in.

Didn't know we'd escalate so fast with me sitting on the edge of her bed while she kneels between my knees to suck me off. I was blindsided actually.

She doted on the dogs. They were happy to see her when we walked in. We chatted while she let them out into her small fenced-in yard to go to the bathroom and fixed their dinner. I filled her in on how Leary and Reeve met while the dogs ate. I told her a little bit about the eccentric senior partner at our firm, Midge Payne, while the dogs went back outside for another potty break.

But when they came in and happily went into the living room to curl up on the couch, Viveka made her move. Stepped right up to me in the kitchen and wrapped her hand around my tie, which was still tight around my neck. She gave a playful tug and went to her tiptoes so she could look me in the eyes.

She licked her lower lip and said, "Ford... I want to suck your cock, and I want you to come in my mouth."

I wasn't even finished letting out a groan before I was kissing her hard.

We somehow ended up in her bedroom with the door shut. I vaguely remember the dogs whining, but once Viveka started working at my belt, my attention was focused solely on her.

She got my cock out and started jacking it while we kissed, using her other hand to work my pants and briefs down past my hips. I was pushed to sit back on the edge of the bed, and then Viveka was doing that move that all men love to see.

She started dropping to her knees.

"Wait," I ordered, and she froze. "Put that hair up… I don't want it obstructing my view."

Wearing a seductively sexy smile, she wrapped it all up on top of her head, tucking the end under in such a way it magically stayed up there.

"Unbutton your blouse," I demanded.

She complied. When she got it open just enough I could see the edge of her lace bra and the swells of her breast, I had her stop.

My last request caused her breath to hitch and those tits to start heaving. "Hike your skirt up around your waist. Put your hand down your panties to play with yourself."

Viveka didn't hesitate.

And now she's kneeling between my legs, sucking me hard and playing with herself at the same time. Tiny mewling noises tickle the head of my cock when it hits the back of her throat. Her breathing is as rough and labored as mine. I can't see the exact details since she's bent over me, but I can tell her hand is moving fast between her legs.

She's close.

Oh so close to coming, and that knowledge gives me some measure of control over my own impending orgasm. I open a curled fist, move my arm out, and flatten my palm on the mattress so I can lean to the side for a better view. I can only see the curve of bare ass—she must be wearing a thong. The gray material of her skirt is bunched up and hiding the actual goods, her entire arm jerking as she fingers herself.

Christ, that's hot.

"Come on, V," I urge in a low, rough voice. "Get yourself off, baby."

Her head rises, my cock dislodging from her mouth. She sets back on her haunches, giving me a clear view of her hand disappearing into her panties as she furiously works at her clit. The muscles in her neck strain and her hips punch upward as she starts to come. Her entire body seems to tremble. The sound she makes is otherworldly, and I stare in fascination as she orgasms really fucking hard.

It takes her a moment for her eyes to open back up and focus on me, her chest still heaving from the exertion of what she did to herself. She gives me a lopsided grin before her eyes drop down to my cock.

"Got sidetracked," she murmurs before she closes her mouth over me again.

Immediately, the pressure starts to cause my balls to ache. It's a testament to how much watching Viveka come just now turned me on. Those few seconds she wasn't sucking my cock did nothing to cool me off.

"Feels so fucking good," I praise softly, letting my hands come to the side of her head. I pet her gently while she blows me.

Viveka nudges her head to the right, almost like a cat demanding attention. She pushes into my hand a little harder, and my fingers reflexively squeeze until I'm holding fistfuls of her hair. She nudges into me again, making a tiny sound of need.

I react without thinking, using my grip on her hair to move her on my cock. She gives a tiny hum of approval as I pull her up and push her back down, moving her no deeper than what she was giving me but taking over the effort for her.

"You like me fucking your mouth?" I ask.

She grunts, and I take that as a yes. There's no controlling my hips. They punch upward as I push her back down, and I wince as she makes a tiny gagging sound. My grip on her relaxes, but she gives a shake of her head.

I hold her still, forcing her to look at me. Her jaw is stretched wide, mouth still stuffed with my cock as she stares up at me.

"Do you want me to fuck your mouth?" I ask, so there is no mistaking what she wants.

Her eyes practically sizzle as she nods, more humming noises of assent tickling the head of my dick as it lays on her tongue.

"Fuck," I mutter hoarsely. It's on.

I stand up from the bed. V's forced to raise up on her knees by the hold I have on her head. She moans all around my cock as I hold her in place. I don't move for a scant second.

I stare down at her as she gazes up at me with trusting eyes. Begging me to have my way with her.

"Mmm," I moan, pulling out of her very slowly. Her cheeks hollow as she sucks, and my knees almost buckle.

"Hold on, Veka," I murmur. "This might get rough, but I won't hold on too tight, okay?"

I get a slight nod.

I ease back into her mouth, testing how far I can go before it's too much for her. The fat, mushroomed head of my cock can breach the opening of her throat without too much of a gag.

"Swallow next time," I say as I pull out.

I push in slowly again, and she does exactly as I instruct. It pulls the head into the top of her throat, contracting tight around me. Her eyes widen with the knowledge she didn't gag.

I smile. "That's right. I think your throat can take me, V."

She responds by bringing her hands to my ass and digging her fingernails in.

"Shit," I bark out, thinking she just drew blood.

But her demand is clear.

She's willing to take whatever I want to give her.

Admittedly, I hold back. I've had some women who want to choke, slobber, and cry all over my dick. Had a few who could take me all the way down their throat without even breaking a sweat. But I'm not going there with Viveka.

Not yet, anyway.

But I do give it to her rough, fucking her mouth. She's a natural, learning how to push away panic by breathing in through her nose. I set up an easy enough pace that she can swallow me every time I thrust in. Each time, I go a little deeper.

She sucks a little harder.

I get a little closer.

When she brings a hand to my balls and gives them a squeeze, my orgasm starts racing toward me. Viveka's eyes lock with mine as I thrust in and out of that perfect mouth, and I know I've never had better than this. Her eyes seem to beg me to give myself over to her, so with a last hard push that goes only deep enough to touch the back of her tongue, I start to come.

She swallows and pushes herself onto me a bit more.

Swallows again and my head disappears down her throat.

Another jolt of pleasure slams through me, harder than the first. My hands grip her head hard, holding her still. I shudder and unload, leaving nothing behind.

She leaves nothing behind, sucking me dry and then licking me clean.

After pulling her off the floor, I lift her up into my arms. I turn and lay her on the bed, then prostrate myself right beside her. She's still fully clothed, although her shirt gapes open and her skirt is still hiked up. I'm still dressed too except for my pants around my waist and my wet dick resting on my stomach.

My head rolls to see she's staring at me. I give her a smile.

"Did I do okay?" she asks hesitantly.

"Jesus fuck, Viveka," I groan as I roll toward her. I wrap my arms around her, and then pull her into my chest. "That was the best fucking blow job I've ever had in my entire life. In fact, I'm thinking it was the best fucking blow job any man has ever had in his entire life."

Her body shakes with laughter but then she pushes back from me. Our faces are inches apart and yet I see her more clearly than ever before.

I don't think two months is going to be quite long enough with this woman.

♦

WE CATCH OUR breaths.

We cuddle.

I grab us some bottled water, and Viveka changes into a t-shirt and new panties.

I strip naked because I'm going to fuck her again before we go to sleep, and I might as well make things easier.

Climbing back into bed, Viveka turns on the TV. We watch the news for a little bit. Not surprisingly, our political leanings are the same so there's not much for us to debate.

I'm feeling mellow, relaxed, and as always around this fascinating woman, filled with a million questions about her. She's complex with many layers, and it will take me quite a while to get through them all.

"You mentioned you didn't know your father growing up, but inferred you did later," I say, and she immediately grabs the remote to mute the TV.

We're both leaning up against the headboard, but she rolls slightly to face me. "Yeah... he wasn't in my life growing up. He was a photographer and had done some work with my mother. Got her pregnant, but he had a wife and kids and wasn't about to leave them for her. She pretty much raised me on her own."

"Pretty much?" I ask.

"We stayed with her parents for a few years when she was having a hard time finding work."

Her words sound dispassionate, almost like she's reading from a textbook. "You didn't have a good relationship with them?"

She shrugs. "They were strict and a little standoffish. My mother left home when she was sixteen. They never forgave her for it, especially when she showed back up years later unmarried and with a kid. They never quite warmed up to me."

Fuck if that doesn't make me hurt for her. I have a really close-knit family.

"What about your father?" I ask, moving away from her grandparents as it's clear there's not much there.

"I finally made my mother give me his name. By 'made,' I mean I gave her some money for the information. It was soon after I was emancipated and still had some income coming in. But I never did reach out to him, not until after I graduated college."

"Why not?"

"I don't know," she says lightly. "I guess because I didn't need a father. He was more of a curiosity. That's all he ever was."

"What happened when you finally did?"

Viveka smiles and pushes up to an elbow. "Nothing happened. He just wasn't all that interested. His kids were grown and out of the house, but he was still married to the same woman. He didn't want to rock the boat with his family. We made loose promises to stay in touch via email and such, but neither ever reached out to the other after that one and only phone call."

"That's… just… sad," is all I can manage to say.

"Only to someone who probably had a great relationship with their own father," she reasons. "But I never felt as if I lacked something. I mean… I didn't even have a great mother figure. I sort of raised myself, you know. And I think I turned out okay."

"You turned out marvelously," I tell her, not even trying to hide the respect in my voice. "I'm still not sure how someone as caring, generous, and humble figured that all out on her own."

"I had some good role models in the modeling industry. Before then, I had some good teachers who took an interest in me."

Reaching a hand up, I wrap it around the side of her neck and give a squeeze. "I think you're pretty incredible, V."

Her cheeks get pink, and her eyes dip away from mine. I give her another squeeze, so she brings her gaze back to me.

"Really, really incredible," I reiterate.

More blushing, but then she narrows her eyes as if doubting my compliments. "Does this have anything to do with that stellar blow job I gave you?"

I snort and pull her into me hard, my hand going down to slap her ass for saying such a thing. It was a fucking fantastic blow job. There's not much I wouldn't do to get another one like it in the future, but shame on her for even asking that.

"I'm glad that stupid pecker took up residence in Drake's pine tree," I reassure her as my hand goes to soothe her stinging butt cheek from my slap. "And now… my pecker would like to take up residence in you."

"Mmm," she murmurs, pressing her lips to my throat. "Get your pecker to nesting, baby. The roost is ready."

Both of us start laughing over our pecker jokes.

Then more jokes start coming.

It's… fun. Lying in bed and laughing.

It's not something I recall doing before. I flip through various women, giving a little bit longer thought to Leary.

No.

None of them.

Sex for sure.

Cuddling, of course.

Chatting before we fell asleep.

All of that.

Never laughter, though.

CHAPTER 12

Viveka

SO THIS IS how the other half lives?

Or rather, practices law.

Knight & Payne is one of the highest-rated law firms in the state of North Carolina. I had heard of it, of course. Probably not an attorney in our state who hasn't.

I also perused their website. They have over sixty lawyers, and I would imagine more than that amount in support staff. The firm takes up the top two floors of the Watts Building in the middle of downtown Raleigh.

The lobby is opulent but not ostentatious. Marble flooring and leather furnishings done in neutral tones. The beautiful receptionist looks like she may have walked beside me in a fashion show at some point with flawless makeup, designer clothing, and perfect hair.

"Miss Jones," a woman says. I turn to see another gorgeous woman leaning into the lobby from a doorway I assume leads into the rest of the law firm. "Mr. Daniels is ready for you now."

Pushing up from the couch I had been sitting on, I put my purse over my shoulder and follow the woman through the door. She's voluptuous and her clothing shows off every curve. Pencil skirt hugging her hips and form-fitting blouse leaving no doubt the size of her D-cup breasts. Spiked heels with fishnet stockings adds even more sex appeal, and I wonder if she works directly for Ford.

"This is The Pit," she says as we enter a large open area filled with desks and people working at the desks. There are no walls separating, and I wonder how people can work without privacy. "The partners have offices on the perimeter, but everyone else works in a cooperative setting."

"And what do you do?" I ask as I follow behind her. She walks around the perimeter.

Glancing over her shoulder, she gives me a professional smile. "I'm one of Mr. Daniels' paralegals."

Okay, I could have done without that information. Knowing he has such a knockout of a woman working for him makes that jealousy I felt when I first met Leary try to come back.

I give her a wan smile in return.

The offices around the edge of The Pit are all done in clear glass. Every single wall—even the ones in between offices—are clear. It makes what is already a hugely impressive workspace appear even larger. I can see through the clear offices that the windows overlooking the Raleigh skyline are all floor to ceiling, so the natural lighting is amazing.

We walk toward a corner office. Ford sits behind a desk, typing on his laptop. As we approach, his head pops up. His gaze first goes to his paralegal, but only for a moment before he focuses on me. A wide smile breaks out on his face, and I forget all about his gorgeous paralegal. He doesn't have eyes for her.

At least not today, anyway.

Ford stands from his desk and motions me in as he walks toward the door. The paralegal sort of melts away. When I step inside his office, he shuts the glass door behind me.

"I want to kiss you," he says in a low voice as we stand toe to toe.

"This would be why glass walls suck," I point out.

He laughs and reaches past my shoulder to press a button on the wall by the door he just closed. Immediately—almost magically—the glass walls turn milky and opaque.

"What was that?" I ask. I turn to place my fingertips against the glass wall beside the door.

"Smoke-filled glass," Ford answers as he steps in close behind me. His hands come to my waist to hold me in place, and he cranes around to press a kiss to the side of my neck. "Now no one can see us in here."

My head falls back onto his shoulder, followed by the rest of my body melting back into him. When he'd asked me out to lunch today, I eagerly accepted. It might have had something to do with the fact he'd woken up in my bed this morning. My eyes close at the memory of how thoroughly he fucked my brains out. I'd woken up with his hand between my legs and finished with an earth-shaking orgasm. I was semi-addled when he asked me to lunch today.

"Ready to go get something to eat?" he asks.

I startle and blink, opening my eyes. He releases his hold, and I turn to face him. "Not until I have a chance to check your office out."

Ford smiles and takes a step back from me, turning toward the interior of his office. He motions his hand for me to come further in.

When we were making plans for lunch, he'd offered to come get me at my office. It was sweet and gentlemanly, but I was going to be downtown for a meeting at the DA's office. Given the proximity to Ford's office, I couldn't resist the offer to come here because I have to admit I'm a little more than curious about this side of Ford.

I know a little bit about art. I attended art galas when I lived in New York, as well as spent a lot of time in the numerous museums there. Every once in a blue moon, I could get Adam to go to an exhibit. Even so, I really couldn't identify particular artists.

I can, however, identify quality.

Ford said the sculptures in this office cost twenty

grand, but I can only see two pieces. In the corner stands a life-sized bronze sculpture of Themis, goddess of justice, with a sword in one hand, scales in the other, and her eyes blindfolded. Another sculpture about two feet high done in what I believe to be white alabaster is placed on a pedestal table. It's an abstract of nothing but waves, curves, and intertwining pieces.

"Impressive," I murmur. I move closer to Themis, although most in our profession refer to her as the scales of justice.

"Still like your basket of puppies picture better," he says from behind me, and my stomach flips over the sincerity in his voice. I turn to him with a smile.

Of the millions of ways I find Ford Daniels to be attractive, this is perhaps top of the list. Telling me he likes my cheap little picture full of memories and meaning over his insanely beautiful but ridiculously priced objets d'art. Not once since I met Ford had I felt he was snobbish or looked down on things, and I didn't need him to say that to confirm my intuition. But what he did do was validate the importance of my art to me, and that makes him… yeah, super hot.

"You want to bang me right now, don't you?" he asks teasingly. I'm guessing the expression on my face was easy to read.

"Not in the slightest," I say with a prim sniff. "But I totally wouldn't say no to lunch at Beasley's."

More formerly known as Beasley's Chicken + Honey,

they make the best chicken and waffles. I don't get downtown a lot, so it's a real treat for me to eat there.

"You got it," Ford says, and I move toward the door. He stops me just as quick though when he says, "While you're here, let me give you this."

He leans over his desk and grabs a document. There's a slight hesitation before he hands it to me.

When I glance down at it, I raise my eyebrows in surprise. It's his designation of expert witnesses he intends to use to evaluate the property for clusters of nests.

There are five of them.

"You work fast," I murmur in awe as my gaze comes up to meet his. "Less than twenty-four hours from the hearing and you have your dream team lined up?"

Ford appears slightly chagrined. "Let's just say I was busy yesterday afternoon."

My eyes cut back down to the document. I recognize three of the names, and they will say whatever Powell wants them to say.

"I'm sorry," Ford says.

My head jerks up and my chin pulls in, completely stunned by the remorse in his voice. "Whatever for?"

"I don't know," he says as he blows out a frustrated breath. "I want to do a good job for my client—"

"You *should* do a good job for your client," I assure him. "The best, in fact. And hiring good experts is doing just that."

"We're going to steamroll over you because we can outspend you." His jaw is locked, his expression hard.

"Ford," I say softly. I lay a hand on his forearm and give it a squeeze. "This case has nothing to do with us, okay? That was our agreement. Please don't let this bother you."

He studies me for a moment, and it's long enough I could totally get lost in his eyes. Finally, he nods in agreement.

"What about you?" he asks as an afterthought. "Have you located any experts?"

"Not yet," I mutter. I fold his designation of experts and slide it into my purse. "At least not any in my price range."

"What's your price range?"

My eyes lift to his. "Free. I need them to do it pro bono."

"And why is that?" he clips out. Once again, he's letting this bother him. He's letting the problems with my case bother him, and I don't want him to have that type of obligation.

I try my best to play it off. "Justice for All Animals doesn't have the funds right now, but I'm sure I can find someone to help. I've got lots of calls out to the wildlife community."

"You do realize if you don't get an expert, you're going to lose this case, right?"

He's not telling me anything I don't know. "I'll find

someone," I say firmly.

Even if I have to dip into my personal savings to do it. Of course, I don't voice that to Ford because I know he would not like that at all. Whatever this is between us, it's clear that feelings are now involved. I think this stopped being just good sex and companionship within the last few minutes.

"Now," I say with a chastising tone. "I'm starved, and you promised me lunch at Beasley's. I want to get my waffle on."

That does the trick. Ford's face evens out and the worry dissipates. Waffles can work some serious magic sometimes.

He takes my elbow, and we move to the door. But before we reach it, the knob turns and it pushes inward.

I swear I hear Ford murmur, "I'll be damned," before we even see who is coming in. Almost as if he knows who it is just by the way the knob is turning and he's surprised to have this visitor.

The door swings in, and a woman sticks her head through the opening.

It's none other than Midge Payne. I've never met the woman before, but everyone knows who this woman is. She's a legend in this state. Plus, when I was looking at the firm's website, I also read her bio. Ford told me a little bit about her, and I knew she was reclusive and eccentric.

She's stunning. No clue how old she is but based on

when she graduated law school according to the website, she has to be in her sixties.

The woman doesn't look it, though. Her face is almost completely without any lines or wrinkles except a tiny bit around her mouth and eyes. She has pale silver hair that's clearly from a bottle and cut into a stylish, sleek bob. It is amazing on her.

She's simply stunning.

Midge glances at Ford, then to me, before she pushes the door all the way open and enters. Her outfit is spectacular. While I don't know a lot about art, I do know about fashion. It's a top-end designer… Versace if I had to take a quick guess.

A pencil-styled skirt in a swirling pattern of light blue and steel blue with black accents. A sleeveless black silk blouse with a big, loose bow at the base of her throat. Thin, spiked sandals in black with straps around the ankle. Not exactly attorney businesslike, but dressy chic for sure. I love this woman's style.

She shuts the door behind her, and I steal a glance at Ford. He's clearly stunned to see her here. Not a little surprised, like oh, what a nice surprise.

But like in his jaw has dropped.

"Midge Payne," Midge says regally as she holds her hand out to me.

"Viveka Jones," I say automatically as we shake. She's a thin woman and the bones in her hand are slight, yet she squeezes my hand firmly and with confidence.

"It's a pleasure." Midge inclines her head at me and releases my hand. She turns to Ford. "Did I interrupt something?"

"Not at all," Ford says, and he seems completely at ease with Midge. So his surprise doesn't seem to be a bad thing, just... surprised. "We were going to lunch. Would you like to join us?"

"That's a lovely offer," Midge says graciously and turns to me. Her stare is appraising and curious. "Maybe some other time. I won't hold you two up."

"Did you need something?" Ford asks. "We're not in a rush."

Midge shakes her head and holds up a hand. "Truly not that important. We'll talk later."

She again gives me a gracious nod of her head and a smile. "A pleasure to meet you, Miss Jones."

"Likewise," I tell her.

When she's gone and the door shuts behind her, Ford says, "Huh," as if in contemplation.

"What's up?" I ask, because something happened here and I'm not quite sure what it was.

"That was just weird," Ford says, still staring at the door that had closed behind Midge.

"The senior partner coming into your office was weird?" I ask confused, because he sounds beyond flummoxed.

"Yes, weird." He turns to me, eyes twinkling. "Midge never leaves her office to visit anyone. And I mean never.

If she needed something, I would have been summoned there. That's how I knew who it was when the door started opening because no one would dare enter my office without knocking first."

"Except Midge," I guess.

"Except Midge, but she never does that."

"She said it wasn't an emergency, but it had to be something important."

Ford starts laughing as if he's just realized something. "That sly fox of a woman."

"What?"

"She wanted to check *you* out," he says, and my mouth falls open in surprise.

"Why?" I gasp.

"She must have seen your name on my calendar," he muses.

"What does my name have to do with it? She doesn't even know me."

"She knows you're the attorney representing Justice for All Animals," he explains. "And because she's about the most perceptive person I've ever known—like creepily perceptive—she knows we're sleeping together."

"What?" I screech, and Ford winces. I lower my voice to a harsh whisper. "How could she possibly know that?"

I'm sidetracked when Ford's hand shoots out, wraps around the back of my neck, and pulls me into him for a hard, penetrating kiss. My hands clutch into his suit jacket, and I'm seeing stars by the time he releases me.

Blinking my eyes to reorient myself, I hold my hands up to Ford, who seems way too amused by this. "Whoa, whoa, whoa. Let's back up a minute. The senior partner of your firm and one of the most respected attorneys in this state knows that you—one of her attorneys—and an opposing lawyer—are sleeping together? Because she's perceptive?"

"Yup."

"And you're not freaked out by this?" I ask. "I mean, what we're doing is bordering on unethical."

"It's not unethical if it doesn't impact the case," he says blandly. "And besides, Midge is more apt to encourage rather than discourage it. She's sort of a rebel and a mischievous meddler at the same time."

"Okay, that's weird on so many levels, but how did she even know who I was? You said she probably recognized my name. Surely this case is far beneath her notice and attention."

Ford can't hide the immediate flush to his face.

"What?" I press. "What aren't you telling me?"

He scratches his head, a sheepish expression on his face. "Midge is following the case because she's involved in the Swan's Mill development."

"Why? Like she's counsel for it or something?"

"Not exactly," he hedges.

"Ford," I say with a frustrated growl. "Just tell me."

"Fine," he says with a sigh. "Midge owns the property. She's an investor in the project."

"You're kidding?" My stomach drops because this puts a new wrinkle in our relationship. It's one thing for Ford to use his best legal skills in battling me for Drake Powell, a man I despise and I don't think Ford is that crazy about either.

But this right here… he's got a serious vested interest in this case. His boss is the one who is going to be a big loser if I prevail.

Ford takes a step toward me, but I take two back until the door prevents me from going further. I hold my hands out to stop his advancement. "Okay, that changes everything."

"It changes nothing." His voice is hard, his expression determined. "Midge trusts me to do my job right. She also trusts if I can't do it right, I'll either eliminate the distraction or I'll step down. I need you to trust I'll do the same."

"So I'm a distraction?" I ask hesitantly, because that stings just a little.

Ford is on me, his fingers sliding into my hair and then grasping my head tight. He bends down, peering right into my eyes before saying, "If by distraction, you mean you drive me crazy and inhabit my thoughts way too much, then yes… that's exactly what you are. Right now, though… I like it. A lot. Don't count on me giving that up any time soon."

Sting is gone. Legs are weak.

I kind of want to give him another blow job right

now.

"Now," he says softly. "Can we go to lunch?"

I nod, but I don't have a chance to voice my assent.

That's because his mouth is on mine and we're both distracted for a little bit.

CHAPTER 13

Ford

SHE'S GENUINELY SURPRISED to see me standing on her porch, but she doesn't hesitate in opening the door wider to let me in. I can hear the scrabbling of dog feet on the tile in the kitchen, so I hurry to step in before Daisy and Butch come barreling out. Daisy wags her tail furiously, and Butch yaps in the most annoying way.

Without thought, I squat to receive their attention, scratching them both behind their ears for a few moments.

"What are you doing here?" she asks curiously.

I stand straight while she shuts the door. The dogs are still running around our feet, but I ignore them now that I've said my hellos. "Well, you see… after lunch today, I was kind of waiting for you to suggest we do something tonight, but you never did."

That doesn't get a reaction from her other than a slightly tilted head to indicate she's waiting for more.

So I give it to her. "I then thought maybe you'd call

or text later to make some plans, but you didn't do that either."

That gets a raised eyebrow and a crossing of her arms across her chest. She's going into battle mode, and it causes a jolt of anticipation to shoot through me. I'm wondering if we'll have our first fight tonight and then have wild, angry make up sex, because that would be totally fine with me.

"Do you really need me to point out that you didn't ask to see me tonight after lunch, nor did you call or text me after?" she asks blandly, but I hear it layered within her voice. She's slightly amused.

"I wasn't the one who freaked out about Midge," I explain. "I decided to leave the ball in your court, but you didn't charge down court. Instead, you sat on the bench, so I'm the one who has to take charge."

Her forehead furrows, and she gives a slight shake of her head. "I have no clue what you meant with that analogy because I know nothing about basketball, but—"

Fuck, that's adorable. I can't help myself. With one long step, I'm in her face.

Then on her face.

With my mouth.

She doesn't pull away from my kiss, and I can even feel her mouth curling upward at the edges as she smiles through my onslaught.

When I pull back, I also admit, "And I thought maybe as a European, you'd be a little more forward, but you're apparently kind of old fashioned, clearly wanting the guy to make the next date plans."

"Is that what you call this?" she asks, her voice so dry it obliterates any hint of her faded accent. "Dating?"

"Aren't we dating?" I turn it back on her, dropping my hands from her face to her shoulders. "We go out, we talk, and we sleep together."

"Otherwise known as friends with benefits," she points out.

"Fine, call it what you want," I capitulate, knowing we really don't need a label for what this is. "But I'm staying tonight. And in the future, I'll be more proactive in making plans with you."

Viveka snickers and moves past me toward the kitchen. "Did you eat dinner? I was just getting ready to heat up a Lean Cuisine."

"I'll pass," I say. "Want to go out for Mexican instead?"

"Oh, you mean like a date?" she smart-asses me.

"Yes, like a date. That ends with me bringing you back here to do all kinds of dirty things to you."

"That sounds lovely," she says genially, and I love the fact she's not irritated I just showed up on her doorstep, nor that I didn't make any formalized plans with her after lunch.

But I was telling her the truth. I was concerned she was upset about Midge's involvement in the pecker case, and I wanted to give her a tiny bit of space. But fuck…

as the day went on and I hadn't heard from her, I knew I needed to alpha-up my game a bit and take matters into my own hands.

I decided to do this after talking to the two main women in my life.

First, I went to Midge's office when I got back from lunch as I needed to know if she was truly okay with me seeing Viveka. Yes, it's probably not completely kosher and well, fine… it's probably unethical. But Midge has always been a rule bender, if not an outright breaker. She's always pushed the envelope and gone after what she wanted. I watched her silently support Leary when she and Reeve screwed around with each other while battling out a very important case that was also worth millions of dollars.

Still, I needed to hear it from her, because no matter how much I like Viveka, I would step back if Midge asked me to.

Luckily, she did not.

"It's not a big deal," she said with a shrug of her shoulders from where she sat behind her desk. I hadn't even bothered to sit down in a guest chair, even though the invitation with a sweep of her hand was there when I first gained entrance to her world. I had walked right up to her desk, bent over to place my palms flat, and asked, "Do you want me to stop seeing Viveka?"

But it was a big deal, and we both knew it. She explained it away, though. To her, it was a matter of risk analysis. "This case is going to boil down to the experts, and we both know that's usually who has the most money. Drake has the most money. Our experts will sway the preponderance of the evidence. We're most likely going to win."

Fuck, it was like a punch to the gut when she said that, and that in and of itself was very concerning to me. I'm a competitive man. I like winning. I hate losing. And yet, the thought of Viveka losing this case caused a visceral reaction inside of me.

I swept that aside and focused on Midge, though. "But that land is worth millions, and you were going to make even more millions on that subdivision. I don't think you should take this that lightly."

Midge gave me a sly smile and sat forward in her chair. She crossed one leg over the other, steepling her fingers in front of her face while her elbows pressed into the armrests. "I'm aware of that, Ford. I appreciate your concern. But you can consider me aware of the conflict. I'm not concerned about it."

Her blue eyes, not like Viveka's but a color that reminds me of denim and steel—tough and beautiful—stare at me appraisingly, waiting for some facial reaction to clue her in on my thoughts. But I've got a poker face, and I'm not about to give away that her answer was very, very important to me, not only to maintain my loyalty to Midge and the case, but so I could pursue Viveka now rather than later.

"I've got work to do," she announced as she snagged a document from her desk and kicked her feet up on her desk. She settled back in her chair and didn't look at me again.

I had been dismissed, but this was typical. I wasn't offended.

We choose a restaurant not far from Viveka's house that she's eaten at before. After we're served margaritas along with some chips and salsa, I tell her about my meeting with Midge.

She listens quietly and when I'm finished, she asks me one very simple question. "Are you sure about us doing this?"

"I'm sure." My answer was just as simple and didn't need any thought. I would have walked away from Viveka—temporarily, of course, until the case was finished—but I really didn't want to.

I have to ask her back. "Still have concerns?"

I get a half-shrug as she picks up a salted chip and scoops up some salsa. "I don't have personal ties to the case other than my love of animals. You're the one with the bigger conflict. If we both understand we're going to work our asses off and are willing to let the chips fall where they may, then I'm good."

"Like it that much, do you?" I tease, puffing my chest out and pointing at my body with both thumbs.

She picks up another chip and throws it at me. It bounces harmlessly off my chest, and there's something remarkably comforting about the fact we can tease each other this way while discussing a serious subject.

"So Leary went down this path, huh?" she asks. "Hard fought battle against her opponent and lover."

I snag the chip that had fallen from my chest to the table, dipping it the salsa. "That was a little different. Leary was deeply and emotionally invested in that case. And when Reeve came after her client in court, well… it got ugly between them for a bit. But they worked it out."

I go on to tell her the details of the case, because she's a lawyer and fascinated by that. It was a medical malpractice case where an unqualified doctor botched a breast reduction surgery on a woman that left her pretty maimed. That woman was a dear friend of Leary's, so it was a lot different from what we're dealing with. While I might empathize a bit with the poor red-cockaded woodpecker's plight, I've got zero emotion tied to this case.

"Leary seems really cool," Viveka says with a smile. She forsakes the chips and drinks some of her margarita, her tongue poking out briefly to swipe at some of the salt. Christ, that's sexy.

And yeah… Leary is the coolest. While I have no hesitation in sharing the details of my meeting with Midge, I will never tell Viveka about the second meeting I had today. It was with Leary, and it had very much to do with this case and my developing feelings for my opponent.

I'd walked into Leary's office, shut the door, and said, "Remember you owe me for the Lamaze class, and I'm getting ready to ask you to pay up big time."

She nodded with a wary gaze, prepared to do my bidding.

I dropped a check for five grand, written from my personal account, on her desk. It was made payable to Leary.

She picked it up and studied it for a second, but then her eyes snapped to mine. "You're paying me for going to Lamaze class?"

My best friend isn't that dense and is teasing, but I didn't feel like engaging in her sport. I just told her what I needed. "Deposit that in your account. After, I want you to make an anonymous donation to Justice for All Animals, and I want you to stipulate that the money has to be used in the pecker case."

Normally, Leary would have snorted over the word pecker because she can still be juvenile sometimes. Instead, her eyes hardened and her lips thinned with dismay.

"That is highly unethical," she said in a low voice. "You cannot help fund a case you're opposing, especially when Midge is directly involved."

"I'm not funding it," I replied simply. "You are. I'm merely giving you a gift, and you can do with it what you want."

Translation: you better give it to Justice for All Animals exactly as I told you to do.

"I can't do that either, Ford," she practically hissed at me, yet she never handed that check back. She kept it pinched between her forefinger and thumb, waving it wildly while she tried to educate me on all the ways it would be unethical and shady for anyone in this firm—much less a partner like herself—to help an opposing case.

When she finally wore herself out lecturing me, I asked, "Will you do it?"

"You know I will," she muttered, and then she called me an asshole under her breath.

"I love you, too," I replied with a smile as I walked out of her office.

As I sit across from Viveka, sharing stories and drinking margaritas, I have not one single regret about what I did. Viveka will be able to hire an expert. She won't get much for five grand, and her expert will never compare to the five I'll be hiring at Drake's direction, but at least she won't be helpless.

Besides, I've come to figure Viveka out over the last week. We've done more than just fucking. We've talked, and talking is so much more than just words. It's about tone, passion, and sincerity. I've also learned a lot about her character, and I know one thing.

Viveka doesn't have a lot of money, but I guarantee she'd pull money out of her retirement to hire an expert witness because that's the type of woman she is. She's going to fight for that little underdog of a pecker, even at her own expense in time, effort, and money.

"Things have got to change," Viveka says, and I blink several times trying to understand what she's saying. I'd sort of zoned out thinking about my meeting with Leary today and my totally shady request for help.

"What needs to change?" I ask carefully, not wanting to do or say anything to ruin any progress we've made together, especially given our unique circumstances as we battle this case out.

"You," she says, pointing a chip at me with a lopsided smile. "We've known each other exactly a week. We've seen each other six of those seven days. You have intimate knowledge of my body, and I yours. But it suddenly occurred to me, in all the talks we've had, we've never really discussed you. You know all about me, my upbringing, my family, my divorce. But I really don't know anything about you other than you used to bang your best friend. Let's remedy that."

I bust out laughing and continue chuckling even as the waiter appears with two sizzling cast iron platters of fajitas. She got chicken, and I got steak.

I wait for all the fixings to get set up and the waiter to leave before I ask, "What do you want to know?"

"Everything," she says with twinkling eyes. "Start with your childhood, though."

I start loading up my first fajita. "I'll give you the simple version because it's not all that glamorous or exciting. Born and raised in Ohio. My dad was a highway patrolman, and my mom was their station's secretary. There was a little hanky-panky there. Mom got pregnant with me, and they got married. Forty-one years later, they're still married, maybe not over-joyously happy but they've got a really good relationship."

"Siblings?"

I nod. "Brother who is a doctor and sister who is a schoolteacher."

And then she has a million questions, and she doesn't hold back peppering me with them. It takes us a long time to eat our fajitas because of it. It's cool by me, though, because talking to Viveka is not a chore. Sharing information about my fairly normal family isn't either. Because she listens with rapt interest, I keep talking.

We stop at one margarita each. We both eat most of our fajitas. It's almost two and a half hours later when we get back to her house.

It's several hours and many orgasms later before we go to sleep.

CHAPTER 14

Viveka

THE MOMENT I pull myself out of my car and stare over the roof of it at my office, I know it's going to be a crappy day.

The hole through the front window is a good indication. Leaning back into my car with a sigh, I grab my purse and briefcase from the passenger seat, then make my way inside to see the extent of the vandalism.

My rent in this strip is affordable because I'm in an area of the city that has a few unsavory characters around. It's something I easily adapted to, especially with Frannie giving me pointers. It usually means I don't walk out to my car if it's dark unless Frannie is watching. If she's not available, I have on occasion called the police. They never seem to mind. I also carry pepper spray, and I stay hypervigilant of my surroundings at all times.

Given all of that, I have sort of lapsed into perhaps a false sense of security because in the eleven years I have been here, my office has never been vandalized.

I unlock the front door, the deadbolt squeaking loudly as I turn the key. The minute I step inside, I see the offending weapon. A brick had come through the window. It managed to land perfectly in the middle of my desk. Thankfully, it missed the computer monitor sitting six inches to its left.

I also immediately realize this is not a typical vandalism as there seems to be a white piece of paper rubber-banded around the brick.

A message?

Minutes later, I'm dialing the police department and asking for someone to come out to take a report. Had it not been for the note wrapped around the brick, I would have merely turned this over to my landlord to fix. But when someone scrawls a personal message—*Die, Cunt*—on a brick that comes through the window, I kind of feel the need to at least have the police acknowledge what happened. That way, there will be a paper trail in case anything else occurs.

The front door of my office flies open, and Frannie storms in. "What in the hell happened?"

I hand her the note I'd been holding onto after I unwrapped it from the brick. Frannie reads it, and her hand flutters at the base of her throat as she peers at me with worried eyes. "Who did you piss off?"

I shrug. In my line of work, I've pissed off a lot of people.

"It could be the man I sued so his wife could have

custody of their dog in their divorce proceeding, or the thug I helped the DA prosecute for animal cruelty because he was running a dogfighting ring, or hey... it could be the real estate developer I just sued to save an endangered woodpecker. Take your pick."

No lie. It could've been any one of those people and probably half a dozen others. My money was on the man who doesn't want to give up custody of the dog in the divorce, though. Divorce proceedings are some of the nastiest types of law anyone will ever practice. Throw the love of an animal in there, and I'm not surprised it's taken eleven years for somebody to throw a brick through my window. I know plenty of domestic attorneys who arm themselves with guns in their desk drawers because there have been some violent people who come after them.

Surprisingly, it doesn't take long for a patrol car to show up. Two helpful but ultimately powerless police officers come in and take the report. They're polite and say they'll check the surrounding businesses to see if any of them had working security cameras they could look at. They are not, however, hopeful this would yield anything because this area is so rundown the people here really can't afford such security. We just have to kind of hope nothing bad happens.

While I talk to the police, Frannie calls the landlord, since he owns the entire strip of businesses on this block. He promises to send out a maintenance crew to at least board up the window until he can get it replaced.

When the police officers leave, Frannie turns to me and says, "What are they going to do to catch the bastard who did this?"

I give her a sympathetic smile and love her even more for her concern. "Not much they can do. No eyewitnesses and probably no security footage."

"But surely they'll investigate the people you might have pissed off in your legal cases?"

I shake my head. Another sympathetic smile. Poor Frannie. "Not really. I can't divulge anything about my clients without breaching confidentiality."

"You're not giving them info on your clients, just the people on the other side of the cases," she points out.

"Yeah, but to do that would reveal who my clients are, and that's getting into a gray zone. I'd rather not."

"You're awful Zen about this whole someone-throwing-a-brick-through-your-window thing," she observes with a skeptical look thrown in on top.

I shrug, a contented and somewhat sly smile curving my lips as I head into the small utility closet where I keep a broom. The broken glass spread over the floor is not going to clean itself up.

Apparently, because I am willfully refusing to explain the smile I gave her, Frannie goes ahead and gets to jumping to conclusions.

"Oh my God. Ford Daniels is the one who put that smile on your face, isn't he?" Her eyes are bright and twinkling, and she is truly excited for me.

I grin as I start to sweep. "He may have stayed over last night."

"You like him," she says in an accusing voice. Not because she would be unhappy I like a guy, but because I am holding all of this too close to the vest and being stingy with details.

A tiny laugh escapes and I assure her, "Frannie... when I figure out what this is with Ford, you are going to be the first person to know. In fact, you will be the only person to know."

Frannie sits down in one of the guest chairs while I sweep underneath my desk. "So do you think this could get serious?"

"I have no clue. But I do really like him."

She leans forward in the chair and pins me with that look. The one that says I can't bullshit my best friend. "You're not telling me something."

I don't even think about holding out on her. I pause in my sweeping, holding the top of the broom handle loosely in one hand and the dustpan in the other. "He's not exactly a long-term relationship kind of guy. He's admitted as much."

Frannie stares at me like I'm nuts. "Who cares? Just have fun while it lasts."

"Easy for you to say," I chastise and turn back to my sweeping. "You've got a man to go home to every night."

"You don't need a man, Viv," she says boldly. "You

are a fierce, independent woman who can take care of herself."

Squatting down, I sweep the glass shards I'd accumulated into a pile into the dustpan and tip it over into my garbage can.

When I stand up, I say, "Put aside his assertion he's not long-term material, Frannie… He's like perfect in every other way. Charming, intelligent, interested in what I have to say, doting, gallant, and oh yeah, the best sex I've ever had in my entire life."

I let that last statement kind of hang in the air because while I've never been one to focus in on that aspect of a relationship when trying to prioritize things that are important, I've come to learn very recently it actually is something incredibly important between a man and a woman.

"You really like him," Frannie says once again, this time reiterating exactly what my fears are by her tone of voice.

"Yeah… I really like him. And I'm probably going to like him more and more as time goes on."

Frannie nods at me sagely, and then finishes my sad prediction for the future. "And when he's decided he's had enough because he's not a relationship type of guy, your heart is going to be broken."

"And there you have it," I say softly.

"Are you going to give up?" she asks with absolute challenge in her voice.

"Fuck no," I tell her. She knows I'm not the quitting type.

Just then, my cell phone rings and I nab it off the edge of my desk. A brief glance at the screen indicates it's Dr. Granger, the veterinarian who first enlisted me to take this case. I tap the screen to accept the call and answer, "Hello, Dr. Granger."

"I've told you to call me Alton," he chides in a voice he tries to make sound charming and even a little flirty, but that's exactly why I call him Dr. Granger and not Alton.

My only hesitation in taking this case when he originally brought it to me was because he was also coming on to me and I wasn't interested.

But the case fascinated me, and my heart went out to this endangered species. Since then, I've made sure that all of my dealings with this man have been overly professional so he gets the hint.

"What can I do for you?" I ask, keeping my voice light and friendly, but making the statement when I don't acknowledge his request that I use his first name.

It's obvious by his voice he's not happy about it because his tone goes cool and professional. "We've had a very interesting donation, and I wanted to let you know about it. Someone dropped off a check today. They wish to remain an anonymous donor to anyone else within the organization, but as the president, I accepted the donation for five thousand dollars."

"And?" I ask, prompting him to get to the meat of the matter.

"The condition of anonymity also went along with a very specific request that the donation go to help fund your case."

My entire body sizzles with adrenaline. With this donation, I can afford to hire a good expert. Or I could hire two mediocre experts. I know quantity is going to be as important as quality when it comes to putting this information in front of the judge, and Ford already told me that he's going to be spending a lot of money on multiple experts.

Another zap of adrenaline hits me, and not in a good way. My face flushes, and the center of my chest burns.

Ford.

He's the only person who knows I can't afford to hire an expert.

We are already skirting a dangerous breach of ethical duty to our clients by sleeping together, but him helping to fund my case? He could get disbarred for that.

"Dr. Granger... I'm going to need to talk to you about this later. I've got something urgent that has just come up."

"Of course," he stammers. "Call me back when you get a moment."

I disconnect the call. "You think you can keep an eye on this place until the maintenance crew gets here?" I ask Frannie.

"Of course," she says. "Just leave me your keys and I'll let them in."

I nod. Quickly scribbling a note to tape to the front door, I direct them to go over to Frannie's when they arrive.

"Where you are going?" she asks.

"Downtown. I need to go see a meddling attorney and rip him a new one," I answer angrily.

IT IS A rare occasion I will pull out my "bitch attorney" persona. But I don't have time to be jerked around by the Knight & Payne receptionist who is somehow managing to look down her nose at me even though she's sitting down and I'm standing up. "I'm sorry, but Mr. Daniels has no appointments available and he's busy right now."

I have no idea if this is true or not, but between clenched teeth, I say, "If Mr. Daniels finds out I was here and you did not let him know, your job is going to be in jeopardy. Now I suggest you pick up your phone to call him and let him know Viveka Jones is here to see him."

Her perfectly arched eyebrows fly up high. She only hesitates a second before her lips thin out and she picks up the handset. I keep a neutral expression on my face even though I want to smirk in victory when she says into the phone, "Mr. Daniels… I'm sorry to interrupt and I've told her you're busy, but there's a Viveka Jones here insisting to see you—"

Her eyes cut sharp to mine, and I go ahead and give her a victory smile.

"Of course, Mr. Daniels," she says in response to whatever it is he said to her. I can, of course, only imagine. "I'll send her back immediately."

The door leading to The Pit is locked, but the receptionist stands up stiffly from her desk and walks over to a key card reader. Her employee identification badge is hanging around her neck on a lanyard, and she bends over slightly to hold it up to the security pad. When I hear the click of the door unlocking, I give her a genuinely grateful smile and say, "Thank you."

She nods stiffly, but she's also already forgotten. I push through the door and enter The Pit.

The noise of so many people talking, moving about and rustling papers is overwhelming at first but by the time I hit Ford's office, I've blocked it out. I'm both angry and frustrated by Ford's behavior, because he has crossed a line. In my opinion, his actions put our entirely short, but amazing, relationship in jeopardy.

He sees me approach through the glass wall. I am almost knocked over by the dazzling smile of joy on his face when he sees me. I have to grit my teeth because my mouth wants to naturally smile back, but we need to get a few things straight first.

Ford walks around his desk to greet me as I push open his door. My hand reaches out and automatically slaps at the button that fills the glass with smoke, so we can't be seen.

I almost feel sorry for him when I see his eyes go dangerously hot and sexy over my bold maneuver. My other hand goes up, palm facing him, and I say, "Stop right there."

Ford does my bidding and his body goes rigid as he takes in my defensive posture and the cool tone to my voice.

"What are you doing here?" he asks in a neutral voice.

I twist to open the purse on my shoulder, and then grab the certified check I just had issued from my bank. It was a quick stop I made on the way to Ford's office.

I pull it out and walk up to him, pushing it up against his chest. His hands come up and automatically grab it from me, but he doesn't look at it. Rather, he locks his eyes onto mine. They're filled with confusion as well as challenge. He knows I'm mad about something, so he's automatically gearing up for a fight.

I pull my hands back, and he finally glances down at the check I have just handed him. I watch his face carefully, but there is no surprise registered there.

But I didn't expect there to be. He knows what it means.

Still, he tries to play it off. "What's this for?"

"Don't play stupid with me, Ford," I hiss as I go to my tiptoes to get in his face. "You gave that money to

Justice for All Animals. And by doing that, you have put yourself in danger with the North Carolina bar. You could lose your license."

Not a single muscle on his face twitches, and his voice is casual. "I didn't give any money to Justice for All Animals."

Yes, I am really pissed at Ford for doing this. I'm also ridiculously charmed and warmed beyond measure that he is trying to help me. But I'm mostly pissed.

"Don't bullshit around with me."

Ford bends down to put his face within inches of mine, and his voice is hard as he clips out. "I did *not* give any money to Justice for All Animals."

I am not falling for his denials. I have come to learn a lot about this man, and I know he likes to play the role of the alpha protector. But I'm not having it right now. Not when he could hurt himself in the process.

I take two steps back from him, crossing my arms over my chest. I nod at the check in his hand and say, "It was either you or Leary, and I don't care which. But that check had better be cashed by the end of the day to reimburse whoever made that generous donation or—"

"Or what?" he growls. It seems Ford doesn't like being told what to do or for it to be insinuated he's done something wrong that he believes was chivalrous.

"Or," I say dramatically as I sweep my hands from my shoulders downward. "You can kiss this fabulous body goodbye, because you are not having any more if you're going to put yourself at risk for me."

Ford's lips start to curl because I've amused the hell out of him. Before I can try to say something to wipe the smile off his face, my phone rings.

"Low Rider" by War belts out from inside my purse.

Frannie's ringtone.

I snag my phone, connect the call, and hold up one finger to Ford to indicate I need to take this but the argument is not over, just on hold. Putting the phone up to my ear, I say, "What's up, Frannie?"

"The workmen are here to board up the window," Frannie says, and I immediately go on guard by the stiffness in her voice. "But they said the landlord isn't going to pay for the repair, and they want assurances you will pay them before they start."

"You have to be fucking kidding me?" I snap into the phone, not at my bestie but at the situation. But it's a rhetorical question. Frannie would not kid around about that. So I tell her, "I'm on my way. I should be there in fifteen minutes."

"All right, sweetie." Frannie gives a little cough and then says in a sly voice. "But I can pay them, and you can pay me back. You don't have to rush out of there if you don't want to."

"I'm on my way," I say firmly.

I disconnect from Frannie but before I can stuff my phone back in my bag, Ford is demanding. "What's going on?"

So bossy. So nosy. Both things are really hot because I can hear within his voice that whatever is wrong on my end, he wants to fix it.

I give a casual shake of my head, trying for a carefree smile as he's tried to fix enough stuff in my life already. "It's nothing. Someone vandalized my office last night."

"What?" Ford shouts.

Oh, wow… he's completely pissed off.

"Someone threw a brick through the window with a colorful message attached to it."

"What was the message?" he demands slowly.

His eyes are now scary dark and murderous.

"It's not important."

"What. Was. The. Message," he clips out.

I swallow hard, because I've never heard that tone from him. I don't even think to lie because I know he'd know it was a lie. "Die, cunt."

Ford spins away from me to grab his suit jacket that had been laid over the back of his chair behind his desk. He shrugs it on. Stuffing the check that he had been holding into the front breast pocket, he swipes his keys off his desk and shoves those in his front pant pocket, taking only a moment to bend over and shut his laptop.

He spares me a very brief glance as he starts to walk toward his door. "I'll talk to you later. I've got something I have to do."

My arm shoots out and my fingers clutch onto his suit jacket, which pulls him up short. He gives me an impatient look.

"I don't think your client did this, Ford, if that's what you're thinking."

He just stares at me, a muscle in his jaw jumping.

Oh yeah, he totally thinks his client did it.

"Not that your client isn't a dick," I tell him softly in the hopes of dissuading him from doing something stupid. "But I have a lot of people who would be higher up on the candidate list than Drake Powell."

Ford's voice is tight as he asks me, "In the eleven years you have been in that office and doing this type of law, has anyone ever thrown a brick through your window with a message that says, 'Die, cunt'."

I have no choice but to admit, "Well… no."

Shadows of retribution flicker in his eyes, but his voice is eerily calm when he says, "Let go of my arm."

I automatically release my grip on him because I can tell there is no stopping whatever it is he is planning to do. Hopefully, he's not going to do something stupid. At the most, I can only imagine him going to see Drake Powell to ask him if he or any of his cronies had anything to do with it.

I'm going to have to trust he won't get himself in trouble. Still, I need to make sure he doesn't forget the most important thing about my visit.

I call out as he opens his office door, "Ford… that check had better be cashed by the end of the day."

I get nothing back but a grunt before he's out the door.

CHAPTER 15

Ford

FROM THE DAY I first met Viv, chained to a longleaf pine, I knew she was different than any other woman I have met before. From that first kiss, I was pretty sure I would not be bored with her within a few months.

From that first time I sank inside her body, I realized nothing had ever felt better.

These were all truths I immediately recognized and accepted. In some way, I knew deep in my gut that Viveka Jones would have a major impact on my life.

Which makes this all very confusing that I'm feeling the greatest doubt in my life when it comes to her.

As I sit here in my car across the street from her office—the front window crudely covered with a piece of plywood—I realize I am at a crossroads with her. Now would be the perfect time to walk away. We've had a great time together, although I sure as shit would miss fucking her. But she wasn't wrong in my office yesterday when she was outraged over the fact I had essentially funded her case. It was a stupid-as-fuck thing to do because I could have killed my entire career had I been caught.

But the truth is, I would do it again if I thought she would let me. Career be damned. This is what is confusing to me because even though I knew Viv was special in so many ways from the other women that inhabited this planet, I am utterly confounded I would be willing to risk the thing I probably hold most dear in my life next to my family.

My law career.

I stare at that plywood covering her office window, and I acknowledge the burning fury within my chest that it was most likely done by my client, Drake Powell.

Oh, he denied it when I went to his office yesterday. Even acted all offended when I confronted him. I made sure to do it in a concerned, professional way—just an attorney looking out for his client's best interest. He insisted he had nothing to do with it.

I don't believe him for a second. He either did it, directed someone to do it, or one of his buddies did it and he knew about it.

I know this mostly because he made a comment to me the other day on the phone when I was telling him how much the expert witnesses were going to cost. He was not happy about the figure I quoted him and after he ranted about how the legal system was designed to screw over people like him, he also added on, "Someone should do something about that uppity cunt."

That choice of words has me convinced.

Drake Powell had everything to do with that brick going through her window.

And that knowledge has caused a burning need within me to look after Viveka. That, in turn, causes me to open my car door and step out. I lock it up, wait for traffic to pass and then trot across the street.

When I try to pull her door open, it doesn't budge because it's locked up tight. I press my face closer to the glass and put my hands up to shield the sun, peering inside. I don't see Viv, and the lights are off.

I twist toward Do or Dye. Maybe Frannie knows where she is.

When I open the salon door, I immediately see Viveka even though she's sitting the farthest from the door, clear on the other side of the space. She's wearing what I have come to learn is her standard attorney outfit for the type of law she practices. Jeans and a casual yet frilly blouse so she retains an air of femininity. Today, she's sporting black rubber rainboots that are streaked with mud across the top of the foot, but the soles appear to be clean.

She's sitting sideways in one of the salon chairs, one leg cocked over the armrest and the other on the floor. She's using it to push herself around in circles. I watch her for a moment as she spins around while surfing on her iPhone.

So gorgeous. Free spirited. Quirky.

Christ, it's such an attractive combination I could stare at her all day.

I tear my eyes away and glance around the salon, seeing three stylists along with their clients in salon chairs all staring at me.

A woman about my age with purple and blue hair gives a loud cough. Without taking her eyes off me, she calls, "Veka... I think you have a visitor."

My eyes slice over to Viveka just in time to see her plant a foot hard onto the tile floor to stop her spinning. Her eyes go wide as she takes me in, before they cloud over with a certain aloofness. She and I have not talked since she showed up at my office yesterday morning. I have no clue what she's thinking but I have to consider she might be surprised to see me here thinking my lack of contact with her was sort of a kiss off.

In all actuality, I was letting her cool off. She was really pissed at me yesterday, and rightly so.

Besides... absence makes the heart grow fonder, right?

Viveka doesn't say a word but just continues to stare at me. I, in turn, stare right back at her.

This goes on for so long it starts to get uncomfortable, and the women watching us start fidgeting.

Frannie mutters under her breath but we can all hear her. "Well, this is awkward."

This makes me turn to the left, and I give Frannie a

short smile. I step forward and hold my hand out to her to shake. "Hi. I'm Ford Daniels. And you must be Frannie."

Her eyebrows rise, and she darts a glance at Viveka. She holds up a gloved hand smeared with something she had been putting in her client's hair. "Sorry. Can't shake hands. But nice to meet you."

I nod at Frannie and turn back to Viv. She stares at me, and I can't read a thing on her face.

"Can we talk privately?" I ask from across the salon.

She doesn't even twitch, but instead asks me, "Did you cash my check?"

I give her a curt nod, and it causes her to propel herself out of the chair. Her face is awash with relief, and it's a testament to how concerned she was for me. Her anger was born out of worry, and that causes a funny feeling to well up inside of me.

She walks across the salon in her jeans and rubber boots, and I know she could sell them on the catwalk. I drink in her long legs and swaying hips as she comes closer.

She doesn't slow down but instead crashes right into me. Her hands dive into my hair, and her mouth slams onto mine. I catch her body weight easily, pulling her in tight as we engage in probably the deepest, hottest kiss we have ever had.

I vaguely hear a woman murmur, "Oh my."

Viveka's tongue practically wraps around mine, and I

groan deep into her throat.

The same woman says in a much more purring kind of way, "Oh my…"

This seems to knock some sense into us because we pull apart, grinning stupidly at each other. Her hands slide to my cheeks, and her thumbs rub along my jaw. Her eyes are swirling with both desire and gratitude. She merely says, "Thank you for cashing it."

"Well, I wasn't about to give up that hot body of yours."

Viv tosses her head back and laughs. I have the insane urge to lean forward and bite her neck.

Instead, I wait for her eyes to come back to mine. "I wasn't ready to give you up. And so if I had to cash the check, I was going to cash the check. I mean, I want to win this case, but fuck it all… I want you to as well. I just went about handling it the wrong way."

"I understand," she replies softly. "But we have to keep the case separated from us."

I lean forward and touch my forehead to hers.

My voice goes low so none of the women straining to hear can. "I just want you to be on an even playing field. It's not fair you're not because of money. I don't like the thought of you struggling even if it is in a case against me. But I know it's wrong and how dangerous it was to do that. My only excuse is you drive me crazy, and I wasn't thinking straight."

I can feel Viv's body melt into mine. She pulls her

head back, so she can look me in the eye. "I get it. And I'm not going to lie, it's kind of swoony that you would do that for me. But please don't worry about me, Ford. I am a scrappy lawyer. I've never been able to afford the best, so I make sure to bust my ass and use the full extent of my brains on every case. Sometimes I win, and sometimes I don't. Sometimes I win when I shouldn't, and sometimes I lose when I've done everything right. It all balances out for me. If I do my best, I can never be truly disappointed with the results. Because of that, I am okay with whichever way this case turns out, and you need to trust in that."

I bring my hands up to the side of her neck and slide my thumbs under her jaw to hold her in place. It's a domineering move, but I can tell by the flicker of heat in her eyes that she likes it.

"Is everything good between us?" I ask, making sure there is no misunderstanding my level of concern over her answer.

Her eyes soften. "We're okay. More than okay."

I lean in and my mouth finds hers, needing to cement everything we said with a kiss. When I pull back, I ask, "Want to go out and grab some dinner?"

Viv glances down at her watch and then at me with a smirk. "It's only four o'clock."

Shrugging, I drop my hands to lace my fingers through hers. I give her a slight tug toward the door, and she easily follows. "Let's go find something else to do."

There's enough innuendo in my voice that I hear that same woman say once again, "Oh my…"

♦

VIVEKA BOUNCING UP and down on my cock, my hands squeezing her tits, and her fingers at her clit.

The most goddamn beautiful thing ever. The hottest thing ever. I want this on video at some point.

There's no surprise when Viv's body tightens and her back arches with an orgasm. I buck my hips upward and start to come violently.

My body sags back down into the mattress, and Viveka collapses on top of me. For several long moments, we are nothing but a sweaty tangle of limbs and hard breathing.

After several more long moments of cuddling and regaining body function, I make my way to her master bathroom to ditch the condom and get cleaned up. She pushes in right behind me and goes over to the shower, leaning in to turn it on.

"Let's go out to eat," she says.

"Okay," I agree easily as I study her ass in the bathroom mirror. It's a fantastic ass. Rounded and toned with ivory skin as soft as rose petals. My hands spend a lot of time there. After peeling the condom off, I chuck it into her trash can.

"Did you go talk to Drake yesterday?" she asks over her shoulder to me. Our eyes lock in the mirror.

"I did."

"And?" she prompts.

"He says he had nothing to do with the brick through your window," I say through gritted teeth.

Lying bastard.

"He probably didn't," she says softly, and that makes me turn around to face her directly rather than talk through the mirror. "Trust me… I've pissed off lots of people in my practice."

I just bet she has. I bet she's induced a lot of men with lust, too. Probably amused a lot of people with her charm and humor. Caused envy and jealousy among women because she's so beautiful, and probably reduced them to embarrassed lumps of apology when they realize how genuine and nice she is.

Viveka, I'm sure, has a strong effect on most people she meets.

But time for a change of subject. "Can I ask you something?"

She tilts her head and smiles. "What's up?"

I step into her, my hands going to her waist. "Is there any reason we have to use a condom?"

She blinks in surprise. "Um… well, I'm not sure. I mean… we can talk about it."

"Let me clarify," I say in a low voice. "I'm safe, and I'll give you the paperwork to back that up."

"I'm safe," she blurts out quickly and a little too loudly, as if perhaps I was doubting that about her.

I wasn't. She hasn't been with anyone in two years since her husband, so I suspected as much. Her experience is so limited, I just didn't think that was the big issue.

"Are you on the pill?" I ask.

She bites her lip and shakes her head. "Wasn't any reason to be."

"Then we'll stick with condoms," I reply easily, and then give her a quick kiss on the corner of her mouth. "We'll buy in bulk."

I start to pull away, but she latches onto my wrist. "I can get on the pill."

While I'd love nothing but to feel my bare cock slide against her wet flesh, I give her a gentle smile. "You don't have to."

"I don't mind," she says with no doubt in her voice. "I've been on them before… when I was married to Adam."

"You didn't want kids?" I ask curiously.

"He didn't. At least not right away," she admits hesitantly. "And then… well, years sort of went by. He concentrated on his career. And by the time I realized the marriage was over, I also realized he probably never wanted them to begin with."

"Do you?" And it occurs to me I've never discussed this subject with another woman other than Leary, and with Leary, it had only been since she got pregnant. I never knew before—in all the years of our friendship or when we were lovers—how she felt about them.

"Yeah," Viveka says in a dreamy voice laced with a bit of sadness. "I do. One day."

I could see Viveka as a mother. She's a nurturer for sure, and I bet we would make beautiful babies—

What. The. Fuck?

I shake my head and take a step back from Viveka. She turns toward the shower, sticking her hand inside to test the water temperature. My expression must not have given away those inane thoughts I had, because her voice is light and teasing. "Want to come soap me down, Mr. Daniels?"

Yes… I want that very much.

I step into the shower behind her. We spend an enjoyable fifteen minutes getting cleaned up, which I feel is a waste since we're going to get dirty again right after dinner.

While Viveka does her hair and makeup, I step back into the bedroom to slip my clothes back on. I'd been in a dress suit when I showed up at Do or Dye earlier, so I put it all back on except the tie.

"Would you mind feeding the dogs?" she asks as she brushes on some mascara. Her blonde hair is slicked back and still so very pale even when wet. She looks like a fairy or something.

"Sure." I sit on the edge of her bed to put on my shoes and socks. It takes me what seems like forever, because while I'm fully clothed, Viveka does her hair and makeup while naked and it's hard to keep my eyes off her.

After I tie my Oxfords, I push from the bed and take one more shameless gander at Viv's beautiful body. She ignores me as she sweeps on some blush.

When I open the bedroom door, I find Butch and Daisy patiently waiting in the hallway. They don't like being shut out, but they've at least stopped howling and barking when we do so.

"Let's get some grub," I tell them both, and their tails start wagging furiously. That's Viveka's word to them for a meal, so they know they're bellies are about to be happy. It's also what I've learned to use to get them to come inside when they're being stubborn.

For example, I just have to call out, "Come get some grub," and they dash inside. Of course, then I'm forced to give them a treat.

It's funny in hindsight how easily I've acclimated to her dogs, and only I know I've made an overly diligent effort in order to impress Viveka. Still, it turns out her mutts are cute and well behaved—for the most part—so it hasn't been all that trying to develop a relationship with them.

One night we were watching a movie, and Viveka had gotten up from the couch to make some popcorn. Butch jumped right up on my lap as soon as she left. I didn't think twice about it, but when Viveka walked back in and saw me unconsciously rubbing his belly while he snoozed on my lap, she became so overwhelmed with the way I'd warmed up to her beasts that she gave me a blow job that fucking almost permanently crossed my eyes.

Of course Butch wasn't happy. He had to get off my lap for that.

I snicker over that memory as we cut through the living room toward the kitchen when there's a knock on the front door.

I don't even think twice, treating this space as my own since I just fucked Viveka thoroughly and had her calling out my name along with God's. Veering toward the door, I pull it open.

And standing on the porch is… Viveka.

Well, an older version of Viveka. The woman's blue eyes—the same pale Nordic shade—sweep up and down my body. When they land back on me, they're sparkling with keen interest.

Her voice is silky smooth when she purrs, "Well, hello there."

The accent is stronger than Viveka's but given the uncanny resemblance, I don't need anything more to tell me that this is her mother standing on her doorstep.

CHAPTER 16

Viveka

I GIVE A critical review of my makeup in the mirror, and I'm satisfied with the outcome. One could certainly argue it's unnecessary because Ford's clearly interested in more than just my looks.

But I can't help it.

I'm a girl who likes to primp. I like pretty clothes, dressing up, and putting forth my best. I'm sure a psychologist would agree that is something left over from my modeling days, but I choose to embrace it.

As I start to reach for my hairdryer I have in a large basket on my vanity, Ford walks into the bathroom. His eyes lock with mine, and they don't even bother to scan my nude body. This alone would indicate something is wrong, but I can tell by the hard lock to his jaw that whatever he's getting ready to tell me is not good.

I reach my hand down to the vanity and brace myself.

"Your mother is here," Ford says quietly.

Of all the things I thought he might say to me that would explain the grave expression on his face, I was not prepared for that.

"My mother?" I gasp. She had said she was going to come visit, but she never confirmed that.

Ford gives a curt nod. "Want me to... um... Do something with her?"

The uncertainty in his voice coupled with the fierce determination to be a buffer for me is adorable and makes me laugh. "What are you going to do—encase her feet in cement and throw her in the Neuse River?"

Ford rolls his eyes. "No, smartass. But if you want me to ask her to leave and tell her you are indisposed, I'll gladly do so."

That would be lovely. That way I can go on having a pleasant evening, and I can pretend that my mother doesn't give me immense heartburn.

Instead, I give a pained sigh as I shake my head. "No. I'll deal with her."

I make my way back into the bedroom, grateful Ford had shut the door behind him. I don't want to think about my mother eavesdropping on us. I'm sure she has a million questions about who Ford is and why he's in my house.

I grab a pair of yoga pants out of a dresser drawer, a loose T-shirt out of another, as well as a clean pair of panties and a bra from yet a third. Ford watches me as I get dressed, a contemplative look on his face.

"What?" I ask.

He gives a quick shake of his head. "Nothing. But it's uncanny how much you and your mother resemble each other. You could pass as sisters."

"Good Swedish genes, I guess." I mutter.

I move to the door but before I can reach for the knob, Ford stops me with an arm around my stomach. "Do you want me to leave?"

God, that is so fucking sweet.

Sure, one might say it's too early to introduce Ford to my mother because we haven't been together long, but my mother is not a typical parent whose opinion matters in these things. She's more like a casual acquaintance. As it stands, I have a deeper relationship with this man I've known for eight days than I do with the woman who bore me.

"Please don't go," I tell him. "I'm going to shamelessly use you as a buffer."

The breath is absolutely sucked out of my lungs by the beautiful smile Ford bestows upon me. If I had to guess, I really appealed to his alpha protectiveness. While I know Ford respects me as a woman and the fact I am independent, it's obvious any opportunity he can use to be the protector in this relationship, he's going to want to take it.

I hold my hand out to him palm up. He places his against mine, and our fingers clasp. "Let's do this."

"I've got your back," Ford says as I pull the bedroom

door open. Then in a lower voice, he says, "And what a gorgeous back it is."

I don't have to look over my shoulder as I lead him down the hallway to know his eyes are pinned on my ass. I can feel the weight of them just fine.

When I step out of my short hallway and into my living room, I can't help that futile moment of longing that hits me when I first lay eyes on my mother. After thirty-six years as her daughter, I have never stopped wishing she could be the type of mother I want.

The type of mother I need.

But when her eyes come to me for a cursory glance that results in a slightly disapproving grimace, and then go to Ford for a lingering look of approval, I know my wishes won't ever be granted.

There is no denying my mother is stunning.

Tilde Sjögren Wroth is fifty-three, and Ford would not be wrong with saying we could pass as sisters. She has never had plastic surgery to my knowledge, but her face is almost completely untouched by time.

Dewy fresh skin, a tall lithe body, and lustrous blonde hair she wears in a sleek shoulder-length bob. Her makeup is flawless, and her clothes are perfection. To the casual eye, her blue chambray shirt tied at her waist paired with white skinny jeans and flats done in a leopard print could be an outfit off the rack from Target. But because it's my mother and I know her, I'd bet my life every stitch of clothing on her is designer label and probably costs more than what I make in a week.

Simply put, she is stylish, stunning, and one of the most beautiful creatures I've ever seen.

I had told Ford one night as we lay in bed about the relationship I had with my mother. He'd already known the basics of how she had dragged me off to the States to relive her glory days as a model. He knew all about me emancipating myself from my mother. Ford is well up to date on what my life has been like since then.

But I didn't bother to tell him much about the woman she became after I left New York and she had to learn to survive on her own.

She's currently married to her third husband since she lost me as a money source. While she loves to dally with younger men, for marriage, the older and richer the better. Stephan totally fit the bill. He's a nice guy, if not a little gullible in believing Tilde married him for his personality.

Even though Stephan is eighty-three, he's in pretty good health and I'm sure that's to my mother's great dismay. Not that it matters. As long as he indulges her with any luxury she could want as well as not be too demanding of her time, she's perfectly happy to ride the marriage out until Stephan dies of natural causes. I have no clue if he's going to leave his wealth to her, but it's also none of my business.

"Viveka," my mother says in a rich, cultured voice that borders on irritation. "Could you please put those dogs up?"

I note that my dogs are being extremely well behaved. They do bark on occasion, but they never jump on visitors. Right now, they are busy sniffing my mother's legs.

I ignore her request. "It's nice to see you again too, Mor."

My mother sniffs at me in an offended way, but she's mollified somewhat that I called her Mor, which is Swedish for mother.

But I'm really not what's important. She's found something far more interesting, and she turns her attention to Ford. This is not surprising in the least. If my mother is in a room with a mixture of people, her attention has always been on the male persuasion. She steps forward and holds out an elegantly manicured hand loaded with sparkly jewelry. "We didn't formally introduce ourselves earlier. Tilde Sjögren."

Ford leans toward her and shakes her hand. "Ford Daniels."

He tries to pull his hand away, but my mother doesn't let go. She brings up her other hand to clasp his tightly. "It is an absolute pleasure."

I want to roll my eyes, but I stopped doing that over my mother's antics around the time I decided to get emancipation. It's when I realized my mother has a true nature, and it won't change.

Tilde turns to me, still clamped down on Ford's

hand, and purrs, "He's quite a catch, Viveka."

And then she leans toward me and gives a little giggle that sounds absolutely ludicrous. She lowers her voice as if Ford can't hear her, but he totally can. "If I was just ten years younger…"

She lets that hang in the air, an invitation to the man who might be interested in what she just offered.

Ford merely pulls his hand away from her. He steps over to me where he puts his arm around my waist. It's an overt move and completely unnecessary if he did it to soothe me. I have never been jealous of my mother's overtures toward other men before.

I watched her try it on anyone I dated as well as my ex-husband. One thing I can say is the modeling business built my skin up very thickly, and I learned how to let a lot of stuff roll off my back. Moreover, I am a confident woman. What I just did to Ford in my bedroom rocked his world, and there was no way he'd be looking twice at Tilde for that.

My mother, of course, does not like this rebuff. She fully expected me to giggle right along with her as if we were the oldest of pals. She also expected Ford to flirt with her, because let's face it… most men do. She's an exquisitely sexy woman.

"What are you doing here, Mor?" I ask lightly, and her attention comes back to me with narrowed eyes.

I've offended her with my cool tone and in my refusal to play her games. She lets her eyes roam over me critically, and I brace for her bitterness.

When she brings her eyes back to mine, she says, "Honestly, Vivvy… What are you doing to yourself? Have you gained weight?"

Ford's body goes rigid beside me at the overt slap my mother just gave me. I hate that Ford doesn't know enough about our relationship to realize this is par for the course. I am sure he's shocked at her behavior.

But if he is going to stick around for any length of time, he needs to learn and the best way is to observe firsthand.

I give my mother a bright smile instead. "I don't know, Mor. I don't own a scale. I stopped worrying about what I weighed years ago. Right around the time I stopped modeling, actually."

And then I dig the knife in because my mother is itching for battle, and I always refuse to give it.

Instead, I give her the most flattering compliment I can. "But you look amazing. I only hope I can be as beautiful as you are when I get to be your age."

Ford makes a choking sort of noise and my mother blinks at me rapidly as if she can't understand what I'm saying. She has no clue if I'm joking or making fun of her.

I'm not. What I said was absolutely true.

My mother gets frustrated that she can't figure me out. The only way she knows how to get the upper hand is to try to tear me down further. She has never forgiven me for abandoning modeling and consequently abandoning her.

My mother turns to Ford as she throws a thumb my way. "That one threw away an amazing career. She could have been famous. One of the highest earning models in history. But her lack of ambition was her downfall sadly."

Again, I struggle to stop the eye roll. This is Tilde's version of mom guilt, and she's laying it on thick. Unfortunately for her, it stopped having an effect on me long ago.

When Ford's body locks tight beside me again, I know he's taken great offense.

I open my mouth to distract my mother as this is starting to get awkward, but Ford is going to have his say. "I think your daughter's ambition is perhaps greater than any I've ever seen before. She put herself through college and law school. Used her brains to get ahead in life. Now I don't mean to malign the modeling industry or to make light of what hard work she put into that early career, but I imagine if you really knew everything your daughter has accomplished, you would indeed be a very proud parent."

Again like an owl, my mother just blinks and blinks, trying to understand what Ford said. In her world, men don't appreciate women with intelligence. They want a sexy body and a beautiful face. It's unfathomable to my mother to think otherwise.

Using a bright, cheery voice I hold in special reserve to irritate the hell out of my mother, I say, "How long are you in town? Because Ford and I were on the way out the door for long-standing plans that we cannot cancel."

My mother sort of jerks as if stunned I'm not canceling my plans to spend time with her. Maybe I'm being an awful child by doing so, but the amount of loyalty I have for my mother due to our blood ties is nominal.

"Dinner tomorrow night?" she proposes in a clipped voice. "I'll be flying out Sunday."

I grit my teeth because there's no way out of this without being a real bitch, and besides… she is my mother. She could still evolve, I suppose. And I never would want any regrets if God forbid something happened to her and I missed an opportunity to spend some time with her—however unpleasant it might be. "That will work."

"And Ford…" My mother turns her charms his way, leaning over and touching his arm. "You simply must come, too."

Um… no.

Not going to let Ford suffer with me. "I'm sure Ford has better things to do than—"

"I'd love to," he says, giving my waist a squeeze, not as a reassurance but more of a warning for me not to argue with him.

Alpha jerk.

Hot jerk.

My mother gives me a gracious incline of her head and a sweet—but fake—smile. "Call me tomorrow and we'll firm up plans. I'm staying at the Renaissance."

Of course she's staying at the Renaissance. There's no way she would ever want to stay at my house because first and foremost, it's not high class enough for her. I can't afford twelve-hundred thread count sheets. Mostly, I know it's because she brought her boy toy to North Carolina with her and she would want privacy.

I pull away from Ford to walk my mother to the door. She turns and gives me an air kiss near one cheek and then another. She doesn't even glance at Ford before she walks out.

I shut the door, turning the deadbolt in case she decides to come back in. Slowly, I turn around to face Ford. I lean back against the door and give a long-suffering sigh.

He grimaces. "So that was your mom, huh?"

I blow out a shaky breath because for all of my confidence I'm able to show my mother when I'm face to face, it's quite draining to deal with her. "That's my mother."

Ford walks to me and pinches my chin lightly between his thumb and forefinger. He tilts my head up to look at him. "How did you turn out so normal?"

I place the palms of my hands on his chest and give him a little pat. "Who's to say I'm not a whack job?"

Ford's grip on my chin tightens, and his eyes darken

slightly. "You are not a whack job. And I'm an excellent judge of character."

"You're sweet," I tell him.

I go to my tiptoes, which dislodges Ford's hold on me, and I press my mouth to his for a soft kiss.

When I come back down to my heels, Ford wraps a hand around the back of my neck. "I think you're amazing. And maybe perhaps your greatest accomplishment wasn't putting yourself through school, but rather deciding not to be the type of person your mother is."

My stomach flops over, and there is a sweetly aching pain in the center of my chest. It's not just that Ford always seems to say the right things, but that he says them without any thought.

It means that what I am hearing is coming straight from his heart.

And I have to say, a girl could really get used to this type of honest talk from a man.

CHAPTER 17

Ford

"WHO CHOSE THE restaurant? You or your mom?" I ask Viveka as we pull up in front of The Second Empire. It's one of the most expensive restaurants in Raleigh, and they have amazing food and the top-notch service to justify it.

She shoots me a smirk as the valet opens her door. "Who do you think?"

I pop my door open as I give her a return grin. "Your mother, of course."

Viveka turns to step out of the car but then immediately looks back to me, reaching out to touch my arm. "I'm getting the bill. No arguments."

"You're what?" I ask, because I think I heard her right but maybe I'm mistaken.

"Getting the bill. My mother won't pay, and God knows it's going to be enough that you have to suffer, so you're not paying for this extravagantly expensive meal and terrible company."

She doesn't even wait for me to acknowledge her command, just slides out of my front seat using the valet attendant's hand he offers. I just watch her. I have to say, Viveka in a sleek dress that comes just above her knees in normal circumstances but rides up to mid-thigh while she sits in the front seat of my Porsche is something to behold. I had thought about driving my G550 but a dress like that deserves a Porsche. My gaze lingers on her ass until the valet shuts the door, cutting me off from sight.

I exit my car and toss the keys to the attendant when he comes around the front of the car to meet me, then push a five-dollar bill into his hand.

"Thank you, sir," the kid says, but I ignore him.

Viv waits for me with a serene expression on her face. That's good. I think mentally she's ready to do battle with her mom if necessary, but she's going to try to take the high road the entire evening.

I also think she's extra adorable given the fact she thinks she can pay for this meal tonight.

My hand goes to Viv's lower back as I escort her into the restaurant. I don't see her mother but that doesn't surprise me. She looks like the type of woman who is always going to arrive fashionably late.

I give the maître d' our name. Within moments, someone appears at his side to escort us to our table. As Viv starts walking away, I lean into the maître d'. "I'm not sure when the rest of our party will arrive, but please go ahead and send the sommelier to our table."

The maître d' dips his head. "Of course, Mr. Daniels."

"And also make sure I'm given the check at the end of the meal. Despite what anyone else at the table says."

I get another gracious smile. "I will see to it."

Sorry, Viveka. You've been overruled.

By the time we're seated at our table, made a wine selection, and peruse the menu, Tilde still hasn't shown up. This is fine by me because that means I get more alone time with Viv.

She sits to my left at the round table designed to hold four. I hold a glass of Pinot Noir up, and she mimics me. We clink our glasses together and she says, "Here's to really good wine getting us through the evening."

"Amen," I say before I take a sip.

When I set my glass down, I reach across the table to take her hand. I like holding her hand. It's as simple as that. "What are we going to do tomorrow?"

I ask this because it's a given I'm going to stay at her house tonight. Tomorrow is a Sunday, and the weather is going to be fantastic. It's ballsy and egotistical for me to assume we'll spend the day together, but when I see something I want, I always go for it as if I'm going to get it.

"I don't know what *you* are doing," Viv says with a sly grin. "But I'm volunteering at a dog shelter tomorrow."

"So what does that mean… volunteering at a shelter? Because if you're talking about playing with puppies, I'm in."

Viveka laughs and shakes her head. "It means we have to clean out cages and give the dogs baths."

I grimace only slightly before recovering with a confident smile. "All right. Volunteering at the dog shelter tomorrow."

Viveka takes another sip of her wine, staring at me over the rim of the glass. When she puts it down, she gives me a very pointed look. "You know you don't have to do that, Ford. That's kind of my thing, and I do it a few times a month. It doesn't have to be *your* thing, though."

This is interesting. Us exploring the boundaries that perhaps as a couple we should put in place. We still need to maintain our own lives for sure, but that doesn't mean we have to.

I poke around the edges to see what she really means. "Do you like to play golf?"

She blinks those baby blues. "Um… I've never tried it. I'm not really into sports."

Yeah, well, I'm not really into cleaning up dog shit, but I'm adventurous.

"Would you go golfing with me if I asked you to?"

She's so fucking cute when she tilts her head as she ponders. "I suppose so."

I give a nod. "That's good. Because you see, golfing is

kind of my thing. And it might be *your* thing, too, but you won't know unless you try it. Just like cleaning dog shit out of cages might be *my* thing, but I won't know unless I try it."

She nods her head. "You know… you're actually making sense to me."

I laugh in response and give her a wink. "I'm glad you see things my way. So cleaning out dog cages and golfing is next on our agenda as a couple together."

"Are we? A couple?"

"Of course we are," I chide, because she should have no doubts. We've decided to fuck bare once she's adequately protected, and she's going to get in to see her gynecologist to get on the pill this week. But then I give her a lecherous grin. "Unless you're into threesomes. That can be hot."

I thought it would embarrass her and I really was only teasing, but she doesn't even blush.

"Me, you, and another guy?" she purrs and then licks her bottom lip. "I can totally be into that."

I have no fucking clue if she's teasing or not, but the tightening of my pants as my dick starts to harden tells me I hope to God she's not kidding.

Before I can fathom the truth, though, I see her mother walking toward us with a man trailing behind her who appears to be in his late twenties.

Tilde is wearing a scandalously low-cut dress that dips well below her breastbone and exposes the interior swells of her cleavage. It's white silk, gathered around her waist, and comes down barely far enough to cover her ass. The man walking behind her has his eyes pinned to said ass, as does about every other male patron she walks by. Tilde is aware of the attention and it's clear she actually thrives on it. I wonder what will happen to her when she reaches the age that she won't get that attention.

I find it fascinating Tilde walks just like Viveka. Long legs in a confident strut with hips swaying and arms swinging. I don't for a second think Viv mimicked her mother's walk just because she was first into the modeling thing. I would bet a year's salary that Viv patented her own walk on the runway and her mother copied it.

I lift my chin up to indicate to Viv that her mother is walking up behind her. She takes in a deep breath through her nose and blows it out through her mouth before she turns to look over her shoulder. Because I'm a gentleman and a lady approaches, I stand. Manners would dictate that Tilde's date pull her chair out for her, but she doesn't give him an opportunity. She walks to the chair to my right—furthest from her daughter—and looks at me almost imperiously.

I cut a glance at Viveka, who is biting back a laugh, before I pull the chair out for Tilde.

"Thank you, darling," she murmurs graciously in response.

I don't respond but take my seat again, cutting another glance at Viv. She's clearly amused, and that makes me feel much better about this evening. Viv has decided she can do nothing more than treat this like a comedy show.

Tilde's date takes the seat right across from me and glances around the table with a genial smile. He's got perfect teeth and a perfect face, and I am quite sure he's a model himself.

When Tilde picks up her menu and starts perusing it without saying another word, I stand up from my chair once again and reach my hand across the table to the man. "Hey… Ford Daniels."

The guy bobs his head and stands up to shake my hand. "Jim Delvecchio."

Tilde's eyes snap up from the menu to glare at her date as our hands break apart and we both sit back down. "It's Carmine," she instructs him with a good deal of censure in her voice. "You have to start using your professional name in all situations."

I turn to raise an eyebrow at Viveka, who just shrugs at me.

I let my gaze travel to Jim a.k.a. Carmine. "Professional name?"

The poor dude opens his mouth to answer me, but Tilde intervenes. "Yes, Carmine is his professional modeling name. So much snazzier than Jim. I'm his manager."

"Manager?" Viveka says with surprise, and I know exactly what she's thinking.

She's thinking of those two years where her mother was her manager and all the ways in which she abused that position. Viv's face is awash with empathy for poor Jim.

Tilde looks across the table at her daughter and acknowledges her for the first time this evening, which is really shitty by the way. "It's something I started doing on the side. You know, to keep me busy and occupied since Stephan still travels so much and is always working when he's not."

I can see the light go on in Viveka's eyes. I understand, too. That way, Tilde is able to travel with her current squeeze with impunity by hiding it under the moniker of a "manager-client" relationship.

Now, I can be a dirty, kinky son of a bitch when I want, but there is something about it that skeeves me out given the massive age difference between them. On the other hand, Tilde doesn't look her age and some dudes are into older women.

Turns out Jim… or Carmine… or whatever, is a nice guy. I'm sure he doesn't have any deep feelings for Tilde and he's using her as much as she's using him, but otherwise, he seems like a decent dude.

From what I can tell anyway as I catch snippets of his conversation with Viveka. That's because for most of the evening, Tilde tries to dominate the conversation, and by that, I mean she tries to talk only to me.

She leans toward me, talking intimately low to try to cut Viveka and Carmine out. I try a few times to include the others, but at one point, Viveka gives me a little shake of her head like "don't bother." The way she smiles at me tells me she's not bothered by this either, and I swear I saw relief on her face when Carmine engaged her in conversation about the modeling business. She'd rather actually talk to him than her mother, and as Viveka predicted, she's using me as a buffer.

This is fine by me.

After the main course is cleared away, the waiter passes out dessert menus, starting with Tilde.

"No dessert for us," Tilde says with a wave of her hand. The waiter pulls the menu back.

"Actually, I'd like to see that," Viveka says, and the waiter appears overjoyed that someone wants to partake.

"Me too," I add. I'm not actually a big sweets kind of guy, but I just instinctively know I need to see that menu. That Viv needs me to order dessert along with her.

The waiter moves to Viveka and hands her one, then gives one to me. He looks to Carmine, who stares longingly but after a quick glance to Tilde, shakes his head. She totally has him by the short hairs.

"I'll be back shortly to take your orders," the waiter says before walking away.

Tilde stares across the table toward her daughter in

disapproval, her lips pressed tight. I can see it on her face… the warring within herself on whether to say something.

When her lips part, I brace for her onslaught.

"Viveka," Tilde says in a falsetto voice in an attempt for this to come off as merely a pleasant piece of advice. "You know carbs and sugar go right to your hips. You and I both have that body type unfortunately, so perhaps you should pass."

My inclination is to jump to Viveka's defense, but I also know my girl waged a war once upon a time to sever her mother's parental ties, at least in the eyes of the law when she was just seventeen. I suspect that in order to keep the boundaries clear, Viveka needs to defend herself and doesn't need her guy to rush in to save her right now.

Viv takes a breath and shuts her eyes—probably asking for grace from above—and when she opens them again, they are lasered onto her mother with a ferocity that makes me actually feel a little bad for Tilde.

"Mor," she says softly, but it's not meant to make her feel safe and protected. It's with warning. "You lost your right to direct what I put in my mouth a long time ago."

Tilde actually appears surprised to hear this news. Her chin pulls inward, and her tone is affronted. "I'm only looking out for your best interests."

"No, you're not," Viveka says firmly. "You're trying to assert power and control over me because you can't stand you lost it long ago. You also delight in trying to put me down in little ways like making comments about my weight. But you need to know it doesn't hurt me. Doesn't piss me off. Doesn't make me feel bad about myself at all. It only makes you look foolish for trying to make me feel bad so you can feel good about yourself."

"Viveka," Tilde says sharply and with warning in her own voice. She's trying to come off as a parent reminding their child of their manners, but sadly, it's sort of whiny. "I did not raise you to speak to me that way."

Viv gives her mom a smile, and there's nothing but empathy there. She understands her mom and feels bad she can't be more than what she is. What's amazing to me is that Viv doesn't feel bad for herself. She feels bad for this woman who is probably missing out on a lot of really amazing things with her daughter if she just opened herself up to true motherhood.

I think perhaps Viveka may continue schooling her mother in the reality of their relationship and the fact it resembles nothing of a mother-daughter dynamic whereby Tilde might have the right to offer advice.

But instead, she turns to her left and says, "Carmine... it was fabulous meeting you. Good luck with your career."

Her head then swings in the opposite direction, bypassing a glance at her mother until her summer-blue eyes land on me. "Let's get dessert on the way home, okay?"

"Okay," I tell her with a smile, and I stand up from my chair. When I hold my hand out to Viv, she places her fingers against my palm. I let mine curl around to grip her lightly as she stands from her chair.

I turn to Carmine, give him a nod. Then to Tilde with a smile. "Lovely meeting you."

Tilde looks absolutely befuddled as her gaze snaps back and forth between her daughter and me.

I see the waiter coming back to take our dessert order, and I pull Viveka around the table to meet him. "No dessert tonight. But if you'll give the bill to that woman right there," I point at Tilde, who still seems a bit shell-shocked, "she'll be glad to pay."

Viveka snickers and then squeezes my hand. She heads for the exit with long strides, pulling me along behind her. I give one last look at Tilde, who is staring after us with an expression on her face like she just smelled a pile of shit.

When we step out onto the sidewalk, Viveka turns and launches herself into my arms. Her hands come to my face, and she grins like a lunatic on a drug high. "Damn… that was fun. I kind of want to go back in and do that again."

"Never got much of a chance before to put your mom in her place, have you?" I ask with a chuckle.

"I always felt icky about doing it," she admits as she drops her hands. "For a very long time, I felt guilty for leaving my career and her behind. There were years where I tried to overcompensate, and by that, I mean I let her run all over me because it made her feel better and that alleviated my guilt. But tonight… it just seemed the right way to handle her."

"It was absolutely the right way," I assure her as I reach into my pocket for my valet ticket. I hand it to the attendant and then take Viveka's hand in mine. "And please don't feel guilty for putting her in her place. Perhaps she'll think twice before she does that again."

"Well, that will be probably in about a year. We don't see each other often."

"I'm sorry," I say as we step to the side as other people exit the restaurant.

Viveka's head turns my way, her eyes round. "Why are you sorry?"

"That you even have to worry about this shit with your mom," I say as I pull her into my side and wrap my arm around her shoulder. "It's absolutely dysfunctional and a stress you shouldn't have to deal with. You're too good a person to have that crap in your life."

"I know," she murmurs as her arm comes around my waist. "And thank you for validating that."

"Anytime," I promise. I'll validate her anytime she wants. "Now… what kind of dessert will we pick up on the way home?"

She cranes her neck to stare up to me. "A few cans of whip cream."

"Just whip cream?"

Her smile is mischievous and erotic, and it punches me in the gut. "We can do a lot of creative things with whip cream, Ford."

CHAPTER 18

Viveka

"WILL THE DEFENDANT rise and face the court?" the judge says.

I twist my neck to the left to watch as the man stands up from his chair and glares defiantly at Judge Barefoot. Melanie Case, the assistant district attorney who I'm sharing the counsel table with, leans toward me and mutters, "The defendant is such a dick."

I look past her to the man I helped Melanie prosecute. Totally a dick.

"Mr. Kramer," Judge Barefoot says in a gruff voice. "I hereby find you guilty of animal cruelty and neglect, and sentence you to four months in county jail with credit for time served, one hundred hours of community service, and restitution for the veterinarian bills."

"That's bullshit," Curtis Kramer says, and his attorney puts a restraining hand on his shoulder. "That dog was my property, and I can treat it as I see fit."

Judge Barefoot isn't impressed by this outburst. "The

law says differently, Mr. Kramer. And I'm going to tack on an additional thirty days in jail for contempt of court because you have seemingly forgotten your manners. If you open your mouth and say one more word, I'll add on sixty days."

The judge bangs his gavel and stands up. The bailiff says, "Court is adjourned."

Melanie and I stand up from the table, and she turns to me to give me a hug. She usually associates with me on all of her animal cruelty and neglect cases. We've also become good friends over the years. "Thank you so much for your help, Viv."

When I pull back, I smile at her. "My pleasure. You did a great job."

I guarantee that the pit bull that we rescued from Mr. Kramer's property thinks she did a fabulous job, too. He's currently being fostered and hopefully will be adopted out very soon. Any man who stakes his animal on a two-foot chain by the neck outside without adequate food and water deserves to be in jail as far as I'm concerned.

Snagging my briefcase off the table, I turn to walk out of the gallery area. I come up short when I see Leary sitting in the front row with her palms resting on top of her rounded belly. She's wearing a dark blue dress that hugs her tummy with a matching jacket.

When she sees me coming, she leans to one side, places a palm to the wooden bench, and uses that to help haul herself up. When I reach her, she gives me a sheepish grin. "This belly is getting a little cumbersome. Can't wait until I can see my feet again."

"How much longer do you have?" I ask as she slides out of the row to meet me.

"Just about four weeks," she mutters. "Or sooner if I can talk my doctor into inducing early so we can get this over with."

"They can do that?" I ask in awe.

She shakes her head and grimaces. "Only in my dreams."

We both laugh for a moment, but then I ask her. "What are you doing here?"

"I was over in the next courtroom arguing a motion. As I was leaving, I glanced in and saw you sitting there. Just thought I would say hello."

"Well, that's nice," I say with a smile, and we both turn to start walking out of the courtroom. "I don't get over here to criminal court very often. But I have to say, I do enjoy watching the bad guys get locked up for mistreating animals."

Leary laughs. To my surprise, she hooks her arm through mine as we walk down the aisle as if we are the best of buds. "Hey… want to go grab some lunch?"

"You realize it's just past ten thirty," I tease.

"Shut up. I'm pregnant and I'm allowed to eat early lunch. Then I'm allowed to eat regular lunch."

"Feel like a hot dog? I always hit up Snoopy's when

I'm downtown."

"That sounds delicious."

We leave the courthouse chatting about the case I had just helped to prosecute. While my dealings with Leary over the last few weeks have been extremely limited, I feel like I've known her forever and that's because Ford talks about her a great deal.

Admittedly, when he first did it, I thought it was a little odd. I also felt jealous. But the more he talked about Leary and the more I really listened to what he was saying, I realized it was no different than how I talk about Frannie. I realized I had to move past the oddity of a man having a woman as a best friend. Once I did that, I tremendously enjoyed learning more about Leary. Believe it or not, it helped me learn more about Ford himself. Because there is nothing like a womanizer—hopefully reformed—having a female best friend to put him in his place when necessary. And by the stories Ford had told me, Leary did that quite a bit.

It's a gorgeous late April day and despite Leary's rotund belly, she insists we walk the three blocks to Snoopy's.

Apparently, Leary's idea to have lunch at ten thirty isn't so strange, because there's already a line of people waiting to get some dogs. After we get ours—both of us choosing chili and cheese—we walk across the street and find an empty bench to sit down on.

"How are things going with you and Ford?" Leary

asks as we unwrap our hot dogs.

This question neither surprises nor offends me. Her tone of voice is light, easygoing, and filled with curiosity. I also detect a slight hint of happiness that she can actually ask a woman this question about her best friend.

Staring at the gooey mess I'm holding in a bun, I contemplate how I'm going to be able to eat it without getting chili and cheese all over me. But before I take that first bite, I answer Leary's question. "The past two weeks have been… well, amazing, I guess."

Leary looks triumphant as if she had suspected this all along. "I have to tell you, I have never ever seen Ford so taken with a woman before."

"How so?" I ask, my chili dog completely forgotten because I would much rather get inside intel on what Ford is thinking. Even though for the past two weeks we have spent every night together but one, I still feel like at any moment he's going to walk away from me.

It is what he's known for doing, and that's by his self-admission.

Leary has no hesitation in digging into her meal. She opens her mouth wide, shoves the hot dog in, and chomps down. Chili and cheese gather at the corners of her mouth and a big dollop starts to fall, but she expertly catches it with a napkin in her hand. She chews and grins at the same time, and when she swallows, she actually groans in ecstasy. "For some reason, this kid likes spicy food. It's like my belly just had an orgasm."

I wrinkle my nose. "That's disgusting."

Leary laughs and shakes her head. "Just wait until you get pregnant."

Leary can somehow make eating a messy hot dog look both easy and classy at the same time, and I have to remind myself I used to walk the catwalk in Milan, Paris, and Rome. I can do this, too.

I open my mouth wide and take a big bite, trying to suppress a moan of pleasure as the spicy chili hits my tongue.

Leary takes another bite as well. For a few moments, we do nothing but chow down on our dogs.

After we manage to mop up our sticky fingers and mouths thanks to the bottled water we also bought, we finally to turn our attention back to Ford.

Leary throws an arm across the back of the bench and leans toward me. "You know I'm the one who made the donation to Justice for All Animals?"

"I figured," I reply dryly. "But Ford gave you the money to do it."

She neither confirms nor denies, but I don't need her to do either. He cashed the check and that was all I cared about.

"I want you to know that is absolutely uncharacteristic of Ford to do something like that. He would never put his law license on the line like that for anyone. Even me."

My body jerks, and tingles break out all over. She's

saying… well, I'm not sure what exactly she's saying except the myriad of emotions coursing through me right now are unlike anything I've ever felt.

"I'm not sure why," I manage to say past the lump in my throat. "We barely know each other."

"It's been my very personal experience that it's quality and not quantity of time you spend together," Leary says with a chuckle. "But really, I think that sometimes the universe just works in very mystical ways to bring soul mates together."

"You think Ford and I are soul mates?" I whisper in disbelief. This conversation just got very deep and slightly weird.

Leary shrugs. "Look… I love Reeve. Fell for him hard and fast, and he did the same for me. Are we soul mates? Maybe, but who knows what that really means. All I can tell you is that he felt "right" from very early on. Sure, we continued to get to know each other as time went on, but the connection was instantaneous and deep. I can't explain it. And I really don't care about the reasons or the why's. I accept it and I'm telling you, I think it's happening with Ford."

"Why exactly are you telling me this?" I ask hesitantly.

She studies me a moment, her eyes hardening slightly. She pulls no punches with me. "Because I can tell he's really falling for you. I've never seen that from him, and I want to know how you feel because I don't want him to get hurt. Ford won't ask you this question. He's the type of guy who is going to trust his gut and roll with it, but I'm not quite so carefree about the thought of my best friend getting hurt."

I look away from Leary, staring across the green expanse of lawn with pockets of shade casting down from the large oak trees. There's no denying our connection was instant, and we gave into it quickly. I also can't ignore the fact there is something between us that's just… natural. And effortless. And… right. It just seems so very right, and that is not something I've ever felt before.

I had suspected Ford giving money to Justice for All Animals was a really big deal. Not just a rogue maneuver he did because he likes playing dangerous games. He acted out of a natural instinct to help and protect me. He put his very livelihood on the line for me, and while I didn't want to acknowledge what that really meant, I have to address it now for Leary.

"I'm falling for him, too," I tell her quietly as my eyes come back to her. "I mean in a way that is really scary and yet, I wouldn't change a thing about what's happening to us."

"I'm glad," she says as her face relaxes with relief. She smiles and moves her hand over to touch my shoulder. "He's a good man. He deserves to have a good woman."

I'm relieved she thinks I'm a good woman. Let's face it, outside of meeting his parents, Leary's approval is probably required if Ford and I are going to go the distance.

Since I have what seems like her blessing, I decide to go ahead and get all nosy. "Ford told me about how you and Reeve met."

She snickers. "You mean in the elevator?"

"Um… no," I say with utter confusion. "He said y'all met on a case… just like us."

Leary's cheeks turn pink. "Oh, well… yes, that's how we met."

"Oh, no you don't," I say with wide eyes as I lean into her. "Tell me about the elevator."

Because clearly that's a really good story and Ford didn't disclose it to me, so it must be all juicy and protected by best friend privilege.

Leary gives a sigh and says, "Well… you're probably going to marry him and bear his children so I guess I can tell you."

I rear back, aghast over her prediction. "Who said anything about marriage and children?"

"Do you want to hear about the elevator or not?" she says slyly.

I grin. "Oh, I absolutely want to hear about it."

Leary then proceeds to tell me the most unbelievable story of how she "tested" Reeve in the elevator before their first hearing against each other. She knew who he was, but he had no clue she was opposing counsel. She did a strip tease in front of him to change out a stocking that had a run in it. She did it to totally discombobulate him when they met in the courtroom minutes later.

"I think you may be the best attorney I've ever met in my life," I say in amazement.

"Ballsy," she corrects me. "I'm ballsy."

"Still, don't you think it's interesting that you and Reeve and Ford and I both met as opposing counsel on a pretty hot button issue case?"

"Yes, but you and Ford have a much better chance at this than Reeve and I ever did. I had a personal stake in the case, and you don't. I took Reeve's diligence to his job as a betrayal, and that was wrong. You and Ford seem to have a bit more perspective about this than I ever did."

"But Midge has a personal stake in this," I point out, a wave of worry hitting me. I'm still having a hard time accepting that while Ford may not care what happens to Drake Powell, he most definitely has concern for Midge's stake in all this.

"You need to let that go," Leary advises me, and I can tell by her tone of voice that she's discussed this with Ford.

"I'm trying," I assure her. "But I don't want Ford to—"

"To what?" she challenges. "If he loses, it's not going to hurt him personally. And Midge knows the risks. She's aware of Ford's feelings for you, and she's fully aware of the conflict. She's waived it. She's told Ford not to think about it, and you should do the same. She'd say that to your face if she was here right now."

"I'm glad she's not," I admit with shame. "She terrifies me."

"Me too," Leary admits with a laugh. "The bottom line… Ford is going to put all his effort into this case. You need to do the same. What happens will happen."

I hesitate a moment before I say. "I'm going to lose. That's why Ford and Midge aren't worried about our 'conflict'."

Leary's face softens, and she scoots a little closer to me on the bench. "I'm not going to make any wager on the outcome of this case, but you are right in that Midge is confident Ford will win and that's why she's not worried. She knows it's going to come down to the experts, but you know that as well, so there are no surprises lurking in any corners."

"Ford isn't confident he'll win, too?" I ask curiously.

Leary shakes her head. "He's never too cocky to think a case is in the bag. He'll be preparing as if he has the worst case in the world. He's one of the best at what he does, and despite the experts, I hate to tell you this, Viv… but he's probably going to kick your ass all over the courtroom."

I snort and lift my chin. "Dream on. You put me on even playing field with money, and I'd totally win this case."

Leary's head falls back, and she laughs so hard she

starts to hiccup. Still chuckling, she gives a shake of her head like she's still in awe over this. "Ford's a lucky guy. I can't wait for this case to be over so you two can really go to town with each other."

"Is that a figurative thing or a literal?" I ask slyly, because I'm pretty sure Ford has already gone to town on me physically.

Leary laughs again, this time snorting. She even wipes a tear out of her eye before saying, "I really, really like you, Viv."

"Well, the feeling's mutual," I assure her.

CHAPTER 19

Ford

THIS SEEMS RIGHT.

Actually, it's more than that.

This seems real.

There's no telling how many dates I've been on over my adult lifetime. Some were casual, destined to be a one-time thing. Sometimes, I would see the same woman for weeks.

Sometime over the last few years, I've enjoyed taking some of those women on double dates with Reeve and Leary.

And yes… For the most part, those were all enjoyable occasions.

Yet as I sit here now with Viveka tucked up against me in the round booth we're occupying with Reeve and Leary, I can't recall a single detail about any of those other times.

Fast forward twenty years into the future and I bet I won't forget what Viv is wearing tonight—a light blue wraparound dress with a pair of strappy, cream-colored sandals that are at least four inches high. They put her almost eye level with me.

Almost.

Nor will I forget that she smells like spiced flowers and her hair is done in a twist at the back of her head that I'll take great pleasure in releasing later. I won't forget I had a decent steak but that her butternut squash ravioli was amazing, and we ended up switching plates.

I sure as shit won't forget that for the entire evening, the conversation among our group was scintillating and without any lull. We laughed and laughed some more. Viveka fits right in with me, Leary, and Reeve. More importantly, they both really like her a lot.

There's no denying I really like her a lot, too.

Leary is tucked into Reeve's side, but she doesn't seem all that comfortable as her belly barely fits in the booth. We'd moved from the restaurant portion into the bar area, choosing a half-moon-shaped booth to sit in and have an after-dinner drink.

Leary gives a nudge to Reeve. "I'm about ready to call it a night, honey. I'm tired, and my back is killing me."

Reeve's expression immediately clouds with worry as his hand goes to her belly. "You sure nothing else is wrong?"

Leary rolls her eyes and swats her husband's hand away. "I'm tired, Reeve. I worked all day and then we had a two-hour meal, plus delicious cake that is sitting heavy in my stomach, and that's because I ate my cake and yours, too. I can't hang on Friday nights like I used to, and I've had about as much joy and frivolity as I can for the evening."

"Well, it is *your* birthday, Leary," I point out with a grin. "You should be able to leave when you want."

"I knew there was a good reason you're my best friend," Leary says with a firm nod. She reaches across the table, and we fist bump.

Viv straightens up, pulling her body away from mine. She reaches forward and grabs a glass of champagne that's half full. I had ordered that along with a sparkling grape juice for Leary, although we haven't touched it much other than an initial birthday toast.

Taking the glass in hand, Viv holds it up toward Leary. Reeve and I scramble to grab our glasses and do the same.

Then Viv proves once again why she seems to fit within our group dynamic. She holds her glass up specifically to Leary. "Well, let me make this last toast. Not only to wish you a wonderful birthday but to thank you for including me. I don't remember the last time I've had this much fun with a group of friends."

Leary doesn't even bother with her glass of juice, but instead pushes away from Reeve to lean over in the booth. She and Viveka give each other a hug, and I can't help but smile. I'd been filled in last night by Viv about her and Leary's lunch yesterday. Assuming Viv and I stay on course, I think those two will have a very special friendship going forth.

Reeve and I both set our champagne glasses down without taking a sip. Neither one of us like the bubbly very much. Instead, we both reach for the highball glasses of scotch we had been nursing.

Reeve tosses his back without regard as he's got a built-in designated driver with his pregnant wife.

I toss the rest of mine back as well, because tonight Viveka is staying at my apartment. The most dangerous thing we have to do is stumble to the elevator that will lead us up.

I was surprised and warmed when I asked Viveka to join us for Leary's birthday dinner and she suggested having Frannie watch the dogs, so she could stay at my place for the evening. I know she's been feeling guilty we've been sleeping at her house because of her dogs, but I don't mind.

Sure, I miss my king-size adjustable bed and my overly large walk-in shower with multiple spray heads, but sleeping with Viv every night in her cramped little queen has its benefits.

When the women end their hug and pull apart, Reeve slides out of his end of the booth and holds his hand out to help Leary do the same. It's painful to watch her struggle to get her girth out, and I try not to laugh. I've had no qualms with teasing her as she's gotten bigger, but I'm going to give her a pass on her birthday.

I put my arm around Viv's shoulder. "Are you ready to leave or would you like to have another drink?"

She grins and then nods at the champagne bottle that is still half full. "Let's stay. I feel terribly guilty there's all that champagne left over, plus I like the way the bubbly makes me feel."

She scoots in closer to me and tips her head back to put her lips closer to my ear. "Besides… I can get really dirty and kinky when I've got a good buzz going on."

Dear God… I did not need to hear that. For there is nothing more I would like to do than toss her over my shoulder and carry her out of here caveman style.

"Okay, you two lovebirds," Leary says as she puts her purse over her shoulder. "I know that look, which means we are really leaving. Like now."

Viv and I turn to her with silly grins as Reeve slips his arm around her waist. Leary inclines her head toward each of us. "Thank you again for a lovely birthday dinner. We should do this regularly."

Reeve adds, "And preferably before the baby comes. I've heard a rumor that our social lives will be flushed down the toilet after the birth."

I laugh at them because that's probably true. "We'll just come hang out at your house instead."

Leary beams a brilliant smile, and I can tell she likes the idea very much. "That's exactly what we'll do."

"But I'm not changing any diapers," I tell her sternly.

God knows I have to deal with enough shit at the dog shelter. I can't say that was my favorite thing to do last weekend, but it didn't suck spending time with Viv.

Reeve and Leary make their goodbyes, and I reach for the bottle of Verve Cliquot I had ordered. I tip it and fill Viv's glass, setting the bottle back on the table. I pick up the flute and hand it to her. "Drink up, baby. I can't wait to see what dirty things you're going to do."

She gives me a coy smile before taking a delicate sip of the champagne. She closes her eyes to savor it as she swallows, and that might be one of the sexiest things I've ever seen.

When she opens them, she says, "Seriously, though… Thank you for inviting me tonight. I felt like I would be an interloper, but it wasn't like that at all."

"Reeve and Leary both like you a lot. More importantly, they know I like you. It was a no-brainer that you would join us tonight."

Viv nods and turns her body slightly to face me. "Tomorrow, I'm meeting my expert witness out at the Swan's Mill site."

I acknowledge that with a nod. The hearing is next week, and we're both finishing up the evaluations. Four of my five experts have already been out there, and I'm waiting for their reports. My last one is also going to be out there tomorrow as well. I am not surprised Viv is going to meet hers there. I had the choice to do the same, but it wasn't really required. Viv is going because she likes to be more hands on and she's diligent in that way.

"And after that," Viv continues, "Frannie wanted to know if I would do a girl's night with her. Her husband's out on the road, and I think she's feeling a bit lonely."

"That's fine by me," I reassure her with a smile. Although honestly, it kind of sucks. I'd much rather be with Viv, but I suppose I can entertain myself for one evening.

"But maybe Sunday we could do something together," she suggests.

"How about golfing?" I suggest. The weather forecast looks spectacular for that day.

Viveka wrinkles her nose dramatically, but she's just teasing. She gave me so much hell for my distaste in cleaning out the dog cages at the shelter that she's going to give me a lot of grief about golfing.

But honestly, I didn't mind volunteering with her because by the end of the day, I felt I had actually done something very good with my life by helping out. Who knows, maybe by the end of Sunday, Viv will enjoy the game of golf and it can become "our" thing.

I watch as Viv closes her eyes and sways back and forth in the seat next to me for just a moment. When her lids flutter open, she gives a dreamy sigh. "I love this song."

To be honest, I hadn't paid a bit of attention to the music that was being played. The bar area we'd moved to has a dance floor, which is where we had our booth sitting near the edge. I listen closely to the slow melody, recognizing Eric Clapton's *Wonderful Tonight*.

No doubt it's a great song.

"Is this your brazen way of trying to get me out on the dance floor?" I tease as I start to automatically slide out of the booth.

She grins and accepts my hand as she follows me out. "I'll only dance with you if you're any good. I don't want you to embarrass me."

I laugh as I pull her toward the dance floor. "It's kind of hard to screw up a slow dance, Viv."

She fits perfectly into my arms as we sway back and forth to the music. Viv rests her head on my shoulder and hums along with the music. I press my cheek to her temple and smell her hair. Fuck, she smells good.

Neither one of us feel compelled in any way to maintain conversation. Instead, I concentrate on the strange proprietary sensation I'm feeling.

As if Viv belongs to me and only me.

When the song finishes its last notes and then moves into *Unchained Melody* by The Righteous Brothers, I lean back to look at Viveka. "Another dance?"

She shakes her head. "Let's finish that champagne and then go up to your place."

There was nothing solicitous or lewd about her suggestion, yet I feel it straight through to the tip of my cock.

Viv coming up to my place.

Viv in my bed. Knowing she absolutely belongs there.

I take her hand, and we wind our way through the dancers back toward our table. Just as we're stepping off the dance floor, a woman steps into our path. I come to an abrupt halt, Viveka doing the same because I'm holding her hand.

For a brief moment, my mind goes absolutely blank. I recognize the woman, knowing her… well, carnally. I also know I should know her name. Like it should be coming to me at any moment.

But it's perhaps the way the woman is glaring at me that is making my memory rebel.

"And what exactly is this?" the woman asks as she waves her hand in between Viveka and me. My hand involuntarily tightens on Viv's, and I take a step to the side to stand in front of her.

Then it hits me. "Allison."

"I'm surprised you remember my name," she hisses, her glance going once to Viv, where she casts a sneering lip curl before looking back to me. "Are you two-timing me with this woman?"

In all my years of dating, which have included many breakups and many times I've had to kiss off a woman who couldn't take no for an answer, I've never been confronted with this brand of crazy. It's been well over a week since I've even received a text from Allison, and I had assumed she'd moved on.

In fact, I actually stare at her expectantly, waiting for her to start laughing and telling me she's just joking.

But she continues to stare daggers at me.

Finally, I'm forced to say, "Allison... You and I aren't dating, so I can't be two-timing you. It's been over a month and a half since our last date."

"You never officially broke up with me, Ford," she snaps.

"Allison," I say gently. "You and I are not dating and are not a couple. We went out a few times, the last one being over six weeks ago. I didn't ask you out again. Now, you have continued to text me in a casual, friendly way a few times. But given I haven't asked you out again, surely you understand what that means."

Even though what I said is the absolute truth and I feel confident I handled things well, it sounds kinda shitty when I say it out loud.

"You never told me you weren't interested in me," she accuses.

Okay... now I'm starting to get pissed, because I shouldn't have to be dealing with this. "When I stopped calling you or responding, you would think that would be a hint."

Allison gasps as if I had just slapped her across the face. "You're an asshole, Ford."

I take a deep breath, rubbing the bridge of my nose for a moment before I say, "I'm sorry you feel that way. And I'm sorry if you felt I should have been doing something more affirmative to make things clear to you. But so there's no misunderstanding, again I'm sorry… but I am not interested in going out with you again."

Allison's face turns bright red with what I think might be anger, and I brace for maybe her next level of crazy. Instead, her gaze cuts to Viv, and she says, "Honey… I wouldn't waste your time with this one."

Allison then spins on her heel and marches off through the bar. I watch her until I lose sight, dragging out the inevitable moment when I have to turn to face Viveka.

"Well, that was enlightening," Viv says with twinkling eyes and an amused smirk.

"Normally, I would laugh that entire encounter off," I admit sheepishly. "But the truth is, I'm embarrassed you saw that. I don't want you to judge me based on that."

Viveka's eyebrows shoot up and she steps into me, placing one hand on my chest right over my heart. "I would never do that, Ford. You've been completely upfront with me, and I don't have any expectations—"

"Maybe you should," I cut her off.

She blinks a few times before slowly drawling, "What do you mean?"

"I mean, Viv, that surely you have to know this is different to me. *You* are different to me."

She tilts her head as she listens.

"I put my law license on the line for you," I tell her.

"And I never gave it a moment's thought. To this day, I don't have one regret about doing it. I've spent almost every night with you for the last two weeks as well as the weekends. I've invited you into my close circle of friends, and I sat through an unbelievably horrid meal with your mother. I think maybe you *should* have expectations of me. I think I've given you enough that you have to know this is not casual, and it is not temporary. At least not to me."

Viv's mouth opens slightly. She just stares at me with wide eyes.

Processing.

For a very long moment.

Finally, she says one word in a breathy voice. "Ford?"

I bend my face closer to hers. "Yeah?"

"Here's an expectation," she murmurs as her hand trails down my chest, over my stomach, stopping just at my belt. "I'd like for you to take me upstairs right now so we can explore this in a little more depth."

"You know if we go upstairs, there's not going to be a lot of talking," I say with a lewd smile.

"I know," she replies. "And I'm completely okay with that."

CHAPTER 20

Viveka

I PARK MY little Volvo that has seen a lot of miles and still keeps chugging beautifully. It is the car Adam bought for me when we first moved here, and despite his offers over the years to upgrade it to newer, I am fine with it. I don't need fancy—just air conditioning in the South—and as long as it runs safely, it works for me.

There's a small strip of grass that borders the edge of the wooded acreage of what is set to be Swan's Mill. Gone are all the backhoes, bulldozers, and dozens of men with chainsaws ready to cut down the trees. Swan's Mill sits on a two-lane road that's peppered periodically with various subdivisions but with plenty of forested areas in between. Because the Triangle—that would be Raleigh, Durham, and Chapel Hill—is rapidly expanding, everything is pushing outward. In a decade, this will be nothing but homes and very little trees.

As I get out of my car, another pulls in right behind me. A nondescript silver economy car that screams rental. My expert witness, Dr. Andrew Mellman, gets out with a wave at me. I recognize him from his picture on Cornell's website. Dark curly hair that's brown but with a liberal amount of gray streaked throughout it and his thick beard. His black frame glasses start to darken in the sunlight.

With the five thousand I essentially donated—via reimbursing Ford—I decided to put all the money into one very good expert. Dr. Mellman is an ornithologist from Cornell and is one of the leading experts in his field. He has a BS and MS in zoology and a Ph.D. in biology, but his entire research and teaching is now focused on birds. Moreover, he has done specific research on the red-cockaded woodpecker by collecting data to see if conservation efforts are working.

Ford could have easily hired Dr. Mellman. Five minutes of research online would have revealed this man's preeminence. And Ford probably did exactly that, but given that Dr. Mellman is a conservationist at heart, Ford knew his money would be wasted there. Dr. Mellman is going to do whatever he can to help preserve the species.

He's dressed for trekking through the woods. Heavy cargo pants, hiking boots, and a thick denim shirt. He pulls a backpack out of the rental car and heads my way. I'm also dressed to tromp through the woods with him. I put on jeans, a pair of old hiking boots I've had forever, as well as an old t-shirt. Even though it might get a little hot, I threw on a denim jacket for protection against any low-lying brush we have to push through. Lastly, I plaited my hair in a tight braid to keep it out of my way.

"Miss Jones," Dr. Mellman says as he sticks out a hand.

We shake, and I smile. "So pleased to meet you. Please call me Viveka."

"And you should call me Andy," he replies.

"I'm really thankful you could help me on this on such short notice. I know it was asking a lot to drop everything and fly here."

"Nonsense," he reassures me kindly, his eyes sweeping the edge of the woods. "You coming in with me?"

"If that's okay," I demure.

He shrugs. "Sixteen hundred acres… about two-point-five square miles. Going to be out there a long time."

"I've got all day," I tell him.

"Then let's do this," he says with a smile.

I snag my iPhone out of my car, along with a clipboard with a yellow pad attached. I push a pencil behind my ear, and I'm ready. I'm prepared to take notes for any helpful nugget of information Dr. Mellman can give me for my argument next week. I plan on using him as a resource to learn more about this endangered species than what I could find on the internet.

Before we enter the tree line, Dr. Mellman sets his backpack on the ground and squats before it. He pulls out a pair of large binoculars I bet cost a fortune, along with a digital camera. Both have straps, and he loops them around his neck.

Lastly, he pulls out a mini hand-held recorder, presumably to take notes of his findings, and tucks it into a side cargo pocket at his thigh.

Patting his pack, he says, "I got plenty of water in here for both of us."

Oh, thank God. I hadn't even thought of that. I might like nature, the outdoors, animals, and wildlife, but I'd probably die if I ever got lost out here.

We spend a little over five hours walking the property in a grid fashion. Dr. Mellman was very prepared with a topographical map of the area where he made tiny little X's and circles in different-colored pens he had tucked in another cargo pocket. He used his binoculars a lot, letting me have a turn when he found a nest. There were moments he would put the recorder up to his mouth and softly dictate his findings, using coordinates on the map to document locations.

When we finally emerge back near our cars, he walks over to the actual pine tree I'd chained myself to over two weeks ago. He'd looked at that one first and confirmed there was indeed a nest in there. He'd spotted a female and several males, most of which he determined were helpers taking turns to incubate the eggs.

Pointing at the tree, he says, "I've got good news and bad news."

"Lay it on me."

"This nest is isolated."

"What does that mean?" I ask as I scribble notes on my pad.

"Of the roughly sixteen hundred acres, I documented one large cluster and one lone nest, which we can call a cluster. This tree has the lone nest, and I expect it was easy to see given it was on the edge of the forested area. And by edge, I mean it's bordered on one side by the road. I suspect there will be other nests across the road that would be considered part of that cluster. It's bordered on the west side by the next property, whoever owns that."

"And the other cluster you identified?" I ask.

He points to what I think is northeast from where we're standing. "About a quarter mile that way. The cluster covers about sixty acres, and I've documented at least seventeen nests, many I believe are active with eggs or hatchlings."

"That's great news, Andy," I say with excitement. No way are those trees coming down no matter what Ford's experts say because that's too many birds that would be killed.

"Well, this is where the bad news comes in," Dr. Mellman replies with a dour expression. "As you know, these birds are cooperative. They work together to create nests, feed each other, and care for the young. This single nest here depends on a co-op that probably exists across the road or to the west on the next property. It's possible the judge may let them take this tree down because of that."

Not if I have anything to do with it, I think.

"Is it possible it could be considered part of the other large cluster? I mean, that acreage in between… could that possibly connect them?"

Dr. Mellman shrugs. "Possibly. If there's no evidence of nests across the road or to the west, the argument could be made this nest needs the other cluster further in to survive."

"And can you check the other property?" I ask.

"Do we have permission to be on it?"

"Not really seeing as how I don't know who owns it," I admit.

He cuts his gaze across the road and seems to consider. No one else is around. He glances at his watch and then back to me. "I could spare another hour maybe. Go in a few hundred yards on both sides and explore a bit. It wouldn't be conclusive evidence, but I can see what's in there."

"That would be awesome," I say with genuine appreciation. I'd kiss him right now if I didn't think it would freak him out.

"You wait here," he says. "I'll move faster without you."

♦

While Dr. Mellman is off trespassing all over the other properties that neighbor Swan's Mill, I lean against the back of my Volvo, checking emails and texts.

We still on for tonight? Frannie had written not long ago. *Not sure if you're still gallivanting around the woods.*

We're still good. See you at seven, I reply.

Frannie's husband is a long-distance truck driver. He works one week on, one week off. Frannie's a generally independent woman, same as me. But with her kids gone, she also likes to have fun, so we've always tried to do at least one girl's night together on a traveling week for Bill.

Because we are kind of lame, that either involves movies at my house so I don't have to worry about the dogs and more often than not, enough wine that Frannie has to stay the night.

There's a text from Ford. *Hey, hot stuff. How's it going?*

I give a quick reply. *Finishing up out here. U?*

Today is one of those days we aren't seeing each other. Not counting, of course, the glorious morning I had when I woke up in his bed this morning. It was brief but world rocking, and then I had to jet out of there. I had to pick the pups up from Frannie's, take them home to get them settled, then shower and change so I could meet Dr. Mellman at Swan's Mill at ten.

Ford is directly asking about how it's going with my expert, but he's not asking details. Just a general inquiry as to my day stomping around the woods.

Heading to the field, he replies. *Wish me luck?*

Always. And I offer up a quick prayer that Ford remain safe. I was surprised and a little bit alarmed that he plays in a rugby league. He's been doing it for about six years now.

In addition to golf, it's just sort of his thing. He's asked me to come to next weekend's game. Like I told him, I don't know much about sports, but I do know rugby is a dangerous game that can often result in cuts, bruises, broken bones, and sometimes burst testicles.

That's what Ford told me, but he could have been joking. He was using it in context last night telling me I should give them extra loving care because they could get seriously damaged in the game today.

"Not sure if you look better in the chains or out of them," a male voice that I find familiar but can't quite place says.

My head snaps up and I push from my car, turning around. My spine stiffens as I see Drake Powell strolling... no, strutting my way. I see a truck he presumably drove parked down the road along with a jeep behind it.

He gives me a genial smile as he approaches, but his eyes roam over me like I'm a piece of meat. It produces no reaction within me. I've been given that look since I was in my early teens, and I've learned not to let it affect me.

"Mr. Powell," I say coolly with a nod.

"You out here with your expert?" he asks, gaze sweeping around.

"I am," is all I provide. "You?"

"Yup," he says as he tucks his hands in his khaki pants and rocks on his heels.

He doesn't elaborate. He doesn't do anything but stare at me, rocking back and forth. His smile has turned almost "cat eating the canary" type of thing, and it hits me in that moment.

This bastard did have something to do with that brick coming through my office window. I can't prove it and never will be able to, but I know it. I think Ford knew it as well.

"I don't get it," he says, the smirk sliding off his face and his eyes going cruel. He takes a step toward me and lowers his voice. "What the fuck could you possibly get out of this case? You practice in a shithole, have taken this case on for free, costing me a lot of goddamn money in the process, and for what? You're going to lose. You'll go on with your pathetic life, and I'll be scrambling to get this project back on track. I'll never recoup the monetary losses you've caused me."

I give Mr. Powell a polite smile. "Technically, Mr. Powell… you and I shouldn't be talking about this case. But I will tell you, I do this to make people like you obey the law and to protect those that can't do for themselves."

"For a goddamned woodpecker," he snarls.

And… I'm done with him. "Well, you have a nice day, Mr. Powell." My voice is overly bright as I turn on my heel and walk to the driver's side of my car where I'll gladly wait for Dr. Mellman to finish up.

"Cunt," Drake Powell says, and he makes no effort to lower his voice. He wanted me to hear that, and I know that word is near and dear to him. It was written on the brick he or someone at his direction threw into my office.

I've been faced with meaner people than him before, and I've had tougher battles. He doesn't scare me. He certainly doesn't hurt my feelings or make me feel guilty for taking on this case. My allegiance is to my client as is my care and loyalty.

Besides… how could I ever feel guilty for causing this prick some inconvenience?

I get in my car and shut the door, shooting another text off to Frannie. *Feel like NY pizza tonight?*

Neither Frannie nor I are big pizza eaters, unless it's New York style with extra grease. There's a joint not far from my house that makes excellent pies.

There's a hard knock on my window that startles me. My gullible side immediately thinks it's Dr. Mellman, although he's not been gone very long.

When I crane my neck left, I see Drake Powell bent over… leering in my window. He's sort of the average middle-aged man. Pleasant face with the slightest of bellies. He has a wedding ring on, and I'm going to guess that midsection is what many women call a "dad bod".

Ford doesn't have a dad bod. Of course, he's not a dad, but he works hard for that six pack he's sporting. It flexes and comes into sharp definition many times when we're fucking.

Drake Powell's ordinariness turns into something bordering on creepy the way he's staring at me. There's something in his stare that speaks to perhaps retribution, but I'm not sure what he could really do to me. The brick through the window has probably exhausted his bag of tricks.

I debate ignoring him, but he seems like the type of guy who could take douchiness to true assholishness if I didn't at least let him have his say.

I roll my window down, which is crank style, so yeah… that's how old my Volvo is, and try to plaster a pleasantly curious expression on my face as to why he's bothering me again.

"You should watch out," he says.

"For what?" I ask, my voice going sharp and unyielding. I don't play threatening games with anyone. Last time I did that was when I was sixteen and just starting to get the idea I could break free of my mother's control.

He doesn't say anything. Just stares at me, waiting to see if his mental intimidation tactic is going to work.

I stare back with what I'm hoping conveys boredom.

Perhaps a little bit of pity that he feels the need to do this with me. What I really want to do is ask him if this is the only way he can get it up? By making himself feel bigger by putting a woman in her place, which I suspect is actually very true.

But I take the high road.

I give him a polite smile and wait to see if he elaborates.

He doesn't.

Instead, he just points at me and says once again, "Watch out."

CHAPTER 21

Ford

"CHRIST, I'M GETTING too old for this," I mutter as I hobble into the locker room, rubbing my left shoulder with my right hand. I glance at Reeve hobbling beside me. "Remind me why we do this?"

"I do it because my wife thinks it's hot," he says in a matter-of-fact tone.

"You did it before you met Leary," I remind him.

"Well, yeah… because I knew it would help me nail a perfect woman like her," he says, and I know that's utter bullshit. Reeve is a lot like me. An adventurer. An opportunist. A man who likes a challenge, the scarier and more dangerous the better.

I sit down on the bench before my locker, groaning with the effort. It's going to hurt ten times as bad standing back up again, but this is the least painful position to untie my cleats.

I'd give my fucking left nut to go to Viv's house right now to beg her for a full body massage. For therapeutic purposes only, of course.

Well, not only. But to start out with.

But she's with her girl Frannie tonight, and I'm doing my dude thing with Reeve and rugby.

We'd both signed up to join a rec league, and we landed on the same team made up mostly of lawyers, judges, and paralegals. We're called the Legal Eagles, which is sort of lame, but I clotheslined a guy out there today who probably won't be able to talk for a week so whatever.

Talk about a small world. I played rugby with Reeve on the weekends and worked at Knight & Payne with Leary by weekday, never once imagining those two would end up together and not by my introduction either.

They met the same way as Viv and me but because that case was so intensely personal to Leary, it got really, really ugly between her and Reeve at one point. It makes me more than grateful that Viv and I don't have that obstacle between us.

I can remember the day Leary told me about her little striptease in front of Reeve in the elevator. She did it as a means to size him up and to rattle him before their hearing. I couldn't believe she'd done such a thing but a big part of me, as her mentor who advocates for dirty tricks in moderation, was kind of proud of her.

She was brutally candid with me and shared that Reeve had cornered her outside the courtroom, not at all happy with the way she'd been playing him. He'd backed her into a corner. Between a lot of flirting, innuendo, and challenge, he felt her up right there in the hallway.

And Leary liked it.

It wasn't too long after Leary told me this story that I was out with Reeve chugging a few beers when he'd happened to mention this hot attorney on a case he had that stripped in the elevator in front of him, and it was then I realized my two friends were involved with each other.

It was then I realized Leary and I were done.

For good.

From the start, I knew those two were going to go the distance and just look at them. A few years and a baby later, I couldn't be happier for the two of them.

There was a time I didn't think they'd make it. Their situation and mine with Viveka is vastly different. The stakes were so much higher in that case, and there came the inevitable moment that Reeve had to resort to some strong tactics to win the case.

He had found some really bad evidence against Leary's client, and he blindsided her with it in open court. Just as Viveka and I have promised to never let this case get in between us, so had Leary and Reeve.

But what Reeve did—even though it was aboveboard and ethical—was too much for Leary to forgive and she threw him out of her life. Leary simply couldn't keep her love for Reeve and her passion for her case separate.

Luckily, I don't see that as an issue here. Viveka doesn't have the same emotional investment that Leary did. This is just another case to her, and she'll have another one like it on the near horizon.

Reeve and Leary obviously overcame their issues, and only because Reeve made a very bold move. He handed her a witness she hadn't known about who actually turned the tables and gave Leary the win. It was the absolute height of ethical breach for him to have done that. Far more egregious than me donating some money to the organization that hired Viv.

To this day, if anyone ever found out what Reeve did, he could kiss his legal career goodbye.

"What are your plans tonight?" Reeve asks as he sort of falls onto the bench beside me. He also groans in pain.

"Probably get some work done," I say as I bend over to unlace my cleats.

"Is everything okay between you and Viv?" he asks, turning slightly toward me.

I crane my neck, cut him a sharp look, and go back to my shoes. "Of course it is."

"Something must be wrong," Reeve says with assurance in his voice. "It's a Saturday night, and you're not going out with her."

I give a sigh, because fuck if I don't want to be with her tonight. I try for a neutral tone, but think I fail miserably. "She's doing a girl's night with her best friend. Old movies and manicures I think is the theme tonight."

Reeve doesn't say anything so after toeing my shoes off, I turn to him. He just stares at me.

"What?" I snap in annoyance.

"You should go over there," he says. "Drop in. Surprise visit. Bring them both some ice cream. Tell them you're just bringing it over, so they think you're all cool and dashing, and trust me… Viv will ask you to stay."

I sit up straighter. This idea has merit. "You think so? That's not like stalkerish or anything?"

"Not if you act like you're really only there to drop ice cream off," he says, and my mouth curves into a very sly grin.

That's exactly what I'll do.

♦

"This is weird," I mutter as I stare straight ahead at the TV. Their chosen movie of the night is *The Goonies*, and I'm seeing it but not really seeing it.

"It's not weird," Viveka says from my left.

"Stop fidgeting," Frannie adds from my right.

I'm not quite sure how I ended up on the couch, sitting in between these women, getting a manicure.

I look at Viveka, wondering how in the fuck I got so lucky to meet her. It was a right place, right time type of thing. She's currently massaging what she said was "cuticle" oil into my fingernails. Feels good, but her hands on me always feel good.

Swinging my head in the opposite direction, I study

Frannie. She's busy filing the nails on my other hand. She grins almost evilly.

It all started an hour ago when I showed up on Viveka's doorstep with Ben & Jerry's and two bouquets of flowers. It was a given I'd bring flowers for Viv, but bestowing the same on her bestie would help to ensure I'd get invited in for the night.

I had also brought some dog friendly cookies from a local bakery, not to enhance my charm in any way, but mainly because those mutts are growing on me.

When Viveka opened the door, I would have given anything to have had a video running to capture the look on her face. Surprise to start out and then absolute delight.

And this was before she even understood I came bearing gifts. She may have been all in for her girl's night with Frannie, but her face told me that she had been missing me.

Truth be told… it was the ice cream that got me the invitation to stay, and that was by Frannie herself. She welcomed me in right away, and never once made me feel like I was impeding on something sacred. If the penance is having a manicure done, then so be it.

"So, Ford," Frannie says as she moves the file briskly around the edges of my nail. "What's your story? I mean… Viv tells me you were essentially a manwhore before she met—"

"I never said that," Viveka practically shrieks from

my other side.

"You said he wasn't about commitment," Frannie points out.

"Well, that's a far cry from saying he's a manwhore," Viveka sputters.

I get whiplash turning left and right to look at them as they argue over exactly what I was before meeting Viv.

"I guess what I'm getting at," Frannie says drolly, "is that here you are… showing up on girl's night because clearly you can't stand to be away from Viveka, and I'd like to know if that's typical behavior from you? Is it because she's different from all the others, or is it because you're slightly stalkerish? Or maybe you're just wanting a little nookie tonight and couldn't stand not having it."

Viveka groans from my left with clear embarrassment, but I don't look at her. Instead, I address Frannie. First, I get her attention by pulling my hand away from her. Her head pops up.

"All the above," I tell her.

"All the above?" Her eyes round in wonderment.

I nod and then shove my hand back at Frannie, so she can finish up. She automatically starts filing again. "Yes, Viv is different from all the others, and yes, I'm being a little bit stalkerish tonight. And why would I deny I want a little nookie from my girl? It's the best nookie ever."

Viveka groans again, and Frannie giggles.

"But there was one other reason I came over," I add,

and Frannie's head pops back up again. "I wanted to get to know Viv's best friend. She talks about you a lot, and you're an important part of her life. Viv's met my best friend and hung out with her, so I thought I needed to do the same."

And that was the moment I won Frannie's undying devotion.

I wasn't bullshitting her either. I've been generally curious about the hair salon owner who befriended Viv when she moved in next door to her. The day I found Viv over there, sitting in one of the chairs and spinning in circles as if it was her second home, I knew Frannie was an integral part of her life. Her importance became even more apparent after I had the pleasure of meeting Viv's mother.

Frannie puts down the nail file and snaps her fingers at Viv. "Cuticle oil, please."

Viv stretches across me—and damn, she smells good—to hand a small bottle to Frannie. As Frannie dabs little drops of oil on my nails and massages it in, Viv does something that rocks me.

She laces her fingers through mine, and unobtrusively... so very naturally as if it belongs there... places our joined hands on her lap before leaning over to rest her head on my shoulder.

I sort of freeze in place, afraid to move. I don't want to jostle her or in any way make her think it's uncomfortable. On the contrary, I want to rip my hand away from Frannie, reach across my chest, and pin Viv in place so she can't ever move.

Slowly… gently… I kick my feet up on Viv's coffee table. "Tell me about your kids, Frannie," I say.

"Both have flown the coop," she says with an equal measure of pride and tenderness. "Aimee is twenty-five and fiercely independent. She's a nurse over at Wake Med. And Shawna is a senior at Appalachian. She's going to be a teacher."

Viv shifts beside me slightly, and she lifts our hands up from her lap. Higher still, until my entire arm raises. Then she's ducking under, snuggling into my side and letting my arm come down around her shoulders. I instinctively tighten my hold and pull her closer.

This right here.

Relaxing.

Talking with Viv's friend.

Cuddling on the couch on her girl's night out that I interloped upon.

Not a single place I'd rather be right now. In fact, I'd go one step further to say I kind of want this night and what we're doing right now to go on and on.

This is how I realize I'm pretty sure she's the one.

CHAPTER 22

Viveka

I LEAN BACK in my desk chair, which squeaks from the movement. Tipping my head back, I close my eyes and rub at my temples.

I'm done.

I can't get any more ready for the hearing, which is set for ten tomorrow morning.

Ford and I agreed not to see each other tonight. I knew I'd be working late, and even when I get home, I'll be going over my oral arguments several times before I go to sleep. I won't be good company.

Besides, Ford is working late, too. He's got more evidence to organize and present since he has more expert witnesses. I've got my one and only Dr. Mellman, who is flying in tonight from Ithaca and will testify tomorrow.

Ford did throw me a tiny bone. He admitted he wasn't going to call any of his experts to testify, but rather was going to present their findings via affidavit.

That prompted me to call Dr. Mellman and ask him if he'd be willing to testify live. It was going to cost me. I had to dip into my own personal savings to get him down here, but I think it's worth it. He could totally sway the case.

I raise my head and look out the new window that got installed today. I had to have a heart to heart—or in other words, threaten legal action—with my landlord last week since he was balking at the cost. Gone is my name from the window in the fancy gold lettering that Adam had done for me all those years ago, but one day I'll dig up some extra money and have it redone.

It's starting to get dark outside, and my eyes cut over to the time on my computer screen.

"Shit," I mutter as I realize I'd been here a lot longer than I'd planned to be. It was nearly eight, and I try to never be in the office this late because it's not the greatest area of town.

An incredible wave of guilt also hits me that my poor pups have got to be starving to death. Their dog door gives them full access to go in and out during the day when I'm not there, and they have plenty of water, but they're probably ready to eat each other.

Or, God forbid, they've decided to eat my pillows in open rebellion.

Granted, they normally eat dinner around six and my brain acknowledges they are not going to die waiting a few hours, but my heart tells me it's time to go.

I log off my computer and pack up my briefcase with the documents I need for tomorrow. That includes an updated pecker brief—yes, it still makes me snicker—to hand up to the judge, as well as an outline of my direct exam for Dr. Mellman.

I shoot a quick text to Ford as I promised to let him know when I was leaving the office. *On my way out the door.*

He responds quickly. *Be safe. Text me when you get home.*

My heart squeezes in response. In the years we were together, Adam never once told me to be safe. It's not that he didn't want me safe, it's that he was always so busy it wasn't efficient for him to say those words.

I hitch my purse over my shoulder, then grab my briefcase in one hand and my keys in the other, which also has a bottle of pepper spray attached to the ring. It's not pitch black out, but it's dark enough that the streetlights are on. I'm always aware of my surroundings, and I look left and right when I step out to lock my door. I'm relieved to see Gary, the locksmith on the other side of Frannie's salon, also locking up for the night.

He lifts his chin at me. "Night, Viv."

"Night, Gary," I call back, and trot to my car parked right in front. Gary watches me, and that makes me feel safer.

Once in, I lock the door and start the engine, secure

within the protective environment of my trusty Volvo. Before I put the car in drive, I grab my phone from my purse and on a whim call Ford.

He answers on the first ring. "You're violating the rules," he says in a low, sexy voice.

"I know," I say with a laugh. Not only did we agree not to see each other tonight, but we agreed not to talk at all so we could concentrate on our cases. "But I'm driving home. I just figured I'd call and tell you good night and good luck with any prep you still need to do."

"I'm done," he tells me in a relaxed voice. I have an image of him lying on his couch, watching ESPN or something. "Say the word, Viv, and I'll get in my car right now to come to you."

A cramp hits me between my legs as images of what Ford would do to me fill my mind. He's become an expert at playing my body. He's figured out how to make me come really fast and hard, and that's always how he starts out. He gets me off either with his fingers, his tongue, or if he's feeling extra playful, my vibrator. He actually tortures me with that thing, making me come over and over again with it before he fucks me.

"I can't," I practically croak with a healthy dose of whine in my voice. "I still have work to do."

"I won't stay all night," he murmurs. "I'll only come over for a little bit. I'll make you feel good, Viv, then I'll leave."

I know my panties are wet. Just soaked from the

promise in his voice. I want to say yes so bad, but I have so much still to do. What I don't have in money and resources, I make up for with hard work. I'll be going over my arguments until late into the night. I don't have a few hours to spare for Ford's magic cock, and we both know he'd probably stay all night.

"Can't, baby," I whisper. "I want to, but I can't."

Ford chuckles. "Okay. I'll leave you alone."

"But tomorrow night—"

"I'm going to destroy you," he finishes my thought. "Wreck you so thoroughly you won't know what hit you. Make you come so many times you'll forget your name. Going to make up for not seeing you tonight, Viv."

Oh, God. Just… how can one man be that sexy? It's like he received all the sexiness in the universe.

I've never been all that great at phone sex. Ford always has me so discombobulated when we're in bed that I'm fairly quiet there, too, unless I'm yelling his name out.

While I can't give promises of rocking his world back to him because they tongue tie me up so much, different words come into my mind that are just as heartfelt.

"I'll miss you tonight," I tell him softly. Not his cock. Not his tongue. I'll miss him, and I hope he understands that's what I mean.

Ford is silent for a bit, and I think perhaps I've gone a little too mushy for him.

But then he gives it right back to me in a voice filled with emotion. "I'll miss you too, Viv."

"I'll text you when I get home," I promise.

"Okay, baby."

By the time I'm pushing my phone back into my purse, my house comes into view. When I pull into the driveway, Daisy's face appears in the front living room window and she starts barking in joy to see me. Butch is too tiny to look out, but he jumps up and down beside Daisy, so his head pops up periodically. He's yapping hysterically.

Those dogs aren't starving. They're just happy I've come home to them.

"Silly pups," I murmur as I step out of my car, pulling my purse and briefcase out with me.

Just as I'm shutting my door, a large hand clamps down on the back of my neck, another on my shoulder. I give a tiny yip of fright, but then I'm being spun so fast I can't get my bearings. Then the roof of my car is rushing up to meet me as my attacker slams me forward. I try to push back, but the effort is wasted. My forehead slams right on the edge where the roof meets the driver's door, and stars explode behind my eyelids. I can actually feel the skin split and the immediate rush of blood dripping down.

Miraculously, a calmness sort of overtakes me. I have a moment of clarity where I realize I need to figure out a way to fight back. Daisy's barks have changed now to big booming barks of anger as she watches me from the window. She seems to be telling me something.

Make noise.

I open my mouth to scream, but he releases me before I can let loose. His hands are gone, and he just… disappears. I turn to try to identify him, but all I can see through the blood dripping down is a dark figure running down the sidewalk and melting into the darkness of the night.

"Viveka?" I hear from across the street, and I turn that way. I can barely make out my neighbor, Art Sneed, but I sure recognize his voice.

I raise my hand, perhaps in greeting or maybe to assure him all is good, but then an absolute draining of all my energy hits me at once and my knees start to give out.

"Jesus Christ," Art mutters, and I hear the pounding of his feet as he runs toward me. He's too late to catch me, but my driveway stops me when my knees slam into it. I can feel his hand on my jaw, lifting my face to inspect it. "Who the fuck did this?"

I've never heard Art cuss before. He's a retired schoolteacher and has always seemed so mild mannered. I shake my head, but nothing comes out. Either I'm too tired to get the words out or there's no need to waste the energy since I have no clue really what just happened.

"Yes, I'd like to report an assault," I hear Art say and this confuses me. I blink through the wetness in my eyes, which I determine is both blood and tears, to see him talking into his phone. "And send an ambulance."

"No ambulance," I finally manage to say.

Art ignores me as he gives my address to the dispatcher.

Within minutes, there are two cop cars with lights flashing and an ambulance on our street. Neighbors have come out to be nosy and watch. One of the officers asks me questions while an EMT cleans the blood off my face to see better. Art goes inside and feeds the pups for me.

"Did you get a look at your attacker?" the cop asks.

"No," I tell him as I search my memory. "It happened so fast."

"Did he say anything?"

"No," I say again… my voice sounding wooden and hollow.

"You're going to need to go to the hospital," the EMT interjects as he starts to place a bandage on my forehead. "This cut needs stitches."

"Shit," I mutter, realizing my night of practicing my arguments has just been ruined.

"Would you like me to call someone for you?" the cop offers kindly. I think he's feeling the need to do something as we both know this will go down as an unsolved crime.

I shake my head. "I can do it. If you can make sure I have my purse, my phone is in there."

The EMT helps me into the back of the ambulance.

"Let's get you on the stretcher."

"I don't need the stretcher," I say.

"It's protocol," he says and points to the bed on wheels.

The officer reappears, and he hands up my purse and briefcase. Art's face also pops up behind the cop, and he calls, "The pups are fine, Viveka. Do you need me to come with you?"

"I'll call Frannie," I assure Art, and he gives me a wave. I think this is the most excitement he's had in a long time. "Thank you so much."

"Anytime," he says with a smile.

Yeah, I hope this is a one-time only occurrence.

Once the ambulance gets underway, the EMT pulls my phone from my purse and hands it to me. There's nothing to do since he's got a bandage on my cut, so I take a moment to call Frannie. She answers in a groggy voice, and I know I woke her up. It's barely nine thirty, but she's not a big night owl.

"What's up?" she mumbles.

"So, I had a little accident. Hit my head and need some stitches. Think you can come to the hospital and hang with me?"

"What?" she shrieks, all signs of grogginess completely obliterated.

I don't want to give her too many details. "Yeah… just a little accident. I'll fill you in on the details there."

It takes a few more minutes to get her off the phone

as she demands the details right now. But finally, she assures me she's walking out her door and will meet me in the emergency room.

The EMT takes my phone and slides it in my purse for me when I disconnect.

I close my eyes and try not to think of what happened to me. Those few seconds… not more than probably ten total… where I was absolutely terrified. I've never felt that before.

So out of control and helpless.

I think about Ford, too. It had crossed my mind a time or two to call him. In fact, he was the first person I had thought of, not Frannie, which tells me I want his comfort the most. But I immediately dismissed it.

I didn't want to burden him the night before our big hearing.

More importantly, I didn't want him to go apeshit and do something stupid.

Because while I know the cops will never find who did this, I think Ford would come to the same conclusion I have.

Drake Powell was behind this somehow. I don't think it was him, but I think whoever attacked me did it at his direction.

Given the speed of the attack and the fact my purse wasn't stolen, it was clearly personal.

Retaliatory most likely.

Yes, Ford would automatically think it was his client,

and he'd do something stupid. There's going to be no hiding this tomorrow, but at least we'll be in court and he won't be able to do anything.

Then it will all soon be over. We'll argue the hearing. One of us will win. One of us will lose.

After, we can move on and be done with this case and the crazy that's apparently started with it.

Then Ford and I can be together and see where this thing is going to go.

CHAPTER 23

Ford

I GLANCE DOWN at my watch.

Crane my neck over my shoulder to stare at the clock on the courtroom wall.

Down to my phone.

They all say the same thing. Five till ten.

And Viveka is still not in court.

This shouldn't alarm me, but for some reason it does. I can't quite put my finger on it, but something feels off for me. I could probably chalk it up to pre-hearing jitters. Even after nineteen years of practicing law, I still get a little tingle in my nerves before I get up before a judge or jury. I think it's even more prevalent today because I'm going up against Viveka, and I don't want her to lose.

Of course, I have to put those feelings aside. Just for at least the next hour it will take us to argue the merits of the case in front of Judge Boyer. Then it will be over.

Then *we* will start.

The sound of the courtroom door opening has me spinning in my seat. I'm disappointed to see Drake Powell walking in. His eyes immediately go to the plaintiff's counsel table where Viveka would sit before sliding over to me. He gives me a wink and a thumb's-up sign. My smile back is lukewarm at best.

He struts up the aisle that separates the two sides of benches and sits in the front row directly behind me.

When I turn my wrist, my stomach churns as I see it's one minute until ten and still no Viveka. I grab my phone, prepared to text her, when the door behind the judge's bench opens and the bailiff steps through, followed by Judge Boyer.

"All rise," the bailiff says, and I push out of my seat, buttoning my suit jacket as I do. Judge Boyer climbs the raised dais and prepares to sit down, but she notices that Viveka isn't at her table. Her eyes cut to me with question, and I'm prepared to argue on Viveka's sake for a small recess when the back courtroom door opens.

Viveka hurries in carrying her briefcase in one hand, her purse hanging over her shoulder. She looks fabulous in a charcoal-gray pantsuit with wide legs and matching heels. Her hair looks beautiful… pulled to one side for a braid to rest over the front of one shoulder, the top swept low across her forehead, just above her brows.

"I'm so sorry I'm late," Viveka calls to the judge without looking at me. Her voice sounds frazzled, and her shoulders are a bit hunched.

"I haven't sat down yet, Miss Jones," Judge Boyer says back easily. "So technically, you're not late."

Judge Boyer has always been known for being fair and easy to deal with, but this is exactly one of the reasons I like working with her so much. She even goes out of her way to be nice to people, and that's something the older judges could learn something about.

The judge sits, and I start to follow suit since I'm allowed to do so. I cut another look at Viveka, see her busy unpacking her briefcase, and—

What the fuck is that on her forehead?

I almost didn't see it the way she had her braid pulled across, but the harder I stare, the more I can see she's been cut and has had stitches. There's also purple bruising she tried to hide with makeup but couldn't quite conceal completely.

Without thought, I step away from my table and take the two steps to hers. I can feel Judge Boyer's eyes on me, but I ignore her.

When I reach Viveka's side, she refuses to look at me, now busy straightening the papers she pulled out. Turning slightly so Judge Boyer has my back, I ask her in the lowest possible voice I can manage. "What the hell happened?"

Viveka refuses to raise her head, and my skin grows tight. "It's nothing."

I'm not sure what makes me do it, but I crane my neck all the way around to look at my client sitting in the front row. His eyes are pinned on Viveka… on her face… and he's smirking.

"Son of a bitch," I hiss under my breath. When I turn back to Viveka, my eyes lock on hers. "I'm going to kill him."

"Don't," she breathes out so I barely hear her, but the pleading in her eyes speaks volumes.

My gaze breaks free, traveling up to take a closer look at the cut. Dead center, not too far below her hairline. I have no clue exactly what happened, but I know Drake Powell had everything to do with it.

"Is there a problem?" the judge asks, and I slowly turn toward her.

"Your Honor." My voice is solicitous and professional, which is amazing given I feel like I'm shaking with fury. "I need a moment to discuss an issue with opposing counsel."

"Make it fast," she says.

I nod at her before turning back to Viveka. Leaning close so she has no choice but to look me in the eye, I repeat, "What happened?"

She just stares at me.

"Tell me what happened, Viv, or I'm going to make a scene," I warn. I put one hand down on her table and notice it's shaking.

"Ford, please," she says whisper soft. "You make a scene, and you're going to out us. And this is my career on the line, too."

Son of a fucking bitch.

I take in a deep breath, close my eyes, and let it out slowly. I try to will myself to calm down, but all I can see in my mind is that cut on Viv's forehead. My eyes pop back open, because if I keep them closed, I'll imagine the worst.

"Just tell me what happened, and I swear I won't make a scene in here," I tell her. "I have to know, or I'll go crazy wondering."

She keeps her face stoic, but I can see the understanding deep within her eyes. No surprise, but she tries to downplay it. "I didn't see who it was. It happened in my driveway when I got out of my car. It was fast, and he slammed my head down onto my car just once before he took off running."

Fire burns in my gut. Deep in that fiery pit of fury, I'm convinced Drake Powell is behind it. He's too cowardly to do it himself, but I bet he set it up.

I know it.

But I have to make sure.

I hold Viv's gaze a moment longer before straightening up and turning to the judge. "Your Honor, if I could indulge the court for just five more minutes. I need to have a word with my client to go over some new evidence I've just learned about. I promise I'll be brief."

Judge Boyer makes a shooing motion with her hand, then turns her attention back to her computer monitor.

I cut another short peek at Viv, and I can see her

visibly tense up with worry. I try to give her an encouraging smile, but it comes off stiff and forced. I can't reassure her because all I can think about is avenging her.

Turning to Drake, I make a jerking motion with my head to the courtroom doors at the back. A silent demand that we talk outside. I made Viv a promise, and I'm not going to do anything in open court.

Drake's brows furrow in confusion, but he stands up from the bench. I march toward the doors, knowing he's following. When I exit, I make an immediate right and enter the stairwell I'd taken just a few short weeks ago with Viv after our first hearing.

When Drake steps through the door, I turn to face him. He doesn't even give me a chance to bait him into the truth because he gives it up all on his own. He starts laughing and throws a thumb in the direction from where we came. "Did you see her face? Can't think of a nicer person for that to happen to."

It's not an all-out admission, but he takes way too much pleasure in it. A buzzing noise fills my ears, and my fingers curl inward. "She says she took a fall down the stairs," I grit out.

Drake snorts. "That's her story, huh? Clumsy, that one."

Fuck this. I don't need him to admit it.

I'm on him fast, taking every bit of violent aggression I normally burn out of my system on the rugby field and direct it right into his face with my fist. I catch him on the right cheekbone with a roundhouse and his head snaps to the left. He goes stumbling into the wall just before the stairs. I reach out and grab him by his collar so he doesn't fall, which I wouldn't mind seeing, and I swing him toward the opposite wall. He goes careening into it, using his palms to catch himself before his face slams into the cinderblock slab.

"You fucking did that to her," I snarl. I grab him by the shoulders and spin him to face me. Drake's hands come up instinctively to protect his head from further attack.

That's fine.

It leaves his throat exposed and my hand goes to it, pushing him back and pinning him to the wall. I squeeze, and his eyes bug out of his head in fear. I lean in close. "Tell me… did you do that to her?"

Drake's hands come to mine, and he tries to peel my fingers away. I release my grip slightly, so he can talk.

"Tell me the truth," I hiss. "If you don't, I'm going to beat you bloody."

"It was just to scare her," he blurts out with wide eyes. "The bitch is costing me money, so I had one of my boys rough her up just to scare her."

I'm not even thinking. My free hand is pulling back and I let it fly, this time catching him dead center in his nose. He howls in pain and doubles over, his hand covering his face.

"Are you scared, Drake?" I ask softly as I bend over

him.

He nods furiously as he pulls his hands back from his nose. No blood, which disappoints me.

"Now you know how she must have felt," I spit as I grab him by his shirt and throw him back into the wall again.

The fucker starts crying like a baby, and I want to beat the shit out of him for that. Hiring someone to do his dirty work because he doesn't have the balls for it and then crying when he takes a few punches.

I lean in, put my face right before his, and curl my hands tight into his shirt. I give him a little shake and say, "Get out of this courthouse. Go back to your office or home or wherever. I'll call you after the judge makes her decision."

Releasing my hold on Drake, I step back and run my hands through my hair. I take some deep breaths to calm down.

"What the fuck is this all about?" he asks, anger now tinging his voice as he gingerly pokes at his nose. "Why the fuck do you care?"

I give him an out-and-out lie without a single care in the world. "Because if the judge ever found out you did that, I'm guilty by association. I'm not about to fucking lose my license because of your games."

"She has no clue—"

"Just shut the fuck up, Drake," I growl and point to the door. "Now get out of here before I get the urge to beat some fucking manners into you."

"We'll see what Midge has to say about this," he says, feeling much more emboldened now that I'm winding down.

"Go for it," I taunt. "Run to Midge like a baby. Make your complaints known. I'll take the ass chewing she'll give me. Then I'm going to get in my car, come to your house, and kick your ass really good like you deserve."

"That's… that's… criminal," he sputters.

"As is hiring someone to beat up a woman," I snarl. "Don't make this nastier than it already is, Drake."

He opens his mouth as if to argue with me, but the stairwell door swings open and the bailiff sticks his head through. His eyes go to Drake, then to me, then snap back to Drake. It's clear he took punches as his right cheek is red and swollen. It will be purple tonight, and his nose is swelling up, too.

"You all right?" he asks Drake hesitantly.

"He's fine," I answer for him, and then turn to Drake for confirmation.

Finally, he nods at the bailiff. "I'm good."

Not buying it for a second, the bailiff stares at Drake for a moment before turning to me. "Judge Boyer would like to get started."

He disappears back through the door, and I grab onto it before it can swing shut. I don't look at Drake, but I tell him the words I think are important to my own set of ethical standards. "I'm going to go back in there and represent you diligently. We've got a good shot at winning, and I expect I'll be calling you with good news after. But if I ever see your fucking face again, you're not going to like what happens. And consider this my termination notice. Find another attorney for any other matters you have."

♦

IT'S A GOOD thing Viveka was first up to give her arguments to the judge. Not only would it let me rebut whatever she said, but it also gave me more of a chance to calm down. I was still wired when I walked back into that courtroom.

I simply told the judge that my client wasn't feeling well, but I was prepared to move forward.

So we did.

Viveka was a pure joy to watch. Passionate and eloquent. She did a superb job with her expert's testimony on the stand, although I was able to rattle him a bit on cross examination.

My argument was easy as the weight of the evidence was in my favor. My expert's findings were vastly different than Viveka's. I don't pretend to even figure out where the truth actually lies. I'm not a bird expert. My job is to put it before the court and let the judge figure it out.

Viveka's approach was to ask for everything for those

poor woodpeckers. She asked for a protective circle around the active cluster Dr. Mellman found, including the area between it and the one lone nest in the tree she tied herself to. Dr. Mellman testified that if the area in between was de-forested, it would discourage communal helpers from coming to the lone nest.

When we're finished, Judge Boyer leans forward in her chair to peer down at us. "I'd like to thank you both for your eloquent arguments and the expert testimony you presented. You both did a fine job for your client. At this time, I'm going to adjourn court, read through your briefs and take some time to consider the evidence. I understand how important this matter is to both of your clients, and I'm trying to balance the federal laws with the private ownership. I should have a ruling by the end of the day, and I'll be calling each of you."

This was not unusual. Often judges can rule on the merits as soon as arguments are done. Many times, a judge will sit on it, sometimes for days. With the ability for lawyers to appeal, it's imperative that decisions not be made rashly, and Judge Boyer understands that.

The bailiff recesses court and in just a few minutes, Viveka and I are left alone in the courtroom. I watch her pack her stuff up, shoulders stiff. I can't tell if she's on edge because we don't have a ruling on the merits or she's upset about the way I behaved. Regardless of the fact I confronted Drake in private and away from the court's eyes, it was still obvious to everyone in the courtroom I was upset about everything.

Add that to the fact I wasn't upset until Viveka walked in late with a cut to her forehead and then I immediately pulled my client out of the courtroom, I'm sure the courthouse gossip is talking about it everywhere right now.

"Viv," I say softly, but my voice still carries in the now-empty courtroom.

She twists her neck, looking over at me slowly. Her expression is guarded. "What did you do to him?"

It sounds almost as if she's worried for the douchebag.

"I punched the bastard," I growl as I walk up to her table. "I guess what I don't get is why that would bother you. Why would you even care about him?"

Viv's eyes flare with indignation. "Why would I care about him?" she hisses. "I don't care about him. I care about you, you big moron. You could have gotten in serious trouble, Ford. Like lost your law license kind of trouble for attacking a client and fucking the opposing counsel. I don't give two shits about him, but you can damn well better believe I care about you—"

She cares about me.

I snatch her to me so hard I get just a momentary image of her eyes going even wider with surprise before my mouth descends on hers. She grunts from the contact, pushes hard at me for just a nanosecond, and then she's kissing me back.

There aren't two fucks given between the two of us that we might be caught. The bailiff could walk back in, or maybe Judge Boyer forgot something on her desk. Hell, any number of attorneys or court personnel could walk by and look inside.

Fuck them all. Nothing is making me break this kiss.

Except when Viv pulls away. She goes up to her tiptoes, and I bend to put a very gentle kiss to the left of the cut on her forehead.

She lets out a shaky breath. "I was so scared you were going to get in trouble. Promise me that you'll let it go. Whatever you did to that asshole, promise me it's over, okay?"

"You can press charges," I murmur. "I'll support you if you want to do that."

I get a tiny shake of her head. "No. This case is over, all but for the ruling. Let's just let it go."

"Okay, Viv," I say as my hands go to the side of her head. I hold her in place. "Letting it go."

"Thank you," she says with a smile.

"So… you care about me, huh?" I ask slyly.

"I kinda do," she admits with a sheepish grin.

"It's mutual," I say. "And I have an idea."

"What's that?"

"Let's take the rest of the day off and go to my apartment, because it's like only three blocks from here." I tilt my head and brush my lips against her cheek. She shivers slightly. "You can tell me all about what happened last night, I can get all kinds of pissed off, and then work my aggression out on your body. Are you with me?"

She nods, and I move my lips down to her neck. My voice goes husky. "We'll cuddle for a bit, let me recharge, and then I'll make love to you… slowly and taking my time."

"Um… yeah, I like that." Her voice is breathy, and her hands drop to my belt where she tucks the tips of her fingers inside.

"Maybe we'll nap after that for a bit, because we deserve it, but more than likely, I'm going to spend the afternoon playing with your body. I feel it's my duty as your boyfriend to take your mind off what happened to you last night, as well as keep you occupied until we get Judge Boyer's ruling."

Viveka pulls back from me so I have to look at her, and her eyes are questioning. "You're my boyfriend?"

I pretend to think about it by staring up at the ceiling in contemplation, but there's no need. I know what I am to her and she is to me. "Yeah… I'm your boyfriend."

"At least for the next few months," she teases.

But it's not funny. I shake my head and run my nose along her cheek, before pulling her in for a simple hug. "I don't see a time limit, Viv. In fact, I really can't see an end for us."

She doesn't respond.

She hugs me back really hard, and that's all the answer I need.

CHAPTER 24

Viveka

THE SOUND OF a phone ringing pulls me from the most delicious sleep I've had in a long time. Perhaps it's because I didn't get any sleep last night, what with being attacked and all. A lengthy emergency room visit, stitches, and coming down from fear-induced adrenaline should have knocked me out last night, but I hardly slept at all. I was worried about the hearing, and more worried about what Ford was going to do when he saw me.

Frannie had urged me repeatedly last night while we were at the hospital to call Ford, and I still don't know if I made the right decision to keep it from him. I didn't like blindsiding him, but I thought the courtroom would keep his emotions in check.

Clearly not.

Regardless, the hearing is over and the chips will fall where they may. Ford wasn't kidding with his game plan for the rest of the day either. He made me sit in his living room and tell him every excruciating detail of the attack.

He did this while holding my face gently with one hand, turning it this way and that to study the cut from every angle.

"How many?" he'd asked.

Stitches is what he was asking, by the way he took my face gently and peered closely at the cut as he counted them out loud.

There are seven on my two-centimeter cut, by the way.

Afterward, when he had exhausted his list of questions and expended himself cussing Drake Powell out, he did indeed use my body so well I forgot all about what had happened to me. How could I think of much of anything when he had me bent all the way over the back of his couch and pounded away inside of me until we both had orgasms that melted into one another?

He came inside of me for the first time ever without a condom, and it felt amazingly right, like it completed something tiny that was missing between us. I'd been able to get into my doctor just the week before and started the pill the very next day after that. Technically, we were still one day short from when the doctor told me I should be good to go for pregnancy protection, but we really just weren't thinking about it.

Ford had driven me crazy by stripping us both, laying back on the couch, and pulling me on top of his face. I had never in my life done that. Nor had that done to me. I came so hard I thought I would pass out.

Then he was hauling me up with a strong arm around my waist, carried me to the back of the couch, and pushed me over it with my ass in the air.

He kicked my legs apart and put one large hand spread out across my lower back. I felt the huge tip of him press against me, and he grunted, "You're on the pill, right?"

He didn't even give me a chance to answer, but just plunged right into me. My mind went blissfully blank, and I didn't even think about the repercussions of only having six days of being on the pill rather than the seven the doctor told me I'd need to be safe.

The phone continues ringing, and I start to really come awake. Ford moves slightly. Since I'm lying on his chest, I move with him. I open my eyes and see his arm stretching out to his bedside table where he nabs his iPhone. We'd moved into his room for round two, which was the slow lovemaking he'd promised.

"Hello," he says into the phone, sounding all gruff and clearly waking up from that nap we'd taken.

"Yeah… she's here," he says, and I lift my head to see him rubbing his fingers over his eyes. His hair is sticking up all over the place, and he's absolutely edible. He winks with one side of his mouth curving upward. To whoever is on the other line, he says, "Hang on a minute. Let me put you on speaker."

My body tenses as Ford hits the speaker button and whispers, "It's Midge."

I immediately fly off his chest, scramble backward, and yank the sheet over me like Midge can see through the phone. Ford stares at me like I'm bonkers and then starts chuckling low.

"Okay, we can both hear you now, Midge," he says into the phone.

Bewildered, I let my eyes convey a very clear message I can't say out loud. *How the fuck does she know I'm here with you?*

He understands and just shrugs.

"Hello, Viv," Midge says in that smoky voice that's both sexy and terrifying at the same time.

"Um… hi," I mutter, clutching the sheet to me harder. Ford smirks and playfully tries to tug it away. I slap his hand hard, and it's loud.

"Two interesting things happened today," she says without any preamble. "The first is that I got a visit from Drake Powell."

"How is he?" Ford asks drolly.

"Got two black eyes and a swollen cheek," she replies dryly, and there's a tiny bit of censure in her voice. "He's terminated our representation of him and his company. Not happy with the way you handled the case."

My stomach drops, and my eyes actually start to mist up. Ford is in so much trouble, and it's all my fault. I should have never gotten involved with him while this case was going on.

Ford doesn't seem upset in the slightest. In fact, he

tells Midge, "Good riddance. I didn't like that fucker anyway."

My jaw drops open, and Ford grins. But he must have some sort of pity for my discombobulation because he takes one of my hands in his to rub the back of it with his thumb in a soothing manner.

To my shock, Midge laughs on the other end of the line. "I didn't like him either. I, of course, made cordial apologies to him and wished him well."

"Thanks, Midge," Ford tells her with pure affection in his voice.

"I also just got off the phone with Judge Boyer," she continues. "She said she left both you and Viveka voicemails with her ruling, but when she couldn't reach you, she gave me a call."

This shocks me almost as much as Drake Powell firing Ford and his firm. I know of no judge who would call an attorney not officially listed on the case, and I'm guessing that's because Midge is one of those attorneys who sort of knows everyone and commands such respect even from judges that she's probably the only exception.

Ford's hand tightens on mine, a comforting squeeze because we're about to find out who won and who lost.

"And?" he prompts.

"Judge Boyer ruled to give just the most basic protection, only prohibiting cutting of the actual trees with nests. She declined to add safety barriers. As such, all the acreage in between the large cluster and the single tree can be deforested. I'm sorry, Viveka."

I'm not surprised by this ruling. I am surprised by Midge giving me sympathies since this ruling is to her benefit.

I finally find my voice. "Miss Payne… you owe me no apologies."

"It's Midge," she says curtly.

"Midge," I repeat, but I continue. "I understand the ruling. I'm not happy about it, but that's the way the law works."

"Yeah, well," she says dryly. "It doesn't always work out fairly, right?"

"At least there's some protection in place," I say softly, grateful the nests will be saved. Whether they'll be able to propagate once the surrounding trees are cut down is another matter.

"There's actually a lot more protection in place," she says vaguely.

"What do you mean?" Ford asks.

"It means I called Drake Powell to give him the news before I called you," she tells us, and I can hear the slyness in her voice. "He was still pissed over the fact you beat him up, and he wasn't overjoyed with the news. I took an earful from him and let me tell you, you know I have no patience for assholes. I promptly informed him I was going to change the layout of the subdivision and add a protected wildlife area. Essentially, I was prohibiting him from building on the acreage in between the clusters, so it looks like Viveka's birds are going to get the utmost protection they can."

My jaw drops open again, this time wider. Ford grins at me before saying into the phone, "You're amazing, Midge."

She laughs and then asks, "You think so, too, Viv?"

I give a slight shake of my head, wanting to make sure I'm not dreaming, before I murmur, "I don't know what to say, Midge. I never expected—"

"Someone to be so generous and awesome as me?" she cuts in. "It's a hard concept, I get it. But there you have it, kiddos. The case is over, and now you two can quit skulking around."

"We weren't skulking," Ford tells her.

"You weren't doing much of anything as far as keeping it a secret," Midge cuts in. "Judge Boyer knew something was up."

"Fuck," I murmur.

"It's all good," Midge assures us.

Well, assures me.

Ford doesn't appear worried at all.

In fact, his eyes sort of get a little hot as he stares at me, and he tugs on my hand that he's still holding. He pushes it down his naked chest and right in between his legs, forcing my fingers around his cock. He squeezes, and in turn, my fingers squeeze him. He starts to thicken in my palm, and my face heats up that he's doing this while Midge is on the phone.

"Well, we have to go now," Ford says thickly, and I give him a hard stroke. He bites down into his lower lip.

"Bye, Midge," he says, and he doesn't wait for her to respond. He disconnects, tosses his phone to the floor, and puts his hand to the back of my head. When he pushes my face toward his lap, I manage a smile just before his cock slips into my mouth.

♦

THE CUDDLING IS nice.

I mean, the sex is amazing, but the cuddling is nice.

I hadn't realized how much I missed it. Adam was a cuddler, but that was dependent on him being around.

And not just cuddling after sex. Cuddling during a movie, or a hug goodbye that lingers. Spooning during the night, or stepping back into Ford's body in the shower while he wraps his arms around me.

These past three weeks, we've cuddled a lot.

Right now is even better.

The case is over, and I got the best possible outcome. Ford says he sees a long future with me, and this makes me happier than the outcome of the case. I hadn't been looking for him but now I found him, I don't want to let him go.

"Do you think the dogs would do well here at the apartment?" Ford asks. I'm once again stretched out across his body, my head on his chest. His hand rests on my lower back where he's idly stroking my skin. His voice is relaxed and mellow.

I smile against the skin of his chest, enjoying the slight tickle of his hair against my neck. "I don't know. We'd have to take them out on a leash to do their business. Given I have a fenced-in backyard and a dog door, they don't get a lot of leash practice."

"I see your point," he says thoughtfully. After a small pause, he says, "Maybe it's time I move out of the city. That way I can have a fenced-in backyard for them, too."

I can't even respond. The fact he'd actually think about selling his downtown condo for a house to make my dogs comfortable is almost more than I can bear.

I finally manage to croak out, "Maybe."

Ford squeezes me, I think understanding the effect his words have had. "You're mine, Viv. Get used to it."

My hold on him tightens, and I burrow into him closer. "I don't want to get used to it. I like everything about the way you make me feel."

"I'm glad, baby." His head shifts, and I feel his lips press against the side of my head. "And we owe it all to those fucking woodpeckers."

"Hail to the peckers," I say with a laugh.

"Hail to the peckers," he agrees.

EPILOGUE

Ford

MY PHONE VIBRATES inside the front pocket of my suit jacket. I pull it out, see it's Viveka calling, and slide out of the bench in Courtroom 10A. I was watching part of a capital murder trial, really for lack of anything better to do. The one afternoon appointment I'd had canceled on me, and I have nothing but a pile of paperwork waiting for me back at the office.

I'm a master at procrastination, so when I'd popped my head inside to see what was going on, it looked interesting enough I had no qualms with avoiding my paperwork for another hour or so. It's one of the perks of being a partner and able to come and go as I please.

I connect the call before I make it out of the courtroom, so my voice is very low when I answer, "Hey, baby. What's up?"

"Leary's in labor," she shrieks into the phone. "There's an ambulance here, and you need to find Reeve and get him to the hospital now."

"Whoa, whoa, whoa," I say as I start to jog toward the elevator. It's opening, and people are boarding. "Where are you?"

"We were having Snoopy's hot dogs in the park, and after eating one bite, her water broke. All over the park bench. And we're too far from either of our cars, both of which are parked a few blocks down, so I called an ambulance. They're loading her up now."

All of this she said comes out in a fluid rush with one word running into the next. Luckily, I'm able to translate most of it.

"Okay, baby," I croon as I slide into the elevator just before the doors close. "Remember… it's deep breaths in and out."

I remember that from the one and only Lamaze class I took with Leary. Viv will now have that job for now until we can get to the hospital.

"How far apart are the contractions?" I ask.

"How the fuck should I know," she shrieks again, and I can't help but chuckle—very, very silently so she can't hear me. I never thought Viv would be the one to freak out in a situation like this.

"I'm on my way to the hospital, V," I tell her gently. "I'll call Reeve, too."

"Okay," she says almost absently before hanging up on me.

"Is your wife in labor?" a woman asks from my right as I'm pulling up Reeve's number in my contacts.

Startled, I turn to her. "No, my best friend. That was my girlfriend. She's with her right now."

"She'll be calmer when she's the one who's pregnant," she assures me knowingly. "Don't worry about that."

I just blink at the woman, wondering how she went from girlfriend to pregnant girlfriend. I wait for a full-body shudder to hit me at the thought, but it doesn't come. Instead, I think about how cute Viv would look pregnant. She'd be one of those women who would show off that bump, too, and I bet it would be sexy as fuck.

When the woman touches my arm—giving me a reassuring pat—I realize I'm staring stupidly at her. It's as if she could read my thoughts because she says, "Such an amazing experience. You'll enjoy every moment of it."

Whoa, back the fuck up. I give a hard shake of my head and a curt smile to the woman before turning away to put in a call to Reeve.

He's much calmer than Viv when I reach him. Because I'm just minutes from the parking garage and my car, as well as only one block away from the office, I offer to pick him up.

He's there on the sidewalk waiting for me, practically bouncing up and down in excitement. He hops in the car and pounds his fists on my dashboard. "Put the pedal to the metal, dude. I've got a baby coming."

Good thing I'm driving the Porsche.

♦

"VIV IS NEVER allowed to be with me if I have another kid and go into labor," Leary says with an affectionate smile leveled at my girl. We're standing by Leary's bed as she holds little Charlie in her arms. Reeve's on the other side, sitting on the edge next to her.

I've got my arm securely around Viv's waist. Her head is on my shoulder as she stares at Charlie with a goofy grin. She doesn't even take offense to Leary's comment.

Instead, she says, "He's so adorable. I can't believe he was just in your belly a few hours ago."

Yes, Leary's labor went super fast, which is apparently abnormal. From the time her water broke on a park bench until the doctor pulled him free was just over two hours.

All three of us look at Viv, who is so enamored with Charlie she really isn't paying attention to anything else.

"I don't know," Reeve says with a wink. "I think he resembles a little troll."

Viv just stares at the baby with a stupid smile on her face.

"Trolls are actually cuter," Leary says with a sly smirk. "The kid's pretty ugly, actually."

Viv doesn't react. She's not even listening to us, and I have to wonder what's running through her head as she stares at the baby and ignores all of us. Whatever it is, I find it ridiculously adorable. At the same time, it makes my chest feel strange—all tight and warm at the same time.

"Think we can exchange him?" Reeve asks his wife, who snorts and then dips her head to kiss the sleeping baby.

When that doesn't get a rise out of Viv, I release my hold on her waist and take her by the hand. "Okay, I think that's my cue to get Viv out of here. She's staring at Charlie like she's going to kidnap him."

That seems to startle her out of whatever reverie she's stuck in because she looks guiltily around at the three of us. "Sorry… it's just… I've never seen a newborn baby before. I'm so happy for you, Leary. And you, too, Reeve. And it was all so miraculous, and I know I freaked out, but I was so excited and scared shitless that I was a basket case… I get it. But I'll be better next time. I swear it."

We all laugh at her silliness, but I'm compelled to pull her in for a huge fucking hug because I'm not sure I've ever liked Viv more than in this moment right now.

No… not like.

I *love* her.

"We gotta go," I say hastily as I start to pull her toward the door. Reeve and Leary share a smirk. They know how fucking cute Viv was in the last few moments, and I'm sure they think I want to take her home and get it on with my girl.

And yes... I do want that, but after...

"No, let's stay a little longer," Viv pleads. She actually digs her heels in and pulls back.

"No, let's go," I say in that alpha-domineering tone that normally gets her to do whatever I want when we're in bed.

"No, let's stay."

"Viv," I say in exasperation. "I just want to have a moment's privacy with you to tell you I love you, but for fuck's sake... I'll say it right here. I don't care if Reeve, Leary, and Charlie hear me. They'd be the first to know anyway."

"Oh, wow," Leary says in the dreamiest of voices, but my eyes stay pinned on Viveka.

She blinks, not in confusion or surprise, but from the pure emotion welling up so fast in her eyes she can't control the tears.

"Aww, fuck," I grumble as I pull her into me. My hand goes to the back of her head, and I press her face into my throat. "Don't cry, honey."

She sniffs hard and mumbles against me. "I love you, too."

"Good to know, baby." My voice is husky with emotion.

It's the first time I've said those words to a woman, and I think I've been feeling this for a while now with Viv, but I hadn't given it conscious thought. This was the right time to say it.

My eyes search out Leary and Reeve, and both are smiling knowingly at me. I can see it on their expressions. Ford has fallen. He's off the market permanently, and there's going to be a day when Viveka will be in that bed with a baby.

First there will be an engagement, a wedding, and more I love you's.

But it has started.

It's when I fell in love for the first and last time, and waiting for Viv was worth it.

If you enjoyed reading *The Pecker Briefs* as much as I enjoyed writing it, please consider leaving a review.

Don't miss another new release by Sawyer Bennett!!! Sign up for her newsletter and keep up to date on new releases, giveaways, book reviews and so much more.
sawyerbennett.com/signup

Check out all the books available from Sawyer Bennett.
sawyerbennett.com/bookshop

Connect with Sawyer online:

Website: sawyerbennett.com

Twitter: www.twitter.com/bennettbooks

Facebook: www.facebook.com/bennettbooks

To see Other Works by Sawyer Bennett, please visit her Book Page on her website.

About the Author

Since the release of her debut contemporary romance novel, Off Sides, in January 2013, Sawyer Bennett has released multiple books, many of which have appeared on the New York Times, USA Today and Wall Street Journal bestseller lists.

A reformed trial lawyer from North Carolina, Sawyer uses real life experience to create relatable, sexy stories that appeal to a wide array of readers. From new adult to erotic contemporary romance, Sawyer writes something for just about everyone.

Sawyer likes her Bloody Marys strong, her martinis dirty, and her heroes a combination of the two. When not bringing fictional romance to life, Sawyer is a chauffeur, stylist, chef, maid, and personal assistant to a very active daughter, as well as full-time servant to her adorably naughty dogs. She believes in the good of others, and that a bad day can be cured with a great work-out, cake, or even better, both.

Sawyer also writes general and women's fiction under the pen name S. Bennett and sweet romance under the name Juliette Poe.

Made in the USA
Columbia, SC
06 April 2018